N.L.

ELSEWHERE

Other novels by Will Shetterly

Cats Have No Lord
Witch Blood
The Tangled Lands

The *Liavek* series, edited by Will Shetterly and Emma Bull

Liavek
Liavek: The Players of Luck
Liavek: Wizard's Row
Liavek: Spells of Binding
Liavek: Festival Week

The *Bordertown* series, edited by Terri Windling

Bordertown
Borderland
Life on the Border

ELSEWHERE

WILL SHETTERLY, P.J.F.

JANE YOLEN BOOKS

HARCOURT

BRACE

JOVANOVICH

San Diego   New York   London

Copyright © 1991 by Will Shetterly and Terri Windling

Bordertown and the Borderlands were created by Terri Windling, with creative input from Mark Alan Arnold and the authors of the stories in the anthologies *Borderland* (NAL 1986), *Bordertown* (NAL 1986), and *Life on the Border* (Tor Books 1991): Bellamy Bach, Steven R. Boyett, Emma Bull, Kara Dalkey, Charles de Lint, Craig Shaw Gardner, Michael Korolenko, Ellen Kushner, Will Shetterly, and Midori Snyder. Borderland is used by permission of Terri Windling, The Endicott Studio.

Requests for permission to make copies of any part of the work should be mailed to: Permissions Department, Harcourt Brace Jovanovich, Publishers, 8th Floor, Orlando, Florida 32887.

Seven lines from "The Second Coming" are reprinted with permission of Macmillan Publishing Company from *The Collected Works of W. B. Yeats: Volume 1, The Poems*, edited by Richard J. Finneran. Copyright 1924 by Macmillan Publishing Company, renewed 1952 by Bertha Georgie Yeats.
Two lines from "Sailing to Byzantium" reprinted with permission of Macmillan Publishing Company from *The Collected Works of W. B. Yeats: Volume 1, The Poems*, edited by Richard J. Finneran. Copyright 1928 by Macmillan Publishing Company, renewed 1956 by Georgie Yeats.
Excerpts from "Down by the Salley Gardens," "The Stolen Child," and "A Coat" from *The Collected Works of W. B. Yeats: Volume 1, The Poems*, edited by Richard J Finneran (New York: Macmillan, 1989). Reprinted by permission.

Library of Congress Cataloging-in-Publication Data
Shetterly, Will.
Elsewhere/Will Shetterly.—1st ed.
p.   cm.
"Jane Yolen Books."
Summary: Ron, a teenage runaway, comes of age among the punk elves and humans of Bordertown, a run-down city on the border between the real world and the magic world of Faerie.
ISBN 0-15-200731-8
[1. Fantasy.]   I. Title.
PZ7.S55454E1   1991
[Fic]—dc20   91-11075

Designed by Trina Stahl
Printed in the United States of America
First edition

A B C D E

For Emma

An acknowledgment:

Terri Windling set the stage,
then let me bring on my troupe of players.
I am eternally grateful.

TABLE OF CONTENTS

ELSEWHERE

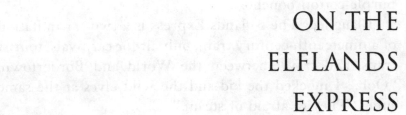

ON THE ELFLANDS EXPRESS

I KNEW I WAS IN THE NEVERNEVER WHEN I SAW A WILD ELF through the train window. Maybe I said something. Maybe I just stared like a tourist. The armless kid in the seat across from me said, "First trip to Bordertown?"

"Did you see—?" I began. Then I caught her tone of voice. "Yeah. Big deal."

I tugged up the collar of the too-big jeans jacket that I wore and scrunched down in my seat. We passed oaks and elms and sequoias, huge things that would've been made into tables or newsprint in the World. Two ravens flew overhead. I saw natural roses in bloom, the color of lips. Through gaps in the trees I could see the red waters of the Mad River. I didn't see any more slim half-naked people with long white hair and pointed ears.

"It is," the armless kid said. When I glanced at her, she added, "A big deal. If you believe in omens, it's probably

1

a good one. The nature types rarely show themselves near the train."

"Yeah. They don't like iron." I didn't care if the folklore was true. I wanted her to be quiet so I could watch the woods for signs of magic.

She shook her head. "They don't like technology." Her hair, a fire-orange mass cut like a monk's, clashed with her purple cotton poncho.

I laughed. The Elflands Express is a two-car imitation of a nineteenth-century train, only fit for carnivals, tourist traps, and travel between the World and Bordertown. "Ooh." I mocked the kid and the wild elves at the same time. "They're afraid of steam."

"Elves aren't *afraid* of technology. Wild ones just don't like the fancier forms of it." She lifted a beaded moccasin to point at my wristwatch, an oddly natural gesture. "Maybe 'cause there's something whimsical about the kinds that work here."

I'd borrowed Dad's watch to pawn or sell if I needed money. It told the time to the sixtieth of a second, had radio and computer functions, and was guaranteed to work underwater or in a vacuum. It must not've been guaranteed to work in the Borderlands. Its face was blank.

"Great." I shook it. The watch blinked to life, promising that it was a little after midnight and about to rain. The afternoon sun and a cloudless sky disagreed.

"It's the nature of the Borderlands," the kid said. "Magic and science wash up against each other here. Makes 'em both fickle."

I stared at her and back at the watch. It squawked, "Who knows what evil lurks in the hearts of men?" then blanked its face again.

2

"I s'pose you knew that."

I nodded. I hadn't thought about it affecting little everyday things like electronic clocks. Bordertown probably wasn't a first-choice vacation spot for people with pacemakers.

"And you wear the watch 'cause you like the strap."

"Yeah." Two snaps held Dad's watch on a studded black band. I unsnapped the watch and held it out. "You think it's funny, it's yours."

"No, thanks."

I nodded and flipped the watch out the window. It made a nice arc, glinting in the sunlight against a backdrop of blue sky and green leaves, and called, "Say good night, Gracie."

The kid pointed her nose in the direction it had gone. "Could've sold that."

"Big market for screwy watches in Bordertown?"

She laughed. "Could've sold it to someone going back to the World. It'd work fine there."

"Thanks for telling me now."

"Hey, you made the grand gesture, not me."

"Check." I looked out the window again. The train tracks still followed the Big Bloody. A blue-and-yellow paddle wheeler churned upriver. Someone sat on its deck, dangling bare feet over the wine-dark waters and lazily strumming a guitar. The only music I could hear was made by the train engine. I smelled wood smoke from the locomotive, dirt and decaying leaves from the forest, and something sweet and decadent from the Mad River itself. Far ahead, a few tall white buildings waited where the slow red river met the sky. I squinted, looking for the Border.

The kid followed my gaze. "Most folks can't see it.

Can't pass it and can't see it. Not that seeing it does you any good, if you're human. You still can't go past it. But those who see it say it's beautiful."

"That wall?" I said. "Going up into the air, all shiny and twinkling like stars?"

"Uh huh."

"It's gorgeous. Words fail me."

"I'm sure." She looked away, down the aisle.

The car was half-full, with business-types in three-piece never-wrinkles off to dicker with Bordertown's merchant princes, and noisy rich kids in this week's styles off for a weekend of slumming in Soho, and even a middle-class family in new sports clothes off a-holidaying to the edge of Faerie. Among them were a few solos like me in scruffy traveling gear, off to the place where magic sometimes works.

I'd taken the seat across from the armless kid 'cause she'd looked simpatico. Shows how much first impressions mean. I said, "You think I can't see it?"

"I didn't say that."

"Yeah, you did. You just didn't use those words."

Across the aisle a tourist looked at me, then made sure her two little darlings were safe beside her.

The armless kid said, "What's it matter?"

"Yeah." I slumped back into my seat. "What's it matter?" I hadn't seen a thing beyond the towers of Bordertown except a rippling green sea where the Old Forest rolled over distant hills.

As we rode on, I watched the woods and the river and the sky. If there were gryphons in the treetops or unicorns behind the bushes, they disguised themselves as squirrels and bluejays. Once I thought I saw a stag, but that must've been two dead branches behind a clump of brush.

4

The kid said, "You running from or running to?"

I looked at her before I could stop myself.

"You get a second chance in Bordertown. You should think about what that means, and what you want."

"Who says I'm running?"

She grinned, glanced at my pack, glanced back at me. With a little shock I realized she must be much older than me, twenty-five or thirty or more. " 'You're coming solo to Soho,' " she said, quoting a song that'd played throughout the World a couple of years back, one of my brother's favorites. "You don't exactly look like an exchange student."

I wore a gray T-shirt, old fatigue pants, and sneakers that were frayed and paint-spattered from months of odd jobs. The black jeans jacket with the phoenix on the back had been in Tony's closet forever. I borrowed it from Mom's shrine to him the same night I borrowed Dad's watch. The green canvas pack beside me was mine. Back when I believed I was being taught to think in school instead of not to, I'd carried textbooks in it.

"What do you care?"

She shrugged. "I was an ass when I was your age, too." She tapped the toe of her moccasin against my pack, where a flat rectangle strained the canvas. "Books help redeem you. Unless it's *Mein Kampf.* Then it depends on why you're reading it."

"You'd like it. It's *The Nazi Babysitter's German Shepherd.* It's the best book I ever read. Course, it's the only book I ever read."

"Right."

Her grin made me say, "Okay, it's a Yeats collection. He was this human poet who lived in Ireland, way before Faerie returned."

She nodded. " 'She bid me take life easy, as the grass grows on the weirs; / But I was young and foolish, and now am full of tears.' " Then she cocked her head and gave me a little smile.

"Yeah! 'And therefore I have sailed the seas and come / To the holy city of Byzantium.' " The book was Tony's, too, but the folks would never notice it was gone. They'd never noticed what he read. When things got really bad and Tony thought no one was listening, he would whisper, *Come away, O human child! / To the waters and the wild / With a faery* . . .

The armless woman laughed. "Bordertown isn't Byzantium. And the sailing's often better than being there. Which might be part of the point of the poem."

I shrugged. "Who's got expectations?"

"Everyone."

She said it very simply, making it hard for me to take offense, but I said, "What're you, a teacher or something?"

"More a perpetual student." She nodded at the bulky canvas satchel on the seat beside her. The strap ran across her chest, molding the poncho to her torso. "I'm a dealer."

I squinted.

She laughed. "Book dealer. Rare and used. There's not much vid in the Borderlands, and since I'm in Soho, I hardly have anything in the way of expenses. I get by."

"There's a *bookstore?* In *Bordertown?*"

She nodded. "Several. There's everything you want in Bordertown. There just isn't everything you need." She grinned. "I'm Mickey. The store's Elsewhere. Hours are as erratic as you can imagine, but word gets out when we're open. A few blocks south of Ho on Mock Avenue."

"I'm Ron. Ron Starbuck."

She lifted an eyebrow. "One kid showed up in Soho,

said her name was Jinian L'Étoile. Everyone called her Jiggle Le Toilet. She cut out for the World after a week. I'm amazed she lasted that long."

"Check," I said. "Just Ron."

"Good to meet you, Just Ron."

I nodded, thinking maybe I liked her.

"You never answered. About running from or running to."

And then I thought maybe I didn't. "Does it matter?"

"Might. Maybe I'm just being sociable."

"Maybe I'm not too sociable, *Mom.*"

"A hit." Mickey rocked back and laughed. "A palpable hit. Well, that's fine, Just Ron. There's plenty of room to hide in B-town, if that's all you want from life."

I inhaled loudly. "I'm going to Bordertown. I'm planning to stay. Good enough?"

"Anything waiting for you? Friends? A job?"

I shrugged.

"It isn't easy."

I rolled my eyes and looked for any sign of magic in the woods of the Nevernever. The trees formed a wall that I couldn't see past.

She said, "Okay, maybe you guessed that. It's still tougher than you think. You planning to find a squat?"

"Yeah." I'd read Tony's copy of *Let's Go: Bordertown.* The main thing I remembered were well-thumbed pages about human and elf kids living for free in the abandoned neighborhoods. Tony must've read that section over and over while he decided whether to run and where to go.

Mickey said, "The best places have all been taken. What's left doesn't have water, gas, or power, either magical or electrical. If a building isn't occupied, it's probably on contested territory. Be in the wrong place at the right time and you're somebody's fun, regardless of your size, sex, or species. There're a lot of gangs in Soho, both human and elf, and the Silver Suits don't come around for anything less than murder."

"Gee." I shrugged. "Sounds rough."

"Not necessarily. There's a community. Every community has its rules. You learn 'em, you won't get hurt."

I wanted to say I don't get hurt anymore. Instead, I said, "Screw the community. I'll get by."

Mickey raised her eyebrows. "Spare me the teen machismo, huh? You don't have to—"

"I'll get by," I said a little louder. "I didn't leave—"

Behind me, someone announced Bordertown as the next stop.

"Oh, great." I slunk a little lower in my seat.

"What's—?" Mickey glanced up as the conductor's shadow fell over me. "Ah."

"Don't think I took your ticket," a dark woman in an iridescent blue uniform told me. I looked tiny and pimply and geeky in the lenses of her mirrored glasses.

"Oh?"

"And I'm the only one who could've."

"It's been pretty busy. Didn't you already—?"

"Nope. Care to show me a seat check?"

"Uh, yeah." I hunted around as if I'd lost my ticket. God, as usual, granted me no miracles. I said, "Huh. Must've fallen out in the john." Which was where I'd hidden for half of the trip, until I decided to ride where I could see more of the Borderlands than the ground under the crossties when I flushed the toilet.

"You have the cash to buy another?"

I did, but then I'd have nothing left for Bordertown.

Besides, I could hear her laughing at me. "I had a ticket, old woman."

"Old woman?" The conductor appeared to be Mom or Dad's age. She looked at Mickey. "He's studying to be a diplomat?"

Mickey cocked her head to one side. "Could be a good idea."

"Hey, screw you both," I said.

"Listen—" the conductor began, losing her smile.

"He's just a kid," Mickey said. "Give 'im a break. We'll be in town in half an hour."

"I don't know." The conductor frowned. "Policy's clear. I can't let—"

"Maybe—" Mickey began.

"You mean, won't let," I said. "Don't hide behind your junior cop suit. You like jerking people around, huh?"

"Not usually." She grabbed my sleeve to yank me to my feet. "You're the charming exception."

Mickey shook her head. "Careful, Just Ron. You get one new start in Bordertown. You rarely get two."

"Oh, wow. Real helpful." I grabbed my pack as the conductor tugged me down the aisle. People stared as if we were hired entertainment. I yelled, "Hey, what's this, a kidnapping? I just lost my ticket! I want to speak to your supervisor! Now, damn it!" At the back of the car I grabbed the doorjamb and jerked free of her. "You can't treat me like this, old woman!"

"No?"

"No!" I shouted so all the petty rich passengers could have their smug little lives broadened. I liked it on the open platform with the wind clutching at my clothes while we rattled along at ten or fifteen miles an hour. "You want to give me to the Silver Suits? Fine. Let 'em send me back to the World. I'll run again. But don't yank me around like some stupid kid. I got rights." In her mirrored lenses I was mean and disdainful and impervious to anything she might do. I looked so good I nearly smiled and ruined the effect.

She reached for my arm. "Rights. Must be comforting."

"Yeah. What'll you do?" I sneered. "Throw me off a moving train?"

She nodded.

"Hey, wait a minute." I glanced both ways. To the west, between us and the Mad River, a line of trees waited to break my fall. None looked particularly soft. To the east, a meadow sloped downward for forty feet or more before climbing uphill.

The conductor yanked my pack from my hand.

"Hey!"

"Probably wouldn't hurt yourself if you jumped and rolled." She tossed the pack into the meadow. The flap opened, spilling my possessions into the long grass. Tony's book fluttered as if it wanted to fly, bounced once, and disappeared. "I'd hate to push you."

I glared at her. I could hit her hard and leap away before she could do anything.

"Ground gets rocky up ahead."

I can never decide if I'm a nice guy or a coward. "Remind me to do you a favor sometime," I told her mirror-shades, and I jumped.

CHAPTER TWO

MOONER

AFTER I PICKED MYSELF UP AND DUSTED MYSELF OFF, I limped along the rails to gather my gear. There wasn't much: a change of clothes, a notebook, a half-full plastic water jug, a can of lentil soup. The Yeats collection had taken a dent and a smudge but no serious damage. Except for a bloody knee, a sprained ankle, and a few more holes in my trousers, I was as fine as I'd ever been.

"Thank you!" I yelled after the train while I snatched up my belongings. "Welcome to the Borderlands! Thank you very much! Delighted to be here!" I smoothed the wrinkled pages of the Yeats, tucked it in my pack, and called to the last distant puffing of smoke, "And wherefore have I crossed the seas and sands / To the shitty city of the Borderlands?"

Behind me, someone applauded. "Author!"

"Yeah, up yours, jack-o," I said, whirling on the hillside with my spare underwear in one hand.

Two people in dusty black leather straddled dustier black bikes on a road maybe two hundred feet uphill. In the shadow of an ancient oak tree, they'd been invisible until one of them clapped. Their skin was almost as dark as their hair, which rose from their heads like raven's wings. Their ears came to perfect points.

"Good pickings?" the second one called. A small difference in pitch or attitude told me that she was female, and the other, male. From where I stood, they looked identical.

He said, "I never knew where underwear grew. Find any with a twenty-eight-inch waist, I could use 'em."

"Love the valentines," said his twin.

I crammed my spare shorts into my pack. "You're, um, you're from Bordertown."

They laughed, baring long teeth. She said, "Whatever gave you that idea?"

"Your, um—" I started to point at my own ears, then snarled and returned to packing my stuff. "Pointy-eared dinks."

"My!" he said. "You do have an attitude."

"Our dinks have pointy ears?" she said. "The man speaks one strange language."

I snatched a rock and chucked it at them.

"No aim." She watched it pass eight or ten feet away. "But an attitude."

"Have we offended you?" he asked me.

"Do we care?" she asked him.

"He has an army hidden in the woods, or he's suicidal." The guy grinned. "He amuses me."

"He bores me. A vicious thing like that isn't a recruit or a meal."

I said, "Imagine how sorry that makes me." When they glanced my way, I wondered how fast I could run into the woods and how far they'd follow. He sat on a low-slung racer and probably wouldn't take it off the road. She sat on a dirt bike and looked like she'd enjoy the chase. They were both lean and strong and bigger than me. I began to wish I'd made a more sincere apology.

"Perhaps"—She raised a mocking eyebrow—"he's the lost heir of Elflands."

The guy laughed at my statement or at hers. "Yeah. I like him."

"You would." She shook her head once. Her neck was longer than his, her hair shorter. "Enjoy yourself." She slipped on a black helmet that'd hung on the back of her bike, and rocketed toward Bordertown. The pale blue exhaust smelled of wildflowers.

Magic. Staring after her, I complimented myself on my usual tact. I'd driven away one of the first two elves I'd met.

Looking at me, the guy said something like "So much for the family outing."

I limped through the long grass toward him. "The ladies adore me." He laughed, so I added, "Look, I don't have an army, and I'm not suicidal. I wasn't trying to hit you guys, anyway."

"Which is like an apology?"

"Yeah. I guess."

"But different at the end."

"Okay, I'm sorry." I walked past him, following the highway and the train toward Bordertown. "It's been a rough day."

"That must be rare for a well-spoken lad like yourself." He rocked his Yamaha off its stand and, still astride it, walked it along. His boots clapped on the gravelly shoulder of the road. I walked faster, ignoring the pain in my ankle. We followed a downward grade, so his bike rolled easily to keep up with me.

Wired into the guts of its stripped-down engine was something that looked like a cigar box sealed with duct tape and painted with Day-Glo pictograms. I pointed at it. "You push your bike up hills and coast down them, saying, 'Vroom, vroom'? No wonder your friend left."

The dark guy grinned. No smoke came from the exhaust, but when he twisted the throttle and lifted his boots from the graytop, the engine growled and the bike crept along beside me.

"Oh," I said cleverly. I'd heard a poem about "the wired bikes of Bordertown, spellbox driven." I'd thought "wired" meant they were always ready to race, and I'd pictured spellboxes as delicately carved cubes of ivory or diamond.

" 'Seas and sands'?" he quoted. His face was pitted like brick, but his bones were as fine as those in paintings of the rulers of Faerie. I'd heard that some elves dyed their hair and their skin to match human hues, but I couldn't imagine one scarring himself. His parents must've been a human and an elf.

"What do you want? 'And therefore from the train I was thrown down / By the buggered suburbs of the border town'?"

A corner of his mouth quirked upward. "We saw you get off the steel dragon."

"Didn't care for the company."

"Mmm. Want a ride to town?"

I didn't slow down. "As a meal or a recruit?"

He kept his smile. "Never heard of an elf or a halfie who liked long pig."

14

"So what're you recruiting me for?"

He shrugged. "You want food and a place to sleep, we've got both at Castle Pup."

I squinted.

"Home of the Strange Pupae. The Pups. We're a mixed bunch, humans and halfies and elves. Meaning neither the Pack nor the True Bloods like us, but they're too busy with each other to hassle us much."

"I don't know." I wanted to ask if his twin would be there.

"Unless," he said with a dismissing wave of his hand, "you've already reserved a suite at the B-town Hilton."

I smiled.

"Or perhaps your agents have purchased a mansion on Dragon's Tooth Hill?" He stroked his chin, which hadn't been shaved for several days. "You might put me up, then."

"No, I don't—" I caught myself.

"No mansion?"

"Sorry."

"And here I was thinking I'd make an excellent house-guest for a season or three. So why B-town?"

"None of—" Something flickered across his face, and I caught myself. The first thing I could think of was the truth, so I said it: "I'm hunting for my brother."

The halfie cocked his head to one side.

I added hopefully, "He looks like me, only older. His name's Tony."

"Has he got a mansion?"

"I doubt it."

"Damn." He frowned, then laughed. "B-town may surprise you; that's why we love it. But your brother won't be easy to find, mansion or no. When did he head out here?"

"He left"—I frowned—" 'bout a year ago."

"A year! Hoy!" The halfie grinned at me like I was the village idiot. "By now he's got a new name, new clothes, and new hair. Course, he might recognize *you*. If you don't change much when you get there. But everyone changes in Bordertown."

I shrugged.

"Castle Pup's a good place to hunt from."

I shrugged again.

He hit the throttle and swung his bike in front of me, blocking my way. "You look a gift horse in the mouth?"

"What'd politeness get the Trojans?"

He opened his jaw wide as if miming a yell. His teeth were long and white and strong like Bela Lugosi's in *Dracula*. "Happier?"

I grinned but said, "Thanks, man. I can walk."

His face closed itself up, becoming an emotionless mask that made me very aware that I was on a deserted road with a creature out of Faerie. "What've you got against elves or halfies, round ears?"

"Hey, not a thing," I said as quickly as I could.

He nodded. "Then I'll ask one last time. Care to visit majestic Castle Pup?" He gave me the deliberately charming smile. "You have five seconds." He rode his bike around me so I could keep walking if I wanted to. "Time."

What could I say? It felt like I was stepping in fire whenever I put my right foot down. If he'd wanted to hurt or rob me, he could've done that already. As his wrist began to cock back on the throttle, I said, "Well, if I won't be any trouble . . ."

He laughed. "Then I'll have erred wildly in inviting you. Hop on!"

I'd barely thrown a leg over the back of the seat when he hit the power. I lurched backward, grabbing his arm to

16

steady myself. The motor wailed like a drunken banshee as we picked up speed.

He laughed, louder than his engine, and yelled, "I'm Mooner—after a habit of my youth rather than the craters of my face! Headed anyplace special in B-town?"

"I'm Ron," I yelled back. "Anyplace special is exactly where I'm headed!"

CHAPTER THREE

BORDERTOWN

THE HIGHWAY TO BORDERTOWN LOOKS LIKE ANY HIGHWAY anywhere. No gold pavement, no will-o'-the-wisps for streetlights, just a broad ribbon of graytop in reasonable repair. I couldn't figure out why it was so beautiful. The hills and the trees were old and wild, but they didn't look weird—not in the old sense of the word, anyway. I wondered if someone had laid a glamour on the countryside so people would see it as exquisite. Then I began to laugh.

"There's a joke? Share it," Mooner called.

"You don't have billboards!" I don't know why that was funny. What did I expect, ads for delivery service by the 7-League Boots Co.? Fast food by Loaves and Fishes? ("When you have to feed the multitudes, remember us.") Exercise footgear by Red Slippers, Inc.? (" 'I couldn't stop dancing!' says typical customer. All shoes guaranteed to last a lifetime!")

18

Mooner's engine died without warning. As we slowed, I wondered if I'd be walking to Bordertown after all. Mooner used the silence to say, "Kids graffitied all the billboards till it wasn't worth maintaining 'em. Call it vandalism for the forces of good."

We were coasting uphill and slowing fast. Behind us, a semitrailer climbed relentlessly, its engine loud and healthy. I looked back to see an immense onrushing front grill painted like a Confederate flag. Mooner leaned the bike toward the side of the road, where we'd fall forty feet over the edge into a rocky stream if the semi didn't smush us into roadkill first. The semi swerved, no one was in the opposite lane, Mooner's bike roared back to life, and we rocketed. I closed my eyes again when Mooner passed the truck. The driver honked her horn and grinned. I began to wonder what people considered normal here.

When I felt ready to speak, I called in bursts over the engine's roar, "Why didn't . . . the truck's motor . . . stop, too?"

"Magic!" Mooner answered with a laugh, as if that explained everything. I suppose it did. Then he yelled, "Plus a redundancy system. Spellbox *and* motor. Expensive!"

His bike coughed several times after that, but each time it fired up before we'd rolled more than a yard or three. Mooner ignored it. Since the stalling happened less and less as we approached Bordertown, I ignored it, too.

In the country we met or passed two semis, a converted ambulance painted all over with murals, a group of kids on stripped-down motorcycles and scooters vaguely like Mooner's, a bicyclist, a pack of skateboarders dressed in rainbow colors, and a couple of hikers. The people who traveled the highway between Faerie and the World seemed an equal mix of elf and human, male and female.

The only thing they shared was an individual taste in clothing.

Near the city we encountered old cars and delivery vans as well as motorcycles. The cars included the kinds of automobiles you expect people with too much money to own, imported sports cars and immaculate antiques. I began to feel uneasy.

When we rounded the last hill, Bordertown sprawled before us. I stared and said, "It looks like any damn city in the World."

Mooner laughed. "It *was* any damn city in the World. Its soul changed, not its shape."

I saw modern housing and ancient malls with shops that sold things and shops that fixed things and restaurants that served food that was "good" because it was fast, schools and churches and libraries and banks and police stations that all looked alike because they had the same purpose of keeping contented citizens content, clean polished buildings furnished with clean polished people who happily transformed every place they lived into the same idealized hometown: some global network videoville where everyone ought to want to live. I saw the place I'd left.

If I'd been on my own bike, I would've turned around and never come back. I couldn't imagine that Tony would've ever wanted to come to anyplace like the city I saw.

Mooner darted between milk trucks and furniture vans, whipped past Ferraris and MGs and Toyotas driven by business-types whose suits wouldn't call attention to them in the World, though their ears would. Brakes squealed in our wake. I heard metal colliding with metal, but I didn't look back.

When I dared open my eyes again, I saw I'd misjudged the fast-food edge of Bordertown. Blocks of businesses had never reopened. Blocks of houses stood empty. Lawns were mowed, but windows were boarded up and only a few neighborhoods seemed to be inhabited. Someone was trying to create an enclave of Worldly normalcy on the border of the Bordertown, but someone was failing.

My first sight of the real Bordertown was an overgrown park where a drummer, a fiddler, and a kid on a Fender Spellcaster made music while people picnicked and danced. I would've joined them in an instant, but Mooner didn't slow or even look their way. All I could do was smile and wave.

The next clue that Bordertown wasn't the place I'd left was a ruined church that twisted around itself as if magic had brought it to life and someone had barely managed to kill it before it could slither away. Then I looked up. Among the older, human structures, strange crystalline forms rose. I yelled, "We're not in Kansas anymore!"

"Do tell, Dorothy? Or is it Toto?"

"*R-rrf! R-rrf!*" I barked. I couldn't see myself in ruby slippers.

We passed parks and wooded streets and old government and university buildings. I began to see that the city must've been beautiful before Faerie returned. Maybe that was why Faerie hadn't swallowed it.

We cut from blocks of mansions to neighborhoods that might've been firebombed. Mooner wove around potholes and bumped over bad spots where road crews had made halfhearted fixes to streets that no taxpaying citizen of Bordertown would ever travel. Here the inhabitants wore rags, and they watched us with wary eyes.

Near the docks the smell of the Mad River was thick

and soporific, sweet and fetid like sweat or blood or the beach after a storm. An old woman pushed a wheelbarrow of tentacled fish across the street. She cursed us when Mooner snatched one.

"Here!" He dropped it over his shoulder into my lap. I almost gagged. The dead fish had two sets of eyes, one above the other, a misshapen mouth filled with teeth like a shark's, and leathery skin instead of scales. "Dinner," Mooner explained. I decided to celebrate my first night in Bordertown by fasting.

"Soho," Mooner yelled as we passed through the gloomy arch of Old Gate and headed up a dusty avenue.

A rusty, shot-out sign said we rode on Ho Street. I grinned and waved the dead fish by its tail in a circle above my head and whooped until Mooner glanced back over his shoulder with a condescending grin.

Soho's air smelled of old garbage and wood smoke. Something drifting from across the Border reminded me of waffles and orange blossoms. Many buildings, clad in fading or shredded coats of paint, leaned on their neighbors for support. Others showed that their inhabitants loved them. One club had a new matte black finish, marred only by graffiti scrawled in glowing faerie dust. Each board of a wooden frame house had been painted a different shade of blue so that its roof seemed to merge with the sky.

I studied the kids in the streets and wondered if I looked like a know-nothing runaway. Some humans wore black leather; some elves, red. Most people seemed to wear what they pleased. Under bright scarves and buttons and studs, clothes showed signs of wear in rips or stains or faded colors, just like mine. Styles of hair ranged from completely shaven to hip-length, braided or tangled or combed,

22

natural or dyed. I couldn't be sure what anyone's natural hair color was: some elves had hair as brown as mine, and some humans had hair as silvery-fine as any elf's.

I saw a kid who, for a second, looked like Tony. It was the glasses and the lock of hair across the forehead and the way he laughed as he hugged a female elf in gray leather. But he was too tall and too thin, and he didn't really have Tony's features at all.

We turned from Ho onto Market and stopped in front of a squat orangish stone fortress with boarded windows on the first floor and mostly cracked glass on the next two. A tarnished plaque beside the front door read: MERCHANTS' EXCHANGE BUILDING.

I said, "I don't have any merchants to exchange."

"Be respectful." Mooner dismounted. "You want a place to stay in town, this is it. Welcome to Castle Pup."

A little kid with silver hair sat cross-legged on the wall by the steps. I couldn't tell if the kid was male or female, human or elf. All I saw were the tangle of hair, tiny shoulders, and an adult's green T-shirt worn as a tunic. A Bowie knife hung like a sword from a thin beaded belt wrapped twice around the kid's waist. The belt had an inscription beginning FL—.

Mooner, flipping the kid a crumpled Good Stuff candy bar, said, "Don't kill him, Florida. Ron's staying with us for tonight, at least. Right?"

"Uh, yeah," I said. "I s'pose—"

Florida nodded, studying me through impenetrable bangs.

"C'mon," Mooner said.

The door stood ajar, so I followed, kicking through leaves and candy wrappers and broken bottles and things I didn't want to study too closely. Florida's head turned to follow us. I lifted the stolen fish a few inches in salute as we passed.

"I hadn't decided—" I began.

"You said someplace special."

"Well, yeah, but—"

The inner hall was dark and cool and smelled of burnt grease, decaying vegetables, incense, and sweat. More litter rustled underfoot, and something ran across the far floor. I decided to think it was a cat or a dog. A murmur of conversation and the bass throb of loud music came from above.

"Doesn't come more special than this. Unless you thought of another place to stay."

"Well, no, but—"

"Then it's decided. I'll introduce you around, find you some floor space. Hungry?"

I thought of the fish that I carried, and wasn't sure how to answer.

"Durward or Wiseguy's probably fixed something, if no one else has."

"Okay." Wide marble stairs curved up to the second floor. As we climbed, I said, "Y'know, there was an accident back on the road."

"Could be."

"I mean, we might've caused it. When you cut in—"

"You can't take the traffic, get off the highway." He stopped on the steps. A bar of light from a broken window fell across his pocked cheek and one pointed ear. The lobe was split where an earring had been torn free. His eyes were in shadow as he grinned.

"Uh. Yeah. I s'pose." I shrugged.

"You'll do." Laughing, he clapped me on the shoulder, and we headed up. The music and talking grew louder as

24

we climbed. The light grew brighter. Hooks lined the stairway for paintings that must've been removed when the owners fled from the return of Faerie. Now the hooks held small animal skulls, an impaled snare drum, a mummified squirrel, a plastic crucifix, a warped laser disk, a few condoms, and a heart-shaped box made of cardboard and red foil. On the banister at the top of the stairs sat a glass bottle that held a large pig fetus floating in cloudy water.

Mooner tapped the bottle's lid as we passed. "H'lo, Festus." It might have bobbed or nodded back. I found myself expecting it to open its eyes, and I kept glancing back over my shoulder until we were far beyond it.

A couple of elves, a large gray dog, and an obese human girl slept in a nest of army blankets in the hall. We walked by them, and the sounds and smells of human habitation grew stronger. Something danceable and distorted blasted from behind a closed door; I thought I recognized a Sins of the Pioneers tune. Two babies cried in a crib in another room, where several children played a game that involved tagging the crib, or maybe the babies, whenever they ran by.

A kid who looked a little younger than me stood in the doorway of the farthest room. He stepped aside as we approached. "Mooner! Good hunting in the Nevernever?"

Mooner's grunt might've been an acknowledgment that the kid had spoken, or it might've just been a grunt. The kid glanced at me, but since Mooner ignored him, I did, too.

"Oh, not again," someone said within the room.

CHAPTER FOUR

CASTLE PUP

MAYBE THIRTY OR FORTY PEOPLE WERE IN THE ROOM, more humans than elves. I didn't have time to sort them out. The room was in chaos as humans and elves and cats and dogs ran frantically around, chasing small brown things across the parquet floor.

Almost everyone yelled at each other. Over the racket of excited people lay a squeaky babble that sounded like "*—un, run, fast—*" "*—ead man, ru—*" "*—me, I'm—*"

"Got one!" someone cried, holding her prize in the air.

I looked, then stared. In the elfin girl's fist a gingerbread man squirmed, still adding his squeals to his brothers' high-pitched chorus: "*Can't catch me! Can't catch me!*"

"Watch it!" An Oriental kid pointed near us.

Mooner stamped his foot down. A gingerbread man fell backward to avoid being crushed. It lay on the floor as if it'd never been alive. When Mooner reached out, it scooted behind a case of laser disks, shrieking, *"Fast as you can, you can't catch me!"*

A tiger-colored cat raced after two of the cookie men. When it almost had them, one turned right and one turned left. The cat slid into the side of a battered couch. The gingerbread men made a sound like hysterical laughter. So did someone else.

In a stuffed chair across the room, a kid in jeans and a black T-shirt, her face half-hidden under a puff of dandelion hair, sat clutching her legs to her chest and rolling from side to side. She seemed to be the only person in the room enjoying this. Besides me, that is.

"Leda!" shouted a redheaded guy in square steel-framed glasses. "It's not funny!" He took a quick step forward, proving that he hadn't noticed two cookie men tying his sneaker laces together. He fell onto a battered couch, and Leda giggled and pointed.

"I'm the gingerbread man!" the two cookies sang triumphantly.

"All right!" I jabbed my fist twice in the air in delight. "Ma-*gic!* Ma-*gic!*"

Mooner's twin held wriggling gingerbread men between the thumb and forefinger of each dark hand. She glanced at me and said to Mooner, "You brought the lost heir. How thoughtful."

She wore a black leather jacket draped with chains, a gray Danceland T-shirt, and dirty purple chinos tucked into low blood-red boots. When she came near, I saw that her skin was as pitted as Mooner's. His made him look dangerous. Hers made her look vulnerable as well, which made her look even more dangerous.

Mooner's grin may've been directed at her, or maybe at three gingerbread men that scampered in front of him, trying to scoot into the hall. I stepped farther into the room to get a better look, and something tugged on my pants.

I glanced down. My leg was half-covered by Mooner's mutant fish. When I shifted the fish, I saw a gingerbread man climbing my pants, clutching the cloth between its fingerless hands. Its squeaks sounded like human speech played in fast-forward: *"Can't catch me, can't catch me!"*

I jerked back, almost dropping the fish, then realized I'd been scared by a five-inch-long cookie with raisin eyes and a sugar frosting tie. No one else in the room was acting afraid of the gingerbread men, not even a diapered two-year-old who chased them, fell over, laughed, and chased them again as if there were nothing more wonderful in the world.

My cookie man clung to my leg like a rodeo rider. Its cries of *"Can't catch me!"* seemed more like begging than bragging. I boosted it into a pocket of Tony's jacket. It squeaked in what might've been gratitude until I made a *shh!* sound.

In the mayhem no one noticed. Mooner's twin had shifted her two gingerbread men to one hand and reached for a third that slipped under a chair. "So who gave her the peca?" she asked, nodding toward Leda, who was still laughing.

"I just got here." Mooner kicked at a cookie man and missed it.

"Uh huh." His twin gave her captive cookie men to someone else and went to the laughing girl. She put her arm around Leda's thin shoulders and spoke too quietly for me to hear.

The redheaded guy in glasses brought out an aluminum soup pot. "Dump 'em in here," he said, and everyone began to drop indignant gingerbread men into the pot. I didn't say anything about the hitcher in my pocket.

The gingerbread men shrieked, *"Can't! Can't!"* until the redhead clapped the lid over them. Then they were as quiet as birds whose cages had been covered.

"That's all?" Red asked, wearily and hopefully.

"I think the dogs got a few," said someone.

"I told her it wasn't funny," said Red.

"She didn't do it on purpose," said Mooner's twin, as though the blond girl weren't sitting right beside her. "She was just trying to make a treat for the little kids."

"Some treat." Red looked at several small children with crumbs on their cheeks.

"Uh, you're not going to cook 'em alive, are you?" I nodded at the big kitchen pot.

Mooner laughed wickedly. "Hah, yes! Cannibal sublimation!"

The young kid that we'd ignored at the door said, "They aren't alive. They're just animated."

"Never eat anything that's thrashing around. That's what I say," said Mooner. "Except for—" A tall plump woman with mixed elf and Oriental features elbowed him, and he gasped something like a laugh.

"Can you undo this?" Mooner's twin asked Leda, flicking her hand toward the captive gingerbread men.

Leda said quietly, "Sure." When everyone around her began to look a little more relaxed, she added, "Wouldn't every magician study how to *unmake* cookies?" She guffawed.

I laughed, too. For some reason everyone stared at me rather than her.

A tall elf I hadn't noticed in the chaos said, "Her magic may undo itself shortly."

"Wouldn't count on it," said the halfie with Oriental features."

"No," the elf agreed. He wore torn blue jeans, black cavalier boots, and a ruffled white silk shirt open almost to his waist. His white hair was tied at the back of his head like a samurai's. His features were elvishly perfect: high cheekbones, flaring eyebrows, lips that seemed ready to laugh, eyes the color of smoke.

I didn't hate him immediately. I pitied him. There are three desirable things that a guy can have: height, looks, and brains. The odds of getting all three are so slim that he probably needed help tying his shoes. Then I noticed the way that the Oriental halfie was looking at him, and I realized that he'd never have trouble finding help if he wanted it. *That's* when I hated him.

"Could eat 'em as they are," said Mooner. " 'Bite they little heads off, Nibble on they tiny feet.' "

"You're such an animal," said an admiring human girl with blue hair.

Leda groaned.

"I better put her to bed," said Mooner's twin.

"Leda go beddy-bye," Leda agreed. That began her next giggling spell. Mooner's twin raised an eyebrow at Mooner, then took her away. As she did, the cloud of dandelion hair swung away from Leda's face.

I'd thought she was human because she was smaller than me, but her ears rose to points and her irises were disks of white gold. She didn't look like a halfie, or if she had any human blood, I couldn't see it. She was simply smaller than any elf I'd ever heard of.

The red-haired guy put the pot of gingerbread men onto a scarred conference table, next to a kettle of black-bean soup simmering over a camping stove. He said, "Well, they're quiet now. I'll check on them later."

"The magic never left the animal crackers," said the kid Mooner had ignored at the door. "They just got old and stiff."

"I saw one that got rained on," someone else said. "It got all mushy and flopped around and sort of disintegrated. It was pretty gross."

That seemed to be the end of the excitement. People moved away to cluster in small groups and chat or nap or nod to the music, an early Cats Laughing album. The dogs wandered among them. A few of the cats watched from or slept on long oak shelves that suggested the room had once been a library. Most of them found me extremely interesting now that the cookie men weren't available to play with. I slung Mooner's fish over my shoulder and tried to look like a bad person to steal a fish from.

"How's Leda?" Mooner asked as his twin returned.

"Communing with her muse." They shared a look I couldn't read, as if they were dueling without words or deeds.

"And here I haven't had the chance to introduce her new servitor."

"A shame," said the topknotted elf in the silk shirt. He also received a look from Mooner that I noticed but wasn't interested in analyzing.

"Excuse me," I said. "What's this servitor crap?"

"Mooner's humor." His twin, glancing at me, stood near me for the first time. Her eyes were pale green, like the sea in the rain on a sunny day. I thought to myself, La Belle Dame sans Merci me hath in thrall! Hot damn.

"Oh," I said. "Um, I'm Ron Starb— Uh, just Ron."

"Come to the Borderlands from a distant, insignificant home in the World." She raked me once with her gaze. "Where you were fed and clothed and educated, but never understood, and mistreated in ways that left no mark."

"Sometimes they left marks." I spoke as matter-of-factly as I could.

She nodded. "Which you hid under your clothing, from the World and yourself, until you could bear it no longer and sought Bordertown and freedom."

"Hey, what is—?" I started to whirl about and march away. "Forget this. Bye, bye, blackbird."

The perfectly manicured hand that caught my shoulder belonged to the topknotted elf. "Wiseguy means nothing by it. That's her nature."

"Her nature? What is she, a dog or something?"

Wiseguy smiled. "Sorry. I always forget how humans respond to hearing what they didn't know they showed."

"Yeah, right," I said.

The topknotted elf said, "No elf would blame another for reading what was writ for all to see." He raised an eyebrow at Mooner. "Though an elf might challenge one who read aloud."

I stared at him. Beside me, Mooner laughed. "Strider's just out of the Elflands. He's explaining that to be kind, not to slap you upside the head again."

"Strider," I repeated skeptically.

The tall elf nodded. "Leda's humor. As good a name as any, and it bears a fine heritage."

Mooner's amusement disappeared as soon as Strider mentioned Leda. I said, "Right." I nodded at Mooner's twin. "Wiseguy." Then at the pale guy. "Strider. Got it so far."

The redhead touched his chest. "Durward." He grinned and held out a hand. "If the elves get too weird, I'm always happy to talk."

As we shook, the woman with Asian and Elflands features said, "And then you'll think the elves aren't weird at all. I'm Sai."

Durward chuckled. I nodded and said to Wiseguy, "Okay. This is your place?"

Wiseguy shook her head. "It's Leda's if it's anyone's. You'll meet the real her when she wakes up. Today wasn't typical."

"Becoming a little too typical," Sai muttered.

"I swear," Durward said, "I was only going to bake some cookies. Did I ask her to help? No way, José. Who could've stopped her?"

Sai put her hand on his shoulder. "Ease on, Durward. No sweat, no fret."

"Uh, I don't want to put anyone out," I said. "Mooner said I could stay here, but—"

"Then stay you shall," said Wiseguy, with another look at her twin. She pointed at the dead fish over my shoulder. "Is that your companion or your luggage?"

"It's somebody's dinner," I said. "We, uh, caught it on the way over."

"Whose work?" Sai asked.

Mooner made a small bow as Durward asked me, "What can you do?"

Wiseguy answered for me, "Swear, with vigor if not imagination. And he has a gift for rhyme of a rude and simple sort. Or perhaps it's only a gift for mockery. And he somersaults from trains."

I shrugged, a little embarrassed. "We all have our specialties."

"We found him out at Stowaway's Bump," Mooner told Sai. "Getting off the Express a little early."

"The soup needs another hour," Durward said kindly. "But if you're hungry now, Sparks scavenged a bag of two-day-old bagels from behind the Delhi Deli. Mixed kinds that all smell like garlic and onion now."

"Garlic and cinnamon-raisin," said Mooner. "My favorite."

"Sounds fine," I said, less because I was hungry and more because I hated being the center of attention.

"You stay, you work." Wiseguy flicked her eyes toward Mooner. "S'posed to be true for everyone."

I said, " 'S cool. You want me burning food or breaking things?"

"You wash dishes tonight," Wiseguy said. "Don't break more than one if you want breakfast."

"There's an extra mattress in King O'Beer's room," Sai said. "You might as well take it."

I felt I was being dismissed, but that was fine. "How far's Mock Avenue?"

"Just a few blocks," Sai said.

"Into elf turf," Mooner added.

"Why?" said Wiseguy.

"I heard there was a bookstore there." I shrugged. "Thought I'd look it over."

Wiseguy and Mooner gave each other a glance. Mooner asked me, "You got money?"

A little in my pocket and more fastened around my ankle, I could've said. "Don't need money to look."

"How'd you hear about Elsewhere?" Wiseguy asked.

"Met the owner on the train."

Mooner nodded. "Bit of a bitch, eh?"

I hadn't thought so, but I said, "I s'pose."

"Mickey's all right," Wiseguy said.

Immediately regretting agreeing with Mooner, I shrugged. "She didn't bug me."

"I'll escort you sometime *mañana*," Mooner said. "The guided tour and all."

Wiseguy looked at him, catching his eye before she spoke. "Mooner."

He grinned. "What else can I do for my protégé? He can't get in trouble looking at books."

"You could," Wiseguy said. The others became quiet. Sai and Durward glanced away, but Strider watched them with amused fascination.

"Sister." Mooner put his hand over his heart. "You misjudge me."

"Never again."

"I'll keep the kid from foolish errors. He'll not walk widdershins around a cemetery nor call a True Blood a fairy while I'm with him." Mooner traced an X across his chest. "Trust me."

Wiseguy looked at me, so I gave her my best grin. She sighed. "Hoy. You probably deserve each other."

CHAPTER FIVE

FUN WITH
FLORIDA

After dinner I learned that King O'Beer was the kid Mooner had ignored when we arrived. Our little room had probably been an office; the basic layout was toto boringo, a box with a couple of windows on one wall. King O'Beer had built or inherited a loft that I admired and desired, a frame of thick wooden beams that you reached by a rope ladder. He'd pasted magazine photos of the night sky on the ceiling and had a low table up there, along with an oil lamp and a potted cactus that must've weighed fifty pounds.

On the floor in the other half of the room, a futon with a purple paisley bedspread lay against one wall. Near that was a small bookshelf with a few paperbacks in it and a pine chest covered with candles embedded in a multicolored lava flow of wax.

King O'Beer lit a lamp by the door with a candle that we'd brought up from the common room. When he turned to me, I nodded and said, "Pretty sharp."

"That's yours." He pointed at a stained narrow mattress in the dust in the shadows under the loft.

"Who's got the futon?"

"Sparks. They sell 'em in the market, but you need cash or good trading stock to get one. They got an arrangement with some truckers to handle things that don't work right here, like computers and electronic stuff. If you've got anything—" He looked at the empty watchband on my wrist.

I said, "Figures. What's Sparks like?"

"We get along."

"Why do they call you King O'Beer?"

"Some joke of Mooner's. Back home they called me Buddy."

"King O'Beer's better'n that."

He grinned shyly. "Yeah."

I smiled back, then decided that I shouldn't get too friendly until I knew more about his status in the Pups. Before I could say anything, King O'Beer stared at his dirty toes or his dirty blue rubber sandals and said, "You're lucky."

"Huh?"

"Mooner likes you."

"Well . . ."

"He doesn't like me much."

I could've told him why: King O'Beer's feelings rose as sloppily to his face as a puppy's. Mooner probably thought I was all right because I was like him, tough. Problem with that theory was the elves hadn't ragged King O'Beer about what his face showed and what it hid. Maybe he'd already gotten the lecture. Maybe his truths were so blatant that they might as well've been in sky-writing, so the elves didn't bother him.

Which made me wonder why Mooner was helping me. "Hey. Mooner's not . . .?" I waggled my fingers.

"Gay?" said King O'Beer.

"Yeah."

King O'Beer laughed. "No!"

"Good." I bent down to dust off the mattress under the loft.

"I am."

I stood up fast and banged my head on a loft beam. "You okay?"

When I looked at him, I could imagine women thinking him cute, with his curly black hair and his lean body. That'd carry over to homosexual boys and men, wouldn't it? I didn't want to think about that. "Uh, yeah. Um, I'm not. Gay, I mean."

He smiled. "That's all right."

"What'd they think when they said I could sleep up here?"

"That Sparks and I had an extra mattress."

"Oh."

King O'Beer laughed. "I won't bring anyone home without your permission if you won't bring anyone home without mine. Sparks and I have the same deal. Fair enough?"

"Uh, yeah," I said, very carefully casual, having never brought a date home with or without anyone's permission.

"If it makes you feel safer, you're not my type. And Sparks likes her men tall and older. Preferably dark-skinned and half-elvish with sweeping black hair."

"Her?"

He heard enough of my emotions to laugh. "The kid with indigo hair."

"The one mooning over Mooner?"

"Yep. Sometimes we sit up at night, trying to decide if his eyes are sea-green or emerald-green."

"If you plan to debate that tonight, you don't need to wake me."

"You think you're immune?"

"Hey, Wiseguy has me ready to ride at a moment's notice. Not her brother."

"Wiseguy?" It was his turn to stare. Then he laughed, clutching his stomach and falling onto Sparks's futon. "Oh, you poor, poor boy!"

"We're not talking the great love of my life here. You think Mooner's cute, that's cool. But I'll take his sister or the short elf any day."

"Wiseguy or Leda." King O'Beer rolled onto his back and shook his head. "I wonder if Sai saw that when she suggested you crash here. You and me and Sparks, we're charter members of the Unattainable Passions Marching Society."

"Mmm." I stood there, wondering if I really wanted to share a room with a gay male and a straight female. Either would be strange, but the combination made me extremely uncomfortable.

King O'Beer grabbed the edge of his loft and swung himself up. "You can get the light?"

"Uh, sure." It was too late to try to find a place to sleep in a park. "Mind if I let it burn awhile?" I went back to dusting off the mattress.

"Treat the room like it's yours. It is, y'know."

"Thanks." As soon as he was out of sight, I put my hand in my pocket. The cookie man grabbed my fingers with his paws, and I almost sighed. Life would've been simpler if he'd turned back into an ordinary cookie, yet I was glad that he was still alive, or animated or whatever. All I wanted was to find a place to let him go where he might survive for however long a magicked cookie lives.

King O'Beer hung his head over the side of the loft, smiling upside down. "G'night, sweet prince."

"Hey! I'm not—" I twisted, hiding the cookie man with my body.

"I know. Thought you might get cold." He handed me a faded army blanket. "Night-night."

I stayed up for an hour or two, reading Yeats by candlelight and thinking about Tony and what I should do next. Those thoughts kept being interrupted by memories of Wiseguy: pale green eyes and high scarred cheeks, long thighs in tight jeans, a haughty smile, a laugh, a smell like wildflowers.

When I was sure King O'Beer was asleep, I cleared out my pack, laid it on its side, and put the cookie man in it. I fell asleep before Sparks returned. I never did decide if I was relieved or insulted that I wasn't King O'Beer's type.

Something woke me in the middle of the night. Huddling in the cold under the rough woolen blanket, I shivered and listened. Someone was playing harpsichord music far away. Maybe that'd woken me. But I thought I'd heard a wail of despair, something that said all things go wrong, something that reminded me of Tony.

Maybe the harpsichordist had broken a string and cried out in frustration. Maybe I'd dreamed the wail, though that wouldn't make sense: I'd made it to Bordertown. I'd found a place to stay. All I had to do was find Tony and bring him back.

Then I heard the cry distinctly, distant and hurt and inhuman. The wind, I decided, and eventually I fell back to sleep.

I woke up alone in the room. The cookie man had crawled out of my pack and gone to sleep by my head. I poked it, and it stretched its limbs, then danced in place while looking at me. Stuffing the Yeats and my gear in my pack, I dressed, wondering what cookies did for breakfast, then tucked him back in my jacket pocket.

Sai had shown me the bathing and toilet facilities the night before. I found my way to the roof and the little wooden outhouse. The whole roof smelled like my aunt's farm. Durward and Sai and some of the others had built composting and gardening bins out of scrap lumber. Wash water came from barrels of cold rainwater. While I was scrubbing my face, a bald elf came up, said "Hi," and took off her shirt to scrub herself, putting a severe strain on my ability to play it totally blasé.

When I entered the common room, Mooner was talking with the blue-haired kid who had to be Sparks and a buck-toothed human girl who looked my age. Mooner'd abandoned his leather in favor of a black tank top. I wore Tony's jacket despite the warm morning, 'cause I'd decided to free the gingerbread man somewhere outside of Castle Pup.

Durward tossed me an orange, which I began to peel and eat. "Yo," I said, nodding to the girls. "I'm, uh, Ron."

"Hi, Aaron, I'm Sparks. Sleep well?" My supposed roomie was skinny, maybe an inch taller than me, with a very round face, a small chin, and a broken nose.

"Oh, yeah, fine." I wondered where she'd slept, but couldn't think of a discreet question that'd inspire her to tell me.

"I'm Star Raven," her friend announced.

"Oh," I said. Behind her, Mooner rolled his eyes.

"My name came to me in a dream," she said.

"Nightmare," Mooner whispered.

"Oh, you!" Star Raven giggled and swatted Mooner.

"C'mon, Ron, save me," Mooner said. "See you," he told the girls, and stalked toward the hall and the stairs. I gave Sparks and Star Raven a nod that undoubtedly made me look spastic. They laughed together as we left, and I felt a little lonely.

I said, "You know King O'Beer's gay?"

"Yeah?" Mooner didn't look at me. "I'm mighty cheery myself sometimes."

"You know. He's a faggot."

"He's a bundle of sticks?"

"He likes guys," I said, exasperated. "I'm s'posed to sleep in his room?"

"He bother you last night?"

"No, but if he does—"

Mooner gave me a heels-to-head scan. "I don't think you've got a lot to worry about, Do-Ron."

"Thanks steaming loads, man."

Mooner grinned his pleased, long-toothed smile. He jerked a thumb at my pack. "Planning to leave us already?"

"Just hate to leave my stuff behind."

The obese woman and the two elves were still asleep, or asleep again, on the mattress in the hall. As we stepped over them, Mooner murmured, "Rat bait."

"Huh?"

"Leda puts up with too much."

"Them?" I jerked my thumb over my shoulder.

"Yeah. Strawberry's hooked on the River, and her boyfriends are always sipping peca. They'll do the lightfingers on someone's goods one day, then make a fast fade to black.

All we'll ever hear is that they've been seen running with Wharf Rats. Who needs it?"

"Leda's got a soft heart?"

"Goes with her head." He slapped the top of the pig fetus's jar on the balcony with a "Later, Festus," and took the stairs two at a time. I caught up with him on the front steps.

Florida lay curled in the shade by one wall. A silver-blue eye opened in the pale mat of hair as we came out, and the kid stood up. Mooner rubbed the top of Florida's head. A grin may've flickered under the kid's dirty nose. "Do-Ron and I're heading elfside. Want to tag?"

Florida stared and didn't give any answer, but as Mooner walked away, the kid followed. After a minute or two of silence I told Florida, "You ought to rest your jaw now and then. Give someone else a chance to talk."

Florida growled and dropped a hand to the hilt of the big Bowie knife. I jumped back.

"Kid's dumb," Mooner said. "In the original sense. *¿Comprende?*"

"Uh." I didn't feel so witty all of a sudden.

We walked on. Mooner led without a backward glance. I put one hand into my jacket pocket to see how the gingerbread man was doing. It clutched my finger between its brittle arms, and I yanked my hand out. Florida looked at me, surprisingly quizzically for someone with a face hidden by hair, and reached toward my pocket. I shook my head, and Florida shrugged.

We passed a few elves in red leather. They only nodded coolly at us. I was disappointed. I wanted duels with magic spells or switchblades carved with runes, impromptu dance challenges or rhyming contests. I couldn't tell anything about Mooner's mood, so I didn't ask why we walked instead of taking his bike. Maybe he wanted the exercise, or maybe he wanted to give Florida a chance to play mascot. Later I realized that he'd been showing me off as the newest member of his personal band, but I never decided if he did that for my safety or his vanity.

"What do you want at Elsewhere?" Mooner called.

I jerked my attention from a hand-lettered sign on the front of a little store proclaiming: FORTUNES TOLD! CHARMS SOLD! SPELLBOXES POWERED! LOVE AND MILK SOURED! CURSES LIFTED, CURSES LAID! ANY SPELL IF WE GET PAID! SHOP MAGIC FREDDY'S FOR DISCOUNT MAGIC! ANYTHING LESS WOULD SURELY BE TRAGIC! "I don't know. To look at the books."

"Not to get a job?"

I glanced at him, but he wasn't looking at me. "Why'd I want a job?"

"You're planning to stick around town."

"For a while."

He shrugged, amazingly innocent. "Nice to have a steady source of cash. Something to contribute to the upkeep of Castle Pup or the occasional special project. Who knows?"

"Hadn't really thought about it."

"Think fast," he said. "We're almost there."

I nearly tripped over Florida when the kid stopped without warning. I began, "Jeez, Flor—," then closed my mouth. Florida was staring down the street, making a high-pitched rasping sound.

Four elf motorcyclists, three male, one female, rolled quietly toward us. They didn't seem to be Soho sorts. They looked too immaculate, as if dust wouldn't settle on them. They rode sleek, expensive bikes imported from the World. Their clothes were new leather and silk and linen. Two of them had hair as pale and long as Strider's. One guy's hair had been dyed red and yellow like fire, and the female's was short and so dark that it ate sunlight.

Mooner smiled. "Bunch of rich kids from Dragon's Tooth Hill. Nothing to worry—"

The elf with the matte black hair nodded toward us, and the bikers swerved onto the sidewalk.

"Hey!" Mooner shouted. "What's—?" Two of the males aimed for him, cutting him off from Florida and me. The other two came straight at me. "Grab Florida!" Mooner shouted. I was already snagging a wrist, just as the dark-haired elf caught the kid's other arm.

Florida writhed between us, unable to reach the sheathed Bowie knife. The elf and I looked at each other over Florida's head. The elf's irises, like her hair, consumed light, reflecting nothing. "Let go!" she whispered. I almost obeyed because it seemed oddly right that I should.

Something wrenched my shoulder: the fire-haired elf tried to pull me over. His attempt worked against him. Florida slipped free of Matte Black's grip, and we fell against the male, toppling his bike. I hit the sidewalk, and Florida fell on me.

Firehair skidded into the road, where a delivery truck screeched to a halt before him. The driver, a big swarthy man, yelled something about "Crazy kids" and waited in his cab to see what would happen next.

Mooner had grabbed a bristleless broom from a trash heap and held it two-handed before him like a samurai sword. Two of the elves circled their bikes lazily in front of him, keeping him away from us. Matte Black waited in the street while Firehair rose, shook himself, and remounted.

The truck driver shouted, "Don't you kids have anything better to do than fight?" which sounded reasonable to me, but the elves ignored him. The female lifted her chin toward us, and Mooner shouted, "Get Florida out of here. I'll hold 'em back."

I hoisted the kid over one shoulder and ran into an alley. Florida kicked wildly. Glancing back, I saw that Mooner stood in the mouth of the alley, keeping the elves at bay. I looked at the backs of buildings as I ran, hoping for an open door or a broken window. If I could cut through a deserted building, I could lose the elves and make it back to Castle Pup. I said, "Relax, Florida, we're almost—"

Gravel sprayed ahead of us. I looked up to see Matte Black leaning her bike into the far end of the alley and racing toward us, grinning coolly. Firehair came a little more cautiously behind her. I looked back. Their friends were still keeping Mooner busy. Every nearby door and window was closed or boarded up.

"Mooner!" I yelled, and leaped for the nearest door, hoping it was unlocked. It wasn't. Mooner turned and ran toward us. As soon as he did, one of the white-haired bikers slipped past him, and I knew Florida and I were trapped.

A wailing arose nearby, quietly at first, then louder. I thought the Silver Suits or fire trucks were coming, then thought I was hearing storm or air raid sirens. The sound grew louder and deeper. I felt as if I'd been swimming in warm water and suddenly been caught by cold currents.

Something like mist swooped toward Matte Black and Firehair. They braked and brought up their arms to bat it away, but their blows passed through it. The wailing intensified within my skull.

"Ignore it," Matte Black shouted.

Firehair stared at her. "*You* ignore it."

"It can't hurt us."

"You know that?"

As I stared, the invisible took form. Mist etched itself into the shape of a tall, slender woman with billowing hair and pale robes. She reached toward the two white-haired elves and screamed in anger and pain and desperate fear.

They fled. Matte Black looked from them to me and whispered, "Very well." As her right hand drew back on the throttle and her left foot lifted from the pavement, I yanked Florida behind me.

Matte Black glanced at us, then at Mooner running hard. She smiled and wheeled her bike. By the time Mooner reached us, Matte Black and Firehair had left the alley. The woman made of mist was nowhere to be seen.

Mooner grinned, dropped the broom, and gasped for air. "Welcome to Bordertown."

I sat on a cracked cement step and tried to breathe normally. "What was that about?"

"Probably nothing. Someone's been snatching little kids and leaving them a few blocks away from where they grabbed 'em. Looks like it's some game for Dragon's Tooth Hill brats."

"You could've told me. I was scared, man."

Mooner shrugged. "They didn't tell me what it was about. And just 'cause the kids we know about turned up okay doesn't mean it's all right. You shouldn't mess with little kids." He set his hand on Florida's head. "You okay?"

Florida nodded once and shook the hand away. I smiled; Tony and I'd played out the same scene when we were younger.

Mooner laughed. "Good. You did all right, Ron."

I shrugged. "Wasn't me. If it hadn't been for that thing—"

"Thing?"

"That woman. The wailing woman. All misty—"

He squinted at me. "The White Lady appeared?"

"I guess. Scared the sh—"

"You see it?" he asked Florida. The kid's head shook quickly. Mooner said, "People've heard it. Sometimes at night, it sounds like it's in our backyard. I don't know anyone who's seen it up close. And I haven't heard of it protecting anyone."

He studied me until I felt uncomfortable and stood.

"Some people just live right," I said. "Where's this bookstore?"

CHAPTER SIX

ELSEWHERE

ELSEWHERE STOOD BETWEEN AN ORIENTAL GROCERY AND AN art gallery. All three looked like most stores in the neighborhood, tiny and dark and run-down. Wu's Worldly Emporium smelled of spices and vegetables and fish and fresh-baked noodles. The Mock Avenue Gallery of Fine and Not So Fine Art smelled of sawdust and oil paint. Elsewhere smelled of dust and the old magic of books.

Wu's was open and busy. An elderly black woman and a Native American kid in biker gear and a few young elves waited to be served by a middle-aged Asian woman, who was measuring powders from a wooden cabinet that looked like an antique library card catalog.

The Mock Avenue Gallery was closed and busy. Behind a faerie abstract painting that filled the front window, several elves and humans hung fluorescent canvases for a new show called "Low Fashion and Faerie Dust."

Elsewhere was open and dark. I would've thought it abandoned if an obese Siamese cat hadn't been sitting on a stack of newspapers in the front window.

Mooner said, "I'll be in Wu's. Don't mention me." He walked on without slowing, whispering just before he disappeared, "Steal something." Florida followed him, mimicking his purposeful stride.

Uneasy, I shoved the door. It opened, setting off a tintinnabulation from the brass bells tied to its back, and I flinched, remembering the woman made of mist. The Siamese looked up, made an annoyed sound more like a parrot than a cat, then ignored me. No one came to see who had opened the door.

I stood in front of high wooden racks filled with books. Several ceiling lights, magical or electrical, disturbed the shadows without dispelling them. To the right was a bin labeled: ABOMINABLE BOOKS. IF YOU MUST STEAL SOMETHING, TAKE ONE WITH OUR BLESSING AND PITY. The selection looked fair. In addition to old bestsellers, biographies of media stars, and "nonfiction" about Atlantis and UFOs and What's Really Across the Border, there were copies of Twain's *Saint Joan* and Shakespeare's *Titus Andronicus*. I stared at them, wondering if one of them would satisfy Mooner.

Someone yelled, "Incoming! Bad book!" Something hurtled toward my head. I ducked. A paperback thwacked against a garish comic book version of *The Count of Monte Cristo* and almost skidded off the Abominable Books pile.

"And they say bad writing hurts no one," I said.

"I can't apologize." A black guy with metallic gold hair came from the back of the store. "That is not a book to be tossed aside lightly. Tossed overboard lightly, perhaps."

I glanced at the upside-down spine. "What's *The Sword of Shanana?*"

"A graceless cannibalization of the twentieth century's only good fantasist."

"Yeats had imitators? What'd they write about, sailing to Philadelphia?"

"J. R. R. Tolkien," the black guy stated patiently, "was a novelist. He wrote *Lord of the Rings.*"

"All fantasy books that weren't written by this Tolkien guy are bad?"

"Not necessarily bad. Silly." He shrugged, an impressive gesture since he had the shoulders of a swimmer or a football player. "The real world's far more interesting."

I considered that. "I like mysteries. Books where people learn what really happened. You can believe that."

He nodded. "We have two mystery sections. Resourceful detectives, and resilient ones."

"Actually, I'm looking for Mickey."

"Ah." His face shifted as he reclassified me from a potential customer to an acquaintance of the boss. "I'll call her."

I followed toward the back of the store. Hand-lettered signs marked the shelves: HISTORY. HERSTORY. HYSTERY. SCIENCE. AMUSING NONSENSE IN THE GUISE OF SCIENTIFIC TRUTH. MISCELLANEOUS NONFICTION/MISCELLANEOUS LIES. FICTION ABOUT IMPOSSIBLE THINGS. FICTION ABOUT IMPROBABLE THINGS. FICTION ABOUT PEDESTRIAN THINGS. FOLKLORE. FAKELORE. RELIGION, MYTHOLOGY, AND AMUSING NONSENSE IN THE GUISE OF OCCULT TRUTH (READER'S CHOICE). PHILOSOPHY/SICKOLOGY/MEDICINE. COMEDY, INTENTIONAL, AND COMEDY, ACCIDENTAL.

The shelves opened onto a small space almost filled by

a large metal desk covered with stacks of books. A circular stairway was beyond the desk; the black guy called up it, "Mickey! Someone to see you! A . . ." He glanced at me.

"Just Ron."

"Ron!" he finished.

Mickey answered, "One sec!" Her feet appeared at the top of the stairs, along with a cinnamon-colored cat that raced by her. Mickey stumbled and threw her hip against the stair rail to keep from falling. She said, "Damn you, Topé," with no particular annoyance and continued down. When she saw me, she was smiling. "Well, hello, Just Ron. Have good luck thumbing?"

"Yeah. A kid picked me up."

"Find someplace to stay?"

I nodded.

Her eyebrows lifted. "Well. You *are* enterprising."

"That's sort of why I came by. I need a job."

"Oh?"

"I mean, I'd like one."

"Uh huh." She gave me the once-over. When I glanced at the black guy, he was grinning. "What can you do?"

"Stuff."

"*Quel coincidence,*" said the black guy. "I also can do stuff."

"Whatever," I said. "Name it. If I can't do it, I'll learn it."

"Well, your attitude isn't hopeless," Mickey said.

"Is," I said. "But I can act like it's not."

"You type?"

I nodded. That was probably the last useful thing that I learned in school.

"Make change?"

Her cash register was huge and old, not one of the

modern ones that dropped the change into your hand as it told you your horoscope. I almost answered, "Creatively," but just said, "Sure."

"Any problem with helping me if I need it?"

The black guy said, "Mickey, there's no need—"

"Who knows what kind of need there might be?"

"You mean, besides store stuff?" I said.

She nodded. "I've lived twenty-seven years like this. I don't have too strong a sense of privacy, or at least, my sense of privacy isn't defined by my body."

"You mean, bathroom stuff?" I probably blushed. I felt extremely middle-class.

"Maybe," Mickey said. "Depends on what I need."

"I wipe myself okay," I said. "Years of practice."

"You little—" the black guy began, but Mickey laughed.

"Relax, Just Ron," she said. "I won't inconvenience you unless I have to. You willing to work under those terms?"

"Inconvenience *him?*" the black guy said, looking at me.

She laughed again. "Did I embarrass both of you?"

"Nah," he said, "I don't—" while I said, "Hey, no way, lady, I'm—"

The black guy squinted at me, then grinned and told Mickey, "Maybe a little."

"Maybe a little," I agreed.

He held out his hand. "I'm Goldy."

I took it. "Just Ron."

"Welcome to Elsewhere, Ron. Hope you stay awhile."

Mickey watched us with a smile, like a teacher pleased that her students were playing together. Suckers, I thought, but I felt good. I wished I'd come for myself rather than Mooner.

The Siamese brushed itself against Mickey's jeans.

Mickey slid one foot out of her moccasins and scratched the cat under the chin, saying, "No, Vado, it isn't time for dinner. You can quit being sweet now."

"When do I start?"

"Tomorrow," Mickey said. "I'm expecting some new books. Show up around noon."

"I don't have a—"

She laughed. "I know. The sun's usually dependable in the Borderlands."

"Okay." I lifted a hand in farewell, then headed out. At the shelf labeled THE GOOD STUFF, I paused. As I reached for a copy of *Huckleberry Finn,* Goldy called, "Help you find anything?"

"Nah." I let my hand drop to my side. "See you tomorrow."

The Siamese watched me leave, as though she thought I might be stupid enough to release something small and defenseless in her domain.

Mooner and Florida were sitting on the broken curb at the end of the block. They looked up as I approached. "Well?" Mooner rose as if his spine were hydraulic.

"Got the job. S'posed to show up around noon tomorrow."

"Mmm." He looked at me. I turned, heading back toward Castle Pup, forcing him to say, "Lift anything?"

I dropped one hand into my pack and drew out the Yeats.

"Well. All right." He took the book from me. I began to open my mouth but didn't. "It's in pretty good shape, too. She'd get good money for it." He flipped through the pages, then handed it back. "Read that."

"Out loud?"

He grinned. "Yeah, Do-Ron. Out loud."

The book had opened to a page where Tony'd drawn a picture of a hawk flying outward in a spiral. I didn't need to look as I recited:

> *Turning and turning in the widening gyre*
> *The falcon cannot hear the falconer;*
> *Things fall apart; the centre cannot hold;*
> *Mere anarchy is loosed upon the world,*
> *The blood-dimmed tide is loosed, and everywhere*
> *The ceremony of innocence is drowned;*
> *The best—*

Mooner snatched the book back, though Florida made a cat's sound of disappointment. "Poetry," Mooner said. "What's it mean, 'mere anarchy'? A little bit of anarchy goes after the world. Heh."

" 'Mere' also means pure," I said. "Like, total anarchy."

"Yeah." He stared at me. "So. I'm a mere anarchist?"

"I guess."

"Good." Mooner pulled a cigarette lighter from his jeans.

I began to feel ill. "What're you doing?"

"Sympathetic magic." Mooner flicked the lighter and put the flame to the corner of the book. "I burn something the slut owned—"

"Hey!" I swatted at the book.

Mooner laughed and lifted it above my head. I tried to reach it but couldn't while Mooner held me away with one straight arm. He kept laughing. "C'mon, Do-Ron, what do you care?"

"You don't need—"

"Relax. It's not really magic. I just got something now that she'll never get back." He let the pages spread. The flames licked among them, curling back the cloth of the cover and blistering the embossed gold lettering on the spine.

"Screw you," I said.

Mooner frowned. "It's just a book."

"Screw you," I repeated.

"Watch yourself," he warned. "If I made a mistake—"

I swung at him, catching his chin with my fist, more by luck than skill. Mooner's head snapped back. He brought his hand to his chin and said, "Oh." Something drove into my side, just under my ribs, knocking me over.

I stayed on the sidewalk, more numb than frightened, expecting him to kick me again and not thinking clearly at all. The Yeats smoldered in front of me, just a bit of half-incinerated garbage. I wanted to cry.

Mooner held out his hand to help me up. "Better now?"

"Screw you." I ignored him and stood. My side hurt, but nothing felt broken. Replaying it in my mind, I saw that Mooner had kicked me with his foot extended, catching me with the curve of his ankle rather than the ball of his foot or his heel.

Mooner grinned. "You must be a lover, Do-Ron. You're sure no fighter."

"Screw you." I had to work to alter the inflection a fourth time.

"Didn't know you had a thing for books."

"It's not— Forget it." I poked the Yeats with my sneaker. It broke up into blackened shards decorated with fragments of words.

Florida picked up one and handed it to me. I read:

I made my song a coat
Covered with embroideries
Out of old mythologies
From heel to throa—

Florida watched me, so I nodded and tucked the scrap into my jacket pocket. Mooner had already begun to walk back toward Castle Pup.

I felt my bruised side through the thinner cloth of the pocket. Just kids fooling around, I thought. Tony had teased me like that. What's a book worth, anyway?

When I drew my hand out of the pocket, my fingers were dusted with something. I held my hand close to my face to see what it was.

Cookie crumbs.

CHAPTER SEVEN

MORE
FUN WITH
FLORIDA

I WIPED MY PALM ON MY TROUSERS, BUT IT DIDN'T FEEL clean. Mooner, at the street corner, watched me. I called, "Hey, I'm gonna explore a little before dinner."

He narrowed his eyes, then shrugged, said, "Be happy, Raygun Ron," and headed toward Castle Pup. His walk was almost a dance, and he hummed some old pop tune. Two adults in never-wrinkles, definitely not Soho-types, frowned as he passed. Laughing, Mooner leaped into the air, clicked his heels together, and laughed again. At another time the mini-show would've delighted me.

Florida came up with another charred page from the Yeats. I said, "Just go 'way, okay?" Florida held out the page. I closed my fist around it without looking at the words. The page felt like a dry leaf, crumbled like one, too. I lifted my fist high; Florida backed off. I opened my hand.

Flecks of paper, white and ash gray, fluttered down the dusty street. I marched away.

A minute later I looked over my shoulder. Florida trailed about a block behind. I yelled, "Go away!" and grabbed up some rocks and flung them. Florida kept following.

I headed on, turning aside for no one, walking as fast as I could. I stuffed my hand in my right jacket pocket and yanked the lining inside out. Cookie crumbs spilled on the sidewalk for birds and squirrels. I didn't slow down. Some crumbs got on my pants, so I slapped them away. I didn't slow down at all. I didn't look back again. A marching band could've paraded behind me. I wouldn't've known.

The neighborhoods changed, but I didn't pay attention to buildings or people. I walked through a few blocks where I saw no elves at all, and a few where I saw no humans. Mostly, I passed kids, older than me and younger. I passed families, too, mostly young ones with parents about my age and little kids who came in crawling or cradling models. I passed street musicians and bums and fortune-tellers and mimes and anyone else you can imagine who wouldn't be working a day job in the World. Stopping for thirty seconds, I listened to blue-jeaned elves doing one of Shakespeare's comedies in the middle of the street. I didn't want to laugh at anything, so I walked on.

A kid in a wide-brimmed felt hat shoved a booklet at me. She said, "Latest issue. Any donation gratefully—" I started to hand it back. She said, "Keep it. You like it, give me something next time you see me."

It seemed simplest to nod, stuff the booklet in my back pocket, and walk on, so I did. She called after me, "We're always looking for helpers and contributors!"

And you can keep looking, I thought. I just lifted a hand to one side to say I heard her.

Everywhere gangs of kids watched me, and sometimes laughed after I'd passed. None of them hassled me. Maybe the afternoon was too nice to hassle a stranger. Maybe my clothes told them that the only thing they'd gain by hassling me was the fun of doing it. Maybe my face told them that hassling me would be hard-earned fun. And maybe I didn't look as tough as I thought. Maybe they let me pass because I just looked like a kid who ought to be passing through, a kid with a destination, though that wasn't the case at all.

No one and nothing stopped me until I came to the Mad River. I halted among boarded-up and abandoned factories and warehouses. No one was on the street. To my left were sounds of industry, a hammer clanging and someone barking directions to someone else. I turned right and found myself walking toward a high rusty bridge.

Weathered sawhorses cluttered the way onto it. A faded handwritten sign said: CLOSED TO VEHICLE TRAFFIC BY ORDER OF THE MAYOR AND, I MOST DEVOUTLY HOPE, YOUR GOOD COMMON SENSE. On the pavement nearby, someone had spray-painted: WARF RATS RAIN!!! Under that, someone else had painted: THE PACK REIGNS. WHARF RATS DRIBBLE.

As I threaded the maze of sawhorses, Florida ran up, ducked under the barriers, and, with furious shakings of pale, tangled hair, mouthed something, a fierce, harsh exhalation. I lifted my fist like before. Florida stood there, glaring up at me, offering the choice of hitting a little kid or staring one down.

"What do you think you are?" I said. "The president of my fan club?" I walked onto the bridge. I heard a last angry exhalation, but I didn't look back.

Though a few blocks of concrete had fallen in and much of the original paint had flaked away, the bridge seemed safe enough if you kept your eyes open. Graffiti covered the easily reached surfaces. Some of it was romantic: WS AND EB: MAY THEIR LOVE LAST FAR, FAR LONGER THAN THESE WORDS." Some of it was tragic: LAKESIDE JEAN IS A 2-TIMING MACHINE. WHY DO I HAVE TO LOSE JEAN AND MY BEST FRIEND TOO?" Some of it was obscure, some of it was obscene, and some of it was illegible. I almost smiled at GET OFF THIS BRIDGE, STUPID, IT'S DANGEROUS OUT HERE!

That made me look back. Florida couldn't've believed that the bridge was too dangerous, I decided. The kid still followed me at a discreet distance of sixty or seventy feet.

The far shore looked boring: factories and housing and, beyond them, the wild woods of the Nevernever. The road climbed into the hills, paralleling the invisible Border. I wondered if anyone took it, and if it eventually ran to the World or Faerie, or if it circled Faerie forever.

Tony might've followed that road. I imagined him on a big blue Harley like he'd always said he'd get, crouching low over the handlebars as he raced the wind, his hair wild, his face ecstatic.

Suddenly I wasn't ready to walk farther. I sat cross-legged on the sidewalk. Florida sat, too, maybe thirty feet away, and watched the riverfront. I looked once at the skyline of Bordertown, crimson in the afternoon sun, and wasn't interested in the city or anyplace where people were.

Below us, the current swirled and eddied around moss-encrusted pillars, etching patterns over and over on the river's dark surface, writing and rewriting something I couldn't read. I watched and I listened. After a while I felt something like peace or forgiveness, or maybe I didn't feel anything at all.

Florida tugged on my shoulder.

"Get lost," I suggested.

The kid tugged again, harder, and pointed toward Bordertown. Six strangers, my age or older, came toward us.

They weren't strange just because I didn't know them. They walked oddly. Several of them drifted, as though half-asleep. Several of them bounced, like the diapered baby that'd chased gingerbread men at Castle Pup. One, a black girl, walked casually along the handrail with her arms outspread and a silly grin on her face. Though their styles were different, they seemed similar somehow, like people walking through a shared dream.

Florida pulled on my jacket sleeve, trying to drag me up and away toward the distant shore, away from the strangers. I stood. Florida yanked even harder. I glanced again at the six. They were all human, and several were the same race as me. That didn't mean they had good intentions.

"Okay." I started following Florida.

"Whoa-ho!" one called. "Don't go!" The voice seemed friendly and amused. I looked back. The nearest and smallest of them, a brown-haired guy in metal-rimmed glasses, grinned at us. I hesitated, Florida tugged again, and the guy in glasses called, "Please!"

If we ran, we might escape, but running might inspire them to attack. They didn't seem to be carrying weapons and they weren't acting threatening, so there wasn't any reason to assume they wanted trouble.

I shook my arm free. "Ease on," I said. Florida darted back, then dropped a hand to the Bowie knife hanging from the beaded tourist's belt.

"Hi," I said to the six newcomers, and nodded, smiling a little for their benefit.

"Enjoying our bridge?" said the guy in glasses. He wore baggy red trousers and a tight white T-shirt made gray by bands of black type. The top one read: A HUNDRED LINES OF COKE ON THE WALL . . . His grin was as much a part of his costume as his glasses.

"Your bridge?" I laughed in the hope that he was making a joke. "It's a great bridge. I didn't know it was your bridge. You guys are lucky to have a bridge like this. It's a"—I heard myself babbling—"great bridge."

"Yeah." The one in glasses nodded. "A great bridge."

"A really great bridge," said the black girl walking the railing. She jumped down to the sidewalk. The other five stood in the street, blocking our way back.

"Yeah," I nodded. "Well, I oughta be going. Sorry if—"

"Come, now," said the one in glasses. "*We* interrupted *you.*"

"Hey, that's cool. Absolumundo copacetic." When they didn't move to let me by, I wondered if they'd let me walk around them. I decided Florida and I'd go to the far shore, then find another bridge to return to Soho, even if that meant walking an extra ten or twenty miles. "Well, see you." I began to turn. My armpits felt slick with sweat. My throat was so dry that I didn't trust my voice.

The guy in glasses dropped a hand on my shoulder, so lightly that I barely felt it through Tony's jacket. I halted. Shrugging off his hand could be even more provoking than running away. He let his hand fall to his side. "You're new to Border City."

I nodded.

"Welcome."

I shrugged. "Thanks."

"You like it?"

The others watched without expression, as did Florida. I wished Mooner was there. Mooner would know how to handle this. "Yeah. It's great."

"You know what makes it great?"

A girl with bleached hair giggled. The guy with glasses glanced at her, a little annoyed, then said, "The river."

"The river?"

He nodded. "The waters of Faerie. The blood of the Elflands. Magic and poetry and song, washing from the source of all magic and poetry and song, breaching the Border to bring wonder to the human world."

"Uh, yeah, sure. That's what I figure."

Tony had told me about the Mad River. It runs from Faerie into the World, where it loses its name and its color and its magic. It follows the course of an older river, or maybe the older river changed back into the Mad River when Faerie returned. People say a single sip enslaves any human who drinks from it. In the World, no drug's that addictive, but the Borderlands are not the World.

"Have you drunk from the river?"

"No," I said slowly.

"Would you drink from the river?"

"I'm not all that thirsty, thanks."

He nodded. "You will be. When you're really, really thirsty, remember that the river is always here and you may drink from it anytime."

"Uh, yeah. I'll keep that in mind."

"You're afraid of getting hooked?"

"Well . . ."

"You will. So?" His grin didn't have any humor in it.

He swept out one arm, indicating the river as if he owned it, or caressed it. "Anything worth having or doing is addictive. Art. Power. Sex. Knowledge. The river's all of those. Like them, it never ends. It gives so long as you're willing to receive. A river of dream for all who would drink. Are you afraid to have your dreams fulfilled?"

I shrugged. "I'll think about it."

He stared in my face, then laughed. "Good!"

"We should—?" I began.

He slapped his forehead, then adjusted his glasses, reminding me of my Spanish teacher, one of the few teachers who thought school should prepare you for something besides prison. "We haven't introduced ourselves!" He jabbed his index finger at each of his companions like a kid with a make-believe gun. "Sugarman, Lurch, Doritos, El Greco, and Marvelous Martha. I"—He bowed—"am the Prince of Spectacles. Specs, for short."

"Just Ron," I said. "This is Florida."

"A pleasure." Specs squatted and thrust a hand toward Florida, who backed away with a grimace and a silent snarl.

"Florida's shy," I said. Specs offered the hand to me. His palm was cool and damp against mine. I forced myself to keep from wiping my skin against my trousers. The others were amused by the handshaking ceremony. They each held out a hand as if standing in a receiving line. I marched down the line, pumping palms and grinning like this was really grand.

Lurch, the largest, had a surprisingly gentle grip, but Doritos, the girl with blue-black skin, nearly crushed my hand. I didn't mind. Florida followed me, not shaking hands but giving a minuscule jerk of the head to each of them like a general reviewing troops, which made them all giggle. At the end of the game of greetings, Florida and I stood closer to Bordertown than any of them.

"Well, it's good meeting you guys," I said, "but we really ought to go. I 'spect I'll see you again sometime."

"What's the rush?" asked Doritos.

"Said I'd be back for dinner."

"Dine with us." Specs beamed at me. "The food's nothing special, but our drink makes up for that, I assure you."

"The River provides," said Sugarman, his doughlike face emotionless.

"Yeah, thanks anyway, but our friends are expecting us, so . . ."

Specs frowned for the first time. "How were you planning to return?"

"Walk. It's not—"

"On our bridge?"

My stomach clenched itself.

"This is a very dangerous bridge," said El Greco, a wiry kid with tight shiny curls. "Amazing how people fall off it all the time."

"But that's not so bad for them. They fall into the river," said Sugarman.

"Yeah," said Marvelous Martha, a totally hairless Asian girl. "Into the river. If you think you can't come up, drink it down." She licked her lips. Her teeth were tiny, as if she still had her baby teeth.

El Greco made a slurping sound and grinned.

"You *can* swim?" said Specs, perfectly disinterested.

"Hey, c'mon, guys." I couldn't estimate the distance to the water. Maybe two hundred feet, maybe three hundred. I could swim, but I didn't think I could dive. I didn't know about Florida. If the fall didn't break my back, if I didn't drown immediately, there were things that were said to live in the Mad River, things that couldn't live in the World, like catfish large enough to swallow a person and the kinds of mermaids who drag swimmers down for fun.

Florida snatched at the Bowie knife. Three of Specs's dreamy crew woke instantly. Flick knives and switch-blades glittered in their hands. My stomach squeezed itself again, and sweat broke out on my brow.

"Don't," said Doritos, one of the knife wielders. Florida let the Bowie slide back into its sheath.

"People walk all over our bridge," said El Greco. "Get it dirty. Dirty people." He stepped toward us. "Who need baths."

"I've got money," I said quickly.

"Ah." Specs smiled. "Care to make a contribution to the High Street Bridge Maintenance Committee?"

"Uh, yeah." I squatted, and El Greco started toward me.

Specs stopped El Greco by placing a hand lightly on his chest. "Be a shame if the pretty money got wet."

I broke the rubber band that'd held an envelope of cash to my ankle. Standing, I pulled out the bills and fanned them like playing cards in my hand, showing off an entire year's savings. "This is like, toll money, right? For both of us. Okay? We have a deal?"

"Of course." Specs held out his hand, palm up.

"Good." I threw the loose bills at his face, grabbed Florida's arm, and ran. The wind caught the money, blowing it around the bridge. Several of Specs's people chased after it. I heard someone start after us, but Specs called, "El Greco! Doritos! Let 'em go!"

"But—" El Greco began.

Specs laughed. "Gotta take care! Be a shame if the little one hurt you!"

At the barricade of sawhorses, I glanced back. No one was chasing us. Specs saw me stop and called, "I like your style! There's a place for you among the Wharf Rats, if you ever want it!"

"You like my style enough to give me my money back?"

"You want your money back enough to come and get it?"

Florida had run ahead when I stopped. The kid returned, looked at me considering this, and jerked on my sleeve. "You're right," I told Florida, then called, "No. Enjoy it, you bas—"

More kids stepped out from the buildings around us. Ten or twelve kids, enough to keep us from getting by. Dirty kids in tattered clothing. Kids who walked like dreamers.

If I hadn't stopped, we would've been past them before they could block the street.

"Let 'em go!" Specs shouted. "Ron'll be back. Won't you, Ron?"

"No way," I whispered.

Several of the Rats stepped aside to let us leave. I hesitated. Florida took my hand and led me between a boy dyed entirely purple and a fat girl who'd replaced her teeth with fangs. The Rats didn't speak. They didn't attack or follow us. They watched, smiling vaguely. I wondered if Specs was right, that I'd return. The Rats seemed very sure of themselves, very superior and contemptuous. Maybe that made me jealous.

As we climbed away from the riverside, I shook my hand free of Florida's. "I get by fine," I said between clenched teeth. "I don't need anyone's help. Especially not some snot-faced little kid's help."

I walked faster. I tightened my fingers into fists, but I couldn't stop my hands from shaking. I wanted to do something to hurt Specs and the Wharf Rats, but I didn't know any way, short of drying up the Mad River.

All I could think of was how helpless I'd felt, trapped by the Rats, staring down at the River, frightened of falling forever but more frightened of falling through the River's bright surface and never coming up again, snared in the darkness in muck and river grasses, concluding my search for Tony—

My stomach knotted itself one last time. I looked around for an alley or a deserted building where I could be sure of some privacy, spotted a low garden wall overgrown with weeds, and ran to it.

Needing toilet paper, I pulled out the booklet from my back pocket to tear off a page or two. *Surplus Art* No. 3 looked like your basic basement magazine: black ink on white typing paper that'd been cut in half, folded together, and stapled. The cover consisted of crude art, sloppy hand-lettering, and what looked like the output of a typewriter with a bent "e" key. But the cover illo, a stick figure whose hairline came to a point between its eyes, winked at me.

I dropped the booklet. Telling myself I was imagining things, I looked at it again. The stick figure winked again. As long as I stared at it, it did nothing, but when I looked away and back, it winked. Finally, I poked the booklet with one finger, then picked it up and looked inside. After the copyright notice, it said, "Printed with ink, faerie dust, arrogance, and humility by the Bordertown Art Guerrillas."

I used some old leaves to solve my immediate problem

and hoped I was right that none of them were poison ivy.

Flipping through *Surplus Art,* I left the abandoned garden. The little 'zine had poetry and prose and art and even a comic strip about the cover character, a magician called Stick Wizard who lived in a wacky version of Bordertown along with two cigar-smoking elf kids named Tater and Bert, who kept playing tricks on the Wizard that backfired. The story wasn't great, but it made me laugh.

Thinking I'd read it to Florida, I looked around and found I was alone on the street.

CHAPTER EIGHT

CUTTING
HAIRS

I SPOTTED WISEGUY'S RAVEN'S WINGS, THEN LEDA'S DANDE-lion puff, then Sai's short black mane. All three were on the front steps of Castle Pup. A seedybox by Wiseguy's feet was playing a psychoactive dance tune, and Sai danced lazily while Wiseguy trimmed Leda's hair with a scissors. I might've walked by if I hadn't recognized the lyrics. "That's Blake! *Songs of Innocence and Experience.*"

Sai opened her eyes, grinned at me, closed them, and kept dancing.

Leda shook her head. "You got the album title, kiddo. But the band's—"

"Not the band! The writer! William Blake. Somebody set his words to music." I listened as a female voice finished "The Clod and the Pebble." The music continued, a quick Caribbean beat with dueling guitars and synthesizers.

Then two voices sang simultaneously. The male repeated the Clod of Clay's lines:

> *Love seeketh not Itself to please,*
> *Nor for itself hath any care,*
> *But for another gives its ease,*
> *And builds a Heaven in Hell's despair.*

The female sang the Pebble's part:

> *Love seeketh only Self to please,*
> *To bind another to Its delight,*
> *Joys in another's loss of ease,*
> *And builds a Hell in Heaven's despite.*

The music climaxed with the singers' last words. Then the last bars of the tune were repeated on a single, stringed instrument, each note like the cry of a mourning dove. As the next song began, I whistled. "Man, that's too transcendent!"

"Been done a lot," Sai said. "You should hear this Canadian's tune for 'The Highwayman.' "

Leda smiled at Wiseguy. "Too transcendent."

I pointed at the sky with my middle finger.

Leda asked Wiseguy, "He's one of Mooner's, right?"

Wiseguy nodded. "Found him the other day. You met him last night, but you weren't entirely present."

"Oh." Leda became almost apologetic. "I shouldn't've mocked you. The music is, um, transcendent." She cocked her head and lifted an eyebrow. "I'm Leda. And you?"

"I'm not." I started up the steps.

"Says his name's Ron." Wiseguy glanced from her haircutting for the first time and gave me a skeptical smile that was a smile nonetheless. "That still the case?"

"Yeah." I stopped at the doorway in case she decided to smile at me again. "Just Ron."

She nodded and continued snipping half-inch lengths of Leda's pale hair. The locks chased into the street like cats at play.

"Find a place to stay?" Leda asked me.

"Uh huh."

"Good."

"He's with Sparks and King Obie," said Wiseguy.

Leda smiled. "Whole third floor's turning into Mooner's headquarters."

"Nope," said Sai cheerily, not missing a beat as she did a complex kick-step during "The Tyger." "Not while I'm living there."

"Thought you had a crush on my little bro," said Wiseguy.

"Had." Sai took the ends of her hair in either hand and held it away from her face. "Should I let my hair grow or shave it?"

"Why?" I asked.

She grinned. "Easier than dieting."

"You should diet," I said. "You'd look great if you lost twenty pounds."

Sai opened one eye. "Well. Thanks loads." The eye closed again.

"Aren't you the sweet-talking fool?" Wiseguy said to me.

"She would!" I protested. "She's got great features. If she'd just lose—"

"It's like watching someone in quicksand," said Leda.

"Glub, glub," said Wiseguy.

Sai did a sudden hip thrust to the music, directly at me. "I forgive you 'cause you're young."

"Thanks loads," I mimicked.

"Oughta be nice to her," said Wiseguy. "Last year Sai was Bordertown's middleweight boxing champ."

"I liked my nose too much to continue," Sai said.

I nodded. "I didn't mean to insult you about being fat."

"Is he stepping back in?" asked Leda.

"No," said Wiseguy. "Leaping."

"Maybe you'd better move on before you make things worse," Leda said.

"Yeah?" I said. "Maybe you—" I stopped myself.

"Yes?" Leda placed her fists on her hips and stared at me.

Sai opened her eyes. "Don't let 'em worry you, Ronzo. I'm not ticked. Yet. Did I say I liked your jacket?"

"Uh. No."

"It's nice. Buy it in the World?"

"No." All three of them were watching. I was especially aware of Wiseguy's gaze. "It was my brother's. He painted the phoenix." I turned around so they could admire it.

"Nice work," Sai said. "Think he'd paint something for me?"

I shrugged and looked away.

"He in Bordertown?" Leda asked.

"I don't know," I said. "Maybe."

"Is he a runaway?" asked Leda.

"You guys ask a lot of questions."

"There're places where runaways hang out when they get to town," Wiseguy said. "Places you could check, put up notices on bulletin boards, like that."

"If he's in town, he's been here awhile."

"He look like you?" Sai asked.

74

"He did." I didn't add ". . . only taller and handsomer and infinitely more relaxed around women."

They studied me more closely. I knew I was going to blush.

"I don't think I've seen 'im," Sai said.

"Nope," said Wiseguy.

"Uh uh," said Leda.

Wiseguy made a last snip at Leda's hair. "Done."

"Mirror!" Leda demanded. Sai passed her a cracked hand mirror in a neon-purple frame. Leda shook her head violently, looked in the mirror, then stood up. If I hadn't seen her get the haircut, I wouldn't have known she'd had one.

"Well?" said Wiseguy.

"I look like the dog's lunch."

Wiseguy nodded. "Before the dog got to it, or after?"

"Before."

"Then it's an improvement." Wiseguy looked at me. "So, Ron, want a hot new Bordertown haircut?"

"I like it long," I said.

"Funny. So do I," said Sai.

"C'mon," Wiseguy said. "I could use the practice."

"I lived." Leda smiled at Wiseguy. "And you do good work, jerk. Thanks."

"Oh, all right." I sat in front of Wiseguy. "Just a trim."

Wiseguy laughed, then clipped the scissors several times in front of my nose so I could see the blades work. "Relax, Ronaway. You agreed to a haircut, not a circumcision." She made a single cut; several inches of hair fell from the side of my head.

"Yii!" I clutched my skull in my arms to protect it from her. All three women laughed. "I'm maimed for life!"

"You'll be gorgeous," Wiseguy said. "Trust me."

"Yeah, right." I couldn't tell her that I didn't trust her a bit and would still let her do anything she wanted to me.

"Your brother much older'n you?" she asked, beginning to cut again.

"A couple of years."

"Hope you find him." Her voice seemed distant as she concentrated on her art. "Never enough attractive men around."

"Speaking of . . ." Leda whispered.

A shadow fell over me. I glanced up. Strider stood there, tall and elvenly enigmatic. His clothes were Bordertown—biker boots, blue jeans, torn red T-shirt—but his long brushed-back moonwhite hair was pure Prince of Faerie material. A smile came to his lips, and he told Wiseguy, "Looks like an excellent idea. Might I be your next victim?"

I glanced at him, but no one noticed. His accent was exactly like Matte Black's and Firehair's.

"Elven vanity," murmured Sai, who'd stopped dancing.

"Oh?" Strider sat beside me and glanced at Sai. "Do you object to elves or to vanity? I am what I am. Given the alternatives, I'll take pride in that, though I take no credit for it."

"Yeah," Sai said. "Look at you. Thousands of years of elven breeding, and now you're ready to be put to stud. Excuse me if I don't get in line." She looked at Leda. "Here the lost heir of Faerie's been hiding among us all along, huh?"

Leda shrugged and looked away.

"I heard," Strider said casually, "that you misliked elves."

"Misliked, disliked, and despised," Sai said.

Leda said, "Gee, thanks."

"You're okay," Sai said. "Heck, sometimes I forget you're elven."

"Heh." Leda pushed her hair back so her pointed ears showed in all their glory, and twisted the hair into a knot at the back of her head. A long strand slipped free to shadow one silver eye.

Sai jerked her thumb at Strider. "Not like him. If you stuck his mind into Ron's body, he'd still be an alien."

"Could get crowded in there," said Wiseguy.

"But aren't you half—?" I began to ask Sai, then said, "Oops."

Wiseguy said, "Hmm. I guess there's plenty of room."

Sai glared at me and told Wiseguy, "Scalp 'im."

Strider laughed. "You deny your heritage?"

"My heritage," Sai said, "denies me."

"Only if you allow it," said Strider.

"Yeah? Think my fine ancestors will let me cross the Border?"

"You wish to visit Faerie?"

Sai gave him a look that would've made me feel stupider than I already felt. "Hell, no."

Strider shrugged. "Then it doesn't matter, does it?"

Leda rested a pale hand on Sai's strong bicep and asked Strider, "You believe that?"

"I believe that it should not matter. I understand that it does."

"Okay," Sai said softly, "you're not a complete elf dink."

Strider grinned. "Thank you."

"I think I've got time for one more haircut before sundown," Wiseguy said, "if you still want it."

"I'm beautiful now?" I patted my skull and wondered if I should've asked Wiseguy to shave it.

She made a last cut and squinted at me. "Done, anyway."

I shook my head to shed loose hairs, then looked at Sai. She gave a thumbs-up. "Extremely Bordertown, Ronzo." She handed me the mirror.

Maybe Wiseguy understood me. She'd cut the hair scraggly, different lengths that fell wildly around my face. I looked like I'd just escaped a terrible fate and was on my way to another one.

"All right." I grinned at them all. "Thanks, Wiseguy."

" 'S right. Well, Strider?"

"You do excellent work," he said. "But I've reconsidered."

"Oh?" She glanced at him, and so did the others. I decided that in addition to height and cheekbones, he had a better sense of theater than I did.

He smiled. "What should I do? Discard my past with a haircut?" He stopped, glancing at me.

"Like little *moi?* Couldn't have that, hey, elf-o?" I stared at him.

"It's just hair." Sai put a hand on my shoulder. "Doesn't mean anything."

"It's how you present yourself to the world," said Wiseguy. "Might mean everything."

"Elf-o?" said Strider, looking at the others.

Sai pointed at Strider and began to laugh.

"Elf-o?" Strider said again, beginning to smile at Sai. "That's an insult?"

I said, "I haven't begun."

"Good," said Leda. "Don't."

"Nothing personal," I told her. "But maybe I'm with Sai when it comes to elves fresh out of Faerie."

78

"Ah." Leda nodded. "Ask Sai about humans fresh out of the World."

Sai winced and glanced away. I stared at her until Wiseguy said, "You're mighty touchy, Ron."

"Yeah," I said. "Humans fresh out of the World are like that." I stalked into Castle Pup. Leda and Wiseguy laughed behind me.

At the top of the stairs, passing the bottled pig fetus, I said, "Don't say anything, Festus." Then I hurried on, just in case it did.

CHAPTER NINE

PLAYTIME

MOONER SUGGESTED WE HIT THE CLUBS THAT NIGHT TO celebrate my new job. I thought it was a great idea: I could see more of the city, have too much fun, and watch for Tony, all at the same time.

The advantage of hanging out with a halfie is you're half-accepted at any club in Bordertown, whether the usual clientele's elf or human. That's the disadvantage, too. Even at the clubs that're neutral ground, like Danceland, where elves and humans and halfies bump into each other in the crowd and no one feels obliged to swear or fight, you still get that quick look from the corner of an eye, then discover you're invisible. Despite that, we had a good time. I think.

We started at Danceland, then hit The Dancing Ferret and The Factory and Homegirl's (a pretty funny name for a place in a town where almost no one's a native) and The

Dreamery and The Lightworks. Saw Flaming Fairies and Starch Rabbits and Drunk, Not Stupid and Poxy Music and The Ground Zero Tailgate Party and The People Who Live in Your Sound System. Or so King O'Beer told me late the next morning.

"We did?" I opened an eye and wished the top of my head would tear itself off and be done with it.

"Oh, yes. You enjoyed yourself a great deal. At least, that's what it seemed like when I helped you to bed. You said you were having a—" He smiled. "Be faster if I leave out the expletives."

I nodded.

"A time," the King said. "And that everyone was wonder—"

"To bed?" I finally registered what he'd been telling me. All I wore, all that I'd woken up in, were my boxer shorts with red valentines.

King patted my shoulder. "Alone, old boy."

"Ah. Good. I mean, thanks. I mean, that's a relie— I mean, I wondered."

The King narrowed his eyes, then shook his head. "God, you are vain."

"I'm not—"

"You keep assuming I'm going to jump your scrawny bones the first chance I get. That wishful thinking?"

"No way!" I sat on my mattress, hugging myself and forgetting about King O'Beer. Disconnected bits of the night before came back: Dancing by myself in a crowd of taller kids in leather. Falling against a lamppost and discovering that it didn't hurt. Knocking my head against a lamppost and laughing because it didn't hurt. Mooner and some other kids laughing, too. Knocking my head again—

I touched my forehead and winced. Someone had bandaged it. That explained part of my headache but not all. What'd I . . . ?

River. Mooner with a Coke bottle half-full of Mad River water. Sipping and laughing and saying the rest of us should stay away from it, that he as a halfie could barely handle the "liquefied essence of Elfdom." Laughing louder when I took the bottle from him. And drank.

"Oh, hell," I whispered.

King O'Beer looked down from the loft. "Thirsty? I've got some o.j. Vitamin C's s'posed to be good for hangovers, though—"

"How much did I drink?" I saw myself as one of Specs's Rats and felt even sicker than before.

"I don't—"

"How much!"

"Ease on, Rondelay! Mooner only let you have a taste. It's prob'ly just the beer you're feeling now."

"Oh."

"And if it's not, Mooner keeps a jug of River in his room. There are worse addictions to have in Bordertown."

I couldn't remember the taste. Was it like cool smoke on the back of my throat? Did it sting? Did it make me want to gag, then seem so wonderful that I forgot its passing and remembered its effects? I only remembered candlelight shining through dark red waters, and I wanted—

"Yeah. Some o.j.'d be nice."

King O'Beer handed me a warm liter bottle. I uncapped it, wondered what germs the King had, and took a long swig.

"Kill it if you want."

"Thanks." I drained it and began to feel more human. "Did I do anything else stupid?" When the King began to look as if he couldn't stifle a giggle, I said, "Oh, great. What?"

"Well, there was this big kid in Pack colors who was talking pretty loud with some friends. You told him you'd tell the bands to turn down so he wouldn't have to yell over them."

"Why'd he let me live?"

"He saw Mooner was with you."

"Oh."

"And you put the moves on Sparks."

"I did?" I saw a bit of that in my mind without any soundtrack: Sparks's head close to mine, her blue-black locks brushing my face. She, smiling and nudging me. Me, snorting in laughter, beer going up my nose. She must've been impressed. "Did I score?" I asked, as if I didn't care.

"She thought you were cute. I think *she* scored."

I glanced at him.

"With Mooner. She's been after him forever. Lucky girl."

"Hmm." It was frustrating, forgetting so much. I could remember the early part of the evening now. Sparks and her pal, the self-named Star Raven, had come along. Gorty, a big quiet human kid who looked like he was assembled from potatoes, had made a deal somewhere or stolen something; he'd had money to treat us all to pizza at Godmom's. I remembered spinach-and-mushroom pizza with extra cheese. My appetite was returning.

Mooner had said something about how happy he was to be eating with us, people he trusted. That'd made me notice who wasn't there: Wiseguy, Sai, Durward, Strider, Leda.

I touched my forehead. "Who bandaged me?"

King O'Beer blushed. "I did. Sparks helped. We both put you to bed, so you have witnesses to vouch for your innocence."

He meant it as a joke. I grinned and shrugged.

"Don't thank me," the King said. "It was nothing. No, really. Hey, you know what time it is?"

I glanced at Dad's empty watchband on my wrist, then said, "Ha, ha. Very funny."

"No. It's just that I told my sweetie I'd meet him at noon, and I might be late."

"Elsewhere!" I slapped my forehead, and knew that was a mistake as soon as my hand hit the bandage.

"Yeah." King O'Beer frowned. "I told you I wouldn't bring anyone here. You okay?"

"I'm late for my first day of work." Ignoring my dizziness, I scrambled into my jeans and looked for my bag and the rest of my clothes.

King O'Beer smiled. "The bookstore. Oh, yeah. Mooner used to go there all the time."

"He did?" I smelled the armpits of the shirt I'd worn the day before. When I made a face, King O'Beer held out a blue workshirt.

"Here, I never wear this. Yeah, Mooner went there a lot until, oh, two months ago. Sai worked there."

"Why'd she quit?"

"Said it was a stupid job for someone who didn't read much."

"Sai and Mooner have a thing?"

King O'Beer laughed. "Sai had the usual Mooner crush. She got over it around the time she quit working at Elsewhere."

"Was that when Strider showed up?"

"No, Strider showed up two or three weeks later. Why?"

I shrugged. "I don't know. Thought I was seeing a picture forming, but I guess I wasn't."

"There's a mystery?"

"Only the usual one of why people act like they do." I tied my sneaker laces and ran for the door, where I hesitated. "Hey, King. Thanks for, well, you know."

"The shirt?" He nodded. " 'S right."

I hadn't meant the shirt. I'd meant for being a nice guy, but compliments have always had trouble passing my lips.

Durward tossed me a bagel and an orange when I ran through the common room. Sparks and Star Raven were huddled over bowls of oatmeal and raisins. Star Raven had a hand on Sparks's wrist, and Sparks might've been crying. Strider and Sai were also having a meal together, but theirs seemed much happier. The night I could only dimly remember must've been interesting for lots of people. Sai grinned at me, and Strider gave me a small nod, which was a major concession, I knew. I waved and kept running.

I tripped over Strawberry and her elf boyfriends in the hall, but they didn't wake up. My bagel landed on top of Festus's jar. If I hadn't been so hungry, I would've left it there. But I brushed off the bagel—pumpernickel, not one of my favorites, maybe because the name sounds so silly— and ate it as I raced toward Elsewhere.

Florida was on the other side of the street, heading for Castle Pup. I yelled, "Mmmph!" swallowed, then yelled, "Hey, it's me!" Florida didn't even look my way, so I kept running.

I'd covered four or five blocks when I heard a bike behind me. In Soho that didn't mean anything; anyone with two wheels and a spellbox could rig up something that worked and sounded like a motorcycle. I didn't even glance back to see if this might be trouble. It was the middle of a sunny day, and all the inhabitants of Soho, old and young, seemed to be out, playing chess on the steps or riding skateboards in the street or just hanging out.

The engine stopped, and the bike coasted up beside me. "Hey, mister, you called for a taxi?"

I glanced over and grinned. "Hey, Mooner. I got to get to work."

"That's why Mooner's Person Movers is at your service." He'd dressed fast. The wings of his hair looked like he'd run his fingers through them once, and he still hadn't shaved. In spite of his appearance, his eyes were bright and his smile was easy.

"Oh. Well . . ." I wasn't sure why I felt reluctant as I swung a leg over the back of the seat.

Mooner wheeled the bike, heading away from Elsewhere, and I knew why I'd felt reluctant. I yelled, "This is the wrong way!"

"Depends on where you're going, doesn't it?" He laughed. "Relax, Rice-a-ronnie. We need to talk. I'll still get you to work faster than if you'd run."

"Okay!" My only real alternative seemed to be to jump off the bike.

We rode several blocks farther from Ho Street. Mooner stopped in an abandoned supermarket's cracked and buckling asphalt parking lot. At one corner someone had dug up the blacktop to start a garden, then given up. Now a jungle of weeds and saplings was slowly reclaiming the entire lot for Ma Nature.

Mooner twisted on the saddle to look over his shoulder

at me. "I didn't tell you anything about Elsewhere. I wanted you to get your own impression."

"It's a bookstore. If you like bookstores, it's a good one."

"And the people?"

"Goldy's cold. I like Mickey."

"Yeah. She wants you to."

I squinted.

He said, "She's good at it. Very likable. Be careful, Ronzo. She uses people. Gets their sympathy, then gets them to like her."

I blinked. "This has something to do with why you wanted me to get a job there?"

He nodded and grinned. "Yeah. You're my secret agent, Ronnie-o."

"I am?"

"If you want to be. If you can handle it. I don't want you to take on anything you can't handle."

"You want me to spy on Mickey?"

He nodded.

"Why?"

"She's got something of mine."

"What?"

"None—" He stopped and laughed. "Hey, I'm entitled to my own secrets. But it's something of mine, no lie."

I shrugged. "Fine. I'll look for something of yours, and you won't tell me what it is. This'll be fun."

He laughed again. "I know where it is. It's in her store. But Mickey buys some of the best security spells in Soho. Your mission, should you decide to accept it, is to learn the password to get me in. That's all."

"Why don't you go to the Silver Suits?"

"Who said it was something legal? Who said I had the

title to it? If she had that handsome jacket of yours in her basement, could you prove you owned it? Mickey's got connections. The only people who'd believe me against her are people who know me."

I nodded, then looked at the ground.

"You don't have to if you don't want to."

"It's not a matter of wanting to. It's . . ." I shrugged.

"Think about it. That's all I ask."

"Well, okay."

"Good man!" He clapped me on the shoulder, almost knocking me from the bike, then turned back to the handlebars. "Next stop, Elsewhere!"

CHAPTER TEN

WORKTIME

H E MEANT THAT LITERALLY. WE ROLLED THROUGH EVERY
intersection between the supermarket lot and Elsewhere.
Halfway to Elsewhere, I closed my eyes, but it was scarier
to hear the horns and brakes without knowing if our luck
would hold, and so I learned what I'd answer if I were
before a firing squad and offered a blindfold: I kept my eyes
open for the rest of the trip.

"Man," I told Mooner when he dropped me around the
block from the bookstore, "next time I ride with you, I got
to wear rubber shorts."

Mooner laughed and raced away. Three female elves in
red leather nudged each other and smiled as he passed. I
swore under my breath, apparently loud enough to make
myself visible. One of the elves said without smiling, "Got
a problem, kid?"

"Not to spare, sorry," I said as I began to run. I left them shaking their heads.

Hurtling into Elsewhere, I banged the front door back on its hinges. Goldy, on top of a rolling ladder with an armload of books, and Mickey, on a couch turning the pages of a book with a carved stick clenched in her teeth, looked up. Goldy wore purple pin-striped trousers, a red tank top, and blue plastic thongs. Mickey wore multicolored harem pants, a man's dress shirt with the sleeves tied behind her back, and her beaded moccasins. Seeing them, I didn't feel so much grungy as unimaginative.

"Uh, hi." I caught the door and closed it gently. "Sorry I'm late. If I am late. I mean, I'm not sure when you expected me—"

Mickey ducked her chin to slip the reading stick into her shirt pocket, stood, and grinned. "You showed. I'm glad."

I shrugged, looking away. In two short sentences she'd made me feel good about coming here and bad about the reason why. "I said I would."

"Didn't know that meant anything," said Goldy from the ladder. "Glad to see it does."

"There's plenty of work," Mickey said. "Got a major buyer coming in next week, so we're taking a complete inventory. Count it all and list it all, then make a proper catalog."

"First step to becoming Elsewhere, Inc.," Goldy said. "Next thing you know, me and the kid'll be backstabbing each other for a vice-presidency."

Mickey smiled. "Easily averted." She pointed a moccasin at Goldy, then at me. "I dub thee V.P. Goldy, and thee V.P. Just Ron."

Goldy looked at me and whistled a long note. "You're

good, kid. I toil for endless months. You stride through the door, and already we're sharing the same rung on the corporate ladder."

"I think," Mickey said, "we ought to let that ladder topple and all be peons for a while."

"You're not about to say the 'w' word?" Goldy said.

Mickey nodded.

Goldy shook his head. "All right, little workers, let's get working." He resumed shelving books.

"What do I do?" I said.

"I like 'im," Mickey said to the shelf. "Doesn't ask about wages."

"Oh, yeah. What do I get?"

"An eighth of the profits," said Mickey.

"Okay."

"I like 'im," Goldy said. "Doesn't ask if there are any profits."

"Oh," I said. "Are there?"

"Usually," said Mickey. "But sometimes you get paid in World currency, sometimes in Bordertown bills, and sometimes in Faerie scrip. Sometimes you take it in food or bought charms or four-leaf clovers. When times are really tough, you take it in books."

I nodded. "I like books."

"We calculate the profits together at the end of the week. Half goes back into the store, for buying more stock or whatever. You start getting an eighth. As soon as you're working as hard as us, you'll get a sixth, just like us."

"If I work harder?"

Goldy, holding a book that he was about to tuck into a far shelf, cocked his arm to show off his bodybuilder's bicep. "Uh huh."

"If I do?" I repeated.

"We'll be grateful," said Mickey. "We'll know I was right to offer you a job."

"Huh," I said.

"Can't expect things to be perfectly fair," said Mickey.

"Can't expect to show me up, either." Goldy shelved the last of the books in his arms and bounced down the ladder, two rungs at a time. "I work at being smarter and stronger than any white boy who comes around."

"Oooh," said Mickey, stamping her feet in delight. "He bad. He bad."

Goldy's face wrinkled in embarrassment. "Okay, kid." He picked up a notebook and whipped it to me like a Frisbee. "Follow the form. Need any help with big words, let me know."

Goldy and I spent the next couple of hours working close together. We each alphabetized a section of books and moved any that were out of place, then listed the books in our notebooks by author, title, publisher, and date of publication. In the time it took me to finish CHILDREN'S AND UNUSUALLY PERCEPTIVE ADULTS' FICTION, he did both POETRY, RHYMING, and POETRY, FACILE AND/OR CHALLENGING.

Six or seven customers showed up before the tea break. The humans ranged from an older woman in a platinum never-wrinkle to a young guy in leather to a small boy hunting for "the good Hardy Boys books with the brown covers." The elves included an ageless woman dressed in classic High Faerie, looking like she kept her wardrobe in the sixteenth century, and a Bordertown kid in ripped and paint-daubed denim. None of them seemed to have any problem with the rest of the clientele. I hadn't seen elves and humans mingle as comfortably anywhere outside of Castle Pup.

Mostly, Mickey jotted things in a ledger with a pencil held in her teeth. Whenever anyone entered, she dropped the pencil, grinned, and said, "Welcome to Elsewhere! Tell me if I can help you." When people needed change, she invited them to come around the counter and take it from the cash register. She always smiled, even at the woman in the platinum never-wrinkle, who seemed rudely monosyllabic. Mickey greeted people as if she liked them and was equally at ease joking with the human boy and the Elflands elf.

Twice she led customers through the maze of shelves to the books they wanted. But for the Elflands elf, she told me to go up to her office and fetch the Burton *Arabian Nights*.

The circular stairs ended in a small living room crowded with low bookshelves, none higher than my waist—as high as Mickey could comfortably reach with her feet, I realized. The walls were hung with original paintings, abstracts and Bordertown scenes by artists with names like Riki-X and Frost and Jackie Chapeau. The furniture, two stuffed armchairs and a couch, had Native American and Mexican blankets thrown over it; these were covered with cat hair. The providers of the hair, Vado and Topé, looked up from the couch. Topé meowed at me. Vado looked annoyed and left the room.

I followed Vado, and Topé followed me. The office wasn't the cluttered room with the waterbed or the extremely neat room with a mattress on the floor. It was the room in which the walls were hidden behind bookshelves, and a huge oak desk was hidden under stacks of books, and a large Persian rug might've been hidden under crates of books, if the bits of carpet revealed by the narrow paths through the crates were all connected.

I found the sixteen volumes of Burton's *Book of the Thou-*

sand Nights and a Night where Mickey had said they'd be, on a shelf near the window. While Topé rubbed against my ankles, I flipped through a volume to see why anyone would want them. By the time I realized that the archaic style, the extravagant fantasies, and the footnotes about Arabian culture and sexual customs were seducing me into reading it, I'd lost five or ten minutes. I snapped the first volume shut and grabbed an empty box to load them all in.

Then I stopped. Through the window I saw Mooner on his bike by a fruit-and-vegetable stand a block away. I couldn't read his expression. All I could tell was that he was sitting in the shadows, alone, staring at Elsewhere.

I ran downstairs with the books and, suggesting an apology, said, "These were the only Burton *Nights* that I could find."

"That's them." Mickey smiled. "Thanks. How about going next door and getting tea and almond cookies? Ms. Wu'll put it on Elsewhere's tab."

"Check." I ran out, not to impress her with my eagerness but to see if Mooner was still watching from the place where I'd seen him. He wasn't.

I liked the smell of Wu's Worldly Emporium: cinnamon and ginger and pepper and garlic, fresh-baked noodles, sandalwood soap, jasmine incense, a hint of cedar from carved boxes. The shadows held bright ceramic dishes, shoes of cotton and rubber, shiny toys of painted tin, bins of fireworks and buttons and polished river rocks, silk flowers, kung-fu comic books, dried fish, strings of garlic bulbs, rolls of cloth, lamps and candles, hammers and screwdrivers, and packages covered with Chinese writing and pictures of dragons and dark-haired people in embroidered robes.

And I liked the look of Ms. Wu. Though she must've

been forty-five or older, her hair was as black as her silk dress, her figure probably hadn't changed since she was seventeen, and her smile was a gentler version of Wiseguy's usual confident grin.

When I told her what I wanted, she said, "You're Mickey's newest, eh? Here." She tossed me a fortune cookie. "Guaranteed true. I write them myself." She laughed.

"Uh, thanks." I broke it open, popped the fragments into my mouth, read my fortune, and frowned. "For nothing."

Ms. Wu laughed. "You don't like the cookie?"

"The cookie's good," I said. "But the fortune . . ."

"Guaranteed true."

"Yeah, right." I didn't see a trash can, so I tucked the slip in my pants pocket. Ms. Wu handed me a lacquered tray loaded with a teapot, a plate of almond cookies, and five cups. I said, "We only need four cups, even if the last customer's still there."

"You'll see." She nodded once to herself, and I decided I no longer liked her smile.

"Okay." I headed back to Elsewhere, thinking what a smug jerk she was. My fortune had read: YOUR BARK WILL BE WORSE THAN YOUR BITE. At least I didn't have to pay for it.

The Elflands elf had gone, but King O'Beer was there. "Ronzoid! How goes it?"

"Uh, okay." Goldy and Mickey glanced at us, and I whispered, "Hey, it's my first day on the job—"

" 'S right." The King opened his hand, showing three old Worldly coins. "I'm a customer."

"Oh." I blinked. "Well, let me take care of this." I carried Ms. Wu's tray to Mickey's desk.

"Thanks," she said. "Want to pour?"

I looked at King O'Beer.

Mickey followed my gaze and smiled. "For everyone in the store at teatime. It's standard policy."

"Ah." I filled four of the five glasses.

"Everyone," Mickey repeated, in a "no, really, it's all right" tone.

"But—" I began.

A skinny blond guy, taller than me, stepped out from the section labeled GAY AND MOROSE BOOKS ABOUT HOMO-SEXUALITY. King O'Beer linked arms with him and said, "Ron, this is Jeff. Isn't he gorgeous?"

I might've frowned. Accepting in the abstract that my roommate was gay was not the same as meeting his boy-friend. I didn't think Jeff was handsome, but it was clear that Jeff didn't think he was, either. He blushed. King O'Beer stuck his elbow in Jeff's side, and Jeff laughed as he doubled over. The whole thing was so much a picture of young love that Mickey grinned, and even Goldy had to smile.

I poured the fifth cup. Handing it to Jeff, I said, "Which way did you guys come here?"

The King pointed toward the art gallery next door. "Why?"

I shrugged. "Just curious." That explained why I hadn't seen them pass Ms. Wu's. It didn't explain how she knew I'd need five cups. I would've credited it to chance or hidden mirrors, then forgotten all about it, if I hadn't had my fortune neatly printed on a slip of paper in my pocket. Bark and bite?

Then I forgot about the fortune. The King hadn't pointed just toward the gallery but also toward the vege-table stand where Mooner had been sitting on his bike.

I smiled, understanding why he'd been there in the shadows. When I was seven years old, the school bully used to hit me after school and laugh with his friends when I ran home crying. I'd told Tony about it. He'd said, "You're on your own, kid. I can't walk you home every afternoon." Then he showed me how to make a fist and how to throw a punch and told me that fighting back was more important than winning. None of that was particularly comforting, but it'd made me realize I'd have to fight back or Tony wouldn't respect me.

The next day, alone and scared, I'd fought. The bully began to beat me pretty badly. Then he stopped, looked behind me, and ran away. When I looked back, Tony was sauntering toward me. He said I'd been doing good but he was sorry I'd chased the bully off so soon; he'd wanted to watch the fight. I had stood there, my face covered with blood and snot and tears, and I felt great.

"Everything's great," I told King O'Beer.

The King nodded. "Good." He glanced at Jeff, who was reading a paperback from the GOOD STUFF section. "For me, too."

"I don't want to hear about it, thank you."

The King laughed. "You're jealous."

"Hah."

More quietly, he said, "Sparks could use someone being nice to her. She thinks you're cute."

I shrugged. I'd very successfully forgotten that part of last night. Now I pictured a gangly girl without a lot of chin, then pictured Wiseguy's dark eyes and proud smile, and I wondered how wasted I'd been to put a move on a kid like Sparks. "What about Mooner?"

"Mooner said he never promised her anything. That's why she could use someone being nice to her."

"I s'pose. Not me."

"Still holding out for Wiseguy?"

His voice was amused, but mine wasn't. "Not for Sparks, anyway."

"She's a good kid."

"I'm sure."

King O'Beer shrugged. "Ah, well. Can't force you."

"Hey!" Goldy called. "The stock won't inventory itself!"

Mickey glanced up from writing at her desk. "You can take another minute if—" I thought that sounded decent of her, but Mooner was an invisible presence at my shoulder, whispering, *Be careful, Ronzo. She uses people.*

"We've got to be going," King O'Beer said.

Jeff brought over two paperbacks from the Good Stuff shelf and set them on the counter. I read the titles upside down: Bester's *The Stars My Destination* and Delany's *Nova*. I said, "The books in the bin up front are free."

Jeff nodded. "I looked. Everything in there's still overpriced. If you're telling me that because you haven't had a chance to read these, I'll lend 'em to you when I'm done with 'em."

"Oh." I turned to King O'Beer. "He's all right."

The King laughed and put his arm around Jeff. "I know." He left the arm there while Mickey said that two of his three coins would pay for the paperbacks, and he kept it there while they went out the door.

"Gay boys," Goldy said to the books that he shelved, and shook his head.

"So?" said Mickey.

"They bounce around like a bunch of damn puppies."

"Not everyone's as cool as you, Goldy."

He nodded. "There is that."

"Well," I said to Mickey. "What do you want me—?"

Someone yelled in the street. More voices joined in, whooping and shrieking. Jeff and the King came running back inside, followed by six guys in Pack colors. The Packers were laughing and yelling. The only clear words in the babel were "queers" and "pooftahs" and "homos." The King's cheek bled, from a rock or a fist, and Jeff kept an arm around him to keep him from falling.

"You can run," said the oldest guy, a thin kid with acne scars, waist-length dark hair, and sideburns. "But you can't hide." He balled his fists and started toward Jeff and the King.

"Welcome to Elsewhere." Goldy's voice rumbled, an octave lower than usual. He stepped out from the bookshelves and placed himself between the Packers and their prey. When he put his fists on his hips, the muscles of his arms gleamed like cannonballs. "Help you gentlemen find a book?"

It might've worked if there'd been one fewer of them, or if the leader hadn't already committed himself to getting Jeff and the King. The Packers glanced at each other, then the leader said, "We're gonna stomp some faggots. We can do it here or we can do it outside."

Goldy looked at the two black Packers. "I'd think you bros wouldn't be so quick to pick on folks just because they're different."

The smaller black Packer seemed a little uneasy, but the other, taller than Goldy and built like a Sumo wrestler, laughed. "They a couple of white faggots, man. What's it to you?"

"Maybe I'm a black faggot, man. What's it to you?"

Goldy locked eyes with the guy, but the Pack leader snorted once, loudly, and said, "Kick 'em out of here, man, or we bring this whole place down."

"Maybe your boys will," Goldy said slowly, "but I'll—"

Mickey ran between Goldy and the Pack leader, shouting, "Stop it! Just stop it!" She pushed Goldy with her shoulder and added, "Please." He let her back him away. Several of the Packers snickered.

Mickey whirled to face their leader. "Look!" She jerked her chin toward the King and Jeff. "You've succeeded. You've hurt two people whose only crime is liking each other. You think they'll hold hands in public after this?" Her voice broke. When she spoke again, it sounded like her anger was the only thing keeping her from crying. "When they won't know if more people like you are waiting to jump them? That's what you wanted, right? So leave us alone now. Just go away and be proud of what big men you are."

The leader brought his hand up as if he'd hit her. Goldy started forward, but before he could do anything, Mickey turned her cheek up to the leader and said calmly, "Is this what you want?"

The moment probably seemed longer than it was. The leader sneered and let his hand drop. "I don't hit women or cripples."

Not in front of your buddies, anyway, I thought, but maybe it was true. Maybe there is a code that tells you who you can honorably beat up and I'm too stupid to figure it out.

The Pack leader glanced at the others. "C'mon. Let's get out of here. Damn bookstore."

When they left, Goldy told Mickey, "You could've been hurt."

She blinked. Her eyes were damp, but her voice was amused. "I hate to tell you this, Mister Machismo, but you were about to get the crap kicked out of you, and then *everyone* would've gotten hurt."

Goldy chuckled. "Very true, Wonder Woman. Thanks." He looked out at the empty street. "I don't know if they heard what you told 'em, but they sure hated being lectured."

"Isn't fail-safe," Mickey said, "but it's a secret most librarians and teachers know." She turned to King O'Beer. "C'mon upstairs. There's something in the medicine cabinet that'll be good for that cut."

King O'Beer touched his face, then stared at his damp fingers. "Oh."

"C'mon." Jeff took King O'Beer's arm. "A bandage will look very rakish."

King O'Beer gave a weak smile. "The things I do for fashion."

As they climbed to Mickey's quarters, she said, "You know, the only way you let those bastards win is if you stop showing affection in public."

King O'Beer's voice trailed down the stairs. "Gee. What a painful duty."

I looked at my hands. I hadn't done anything, and I felt horrible. I didn't know what I could've done, and Mickey had managed things better than I could've. Yet I felt like a coward because I hadn't stepped up beside Goldy to take the first blow from the Pack leader. Which would've just gotten us all beaten up and the store trashed. Still, knowing that didn't make me feel better.

Goldy had already returned to shelving books. I stared at his back and considered asking him why he'd defended Jeff and the King when he didn't approve of them, then decided I knew the answer. I found my notebook and continued taking inventory.

After Jeff and the King had gone, Mickey told Goldy, "If I'd called up the security spell, we wouldn't've had to go through that."

"The Packers were right on their heels," Goldy said. "Wasn't time."

"Still makes me shake to think about it."

He put his arms around her. "So shake. It's okay now. It's over."

But, of course, it wasn't, because now I had the solution to Mooner's problem.

CHAPTER ELEVEN

KNIVES
AND
LITERATURE

A	T THE END OF THE DAY, I ASKED MICKEY FOR AN ADVANCE
on my pay. She glanced at Goldy. "Gee, I guess he's planning to come back."

"You didn't think I would?"

"Had a little bet going," Goldy said. "I lost a little when
you showed up, and a little more when you lasted the day.
My wallet and I'd be grateful if you left 'fore the end of the
week."

I laughed. "Start saving your pennies, man. I'll last."
Then I wondered how much money was wagered and how
badly he wanted to win.

Goldy saw my look and laughed. "Relax, my man. I
rarely expect much of people; I like being pleasantly surprised. You're doing fine so far."

"Well." Embarrassed, I looked away.

Mickey said, "What'd you have in mind for an advance?"

"Um, a book." I held it up.

Mickey laughed. Goldy said, "There are sides to you I never suspected, Ron."

I shrugged.

"Sure," Mickey said. "Anytime you want to borrow something overnight, go ahead."

"That's great. Thanks." I slipped the book into my canvas bag, nodded at Mickey and Goldy, and left.

Elves and humans passed on the sidewalks and in the streets, more than I'd seen so far. This was Soho's rush hour, when the daytimers headed home for supper and the nighttimers headed out for breakfast. It was all candy for my senses: the sights of strange people in even stranger clothes, the sounds of conversation and music from passersby and street musicians, the smells of traffic, perfume, wood smoke, roasting corn, and clove cigarettes.

I'd gone a couple of blocks when a familiar motorcycle drew up alongside me.

"Hear you had some excitement," Mooner said.

"A little."

"Want a ride?"

"I'm not wearing my rubber shorts."

He laughed. "Y'know, I've never played taxi for anyone as ungrateful as you."

"It's just a nice time of day to walk."

He surveyed the street. "I can understand that." Long shadows made Bordertown a place of beauty and mystery. The flames of the sunset reflected in broken windows, chrome mufflers, mirrorshades, and Mooner's naked eyes.

"You don't have to watch over me," I said. "I carried

books up from the basement and down from Mickey's apartment. If there's a torture chamber in there, it's mighty well hidden."

"You saw me?" The tone of his voice was very casual.

"From Mickey's office. I had to get something for her."

"Ah. Decide anything about the password?"

"I doubt she keeps it written down anywhere."

"If you showed up early, before she turned off the security spell, you might overhear it."

I shrugged. "I'd need a reason to show up early. And I doubt she'd yell the password for anyone to hear."

"Prob'ly true."

We continued on. Mooner's bike purred, no louder than a cat. I wished he'd gun it and be gone. His presence kept me from playing sightseer and gawking at the people and places I passed. Yet I was glad to have company, too.

"I can't imagine Mickey stealing anything," I said. "She seems nice."

"Oh, yeah. She's good." He added, "You can usually spot the bastards. It's the nice guys who always get you."

"I s'pose." I felt cold, probably because of the coming night, and pulled Tony's jacket from my bag. As I put it on, I said, "So all you want is to get this thing back, whatever it is."

"You got it."

"And then you'll leave her alone?"

Mooner laughed. "Why would I bother her when I have what's mine?"

I nodded. "Okay."

"Okay?"

I'd already begun to agree, right? I couldn't back out then, right? I told him my idea.

He laughed. "I like you, Ron." I grinned, but when he tore away on the bike, I didn't like myself at all.

I walked the rest of the way without an interruption. Around me, the dying sun dyed everything red and shadows slowly ate Bordertown.

I didn't know most of the kids watching the sunset from Castle Pup's steps, but I spotted Durward's red hair and square steel glasses, then saw that he was rubbing the shoulders of Sparks's friend, Star Raven, who sat on a step in front of him. Durward lifted a hand in a wave. "Hi! John, isn't it?"

Star Raven raised her head when Durward's hand left her back. "Ron. Great sunset, huh?"

"If you say so."

"Ron," said Durward. "Right. I'm bad with names."

" 'S right."

"How was work?"

"Like work."

"You came to Bordertown and got a job right off?" Star Raven shook her head. "Too weird."

"Didn't plan on it. It just fell into place."

"You don't need to work in Bordertown." She spoke like the pro advising the novice.

"Oh?" I said. "People give you food and money 'cause you're so cute?"

A hit: Star Raven looked away. Durward began rubbing her shoulders again, saying to me, "Y'know, John, we're all beautiful inside."

"Sure. If you're into meat."

"I didn't say we're all alike inside."

I glared at him. He regarded me calmly. His glasses turned his eyes into small green beads in his long soft face.

"Yeah," I said. "I'm beautiful. The Wharf Rats are beautiful. Caligula was beautiful, Genghis Khan was gorgeous, and Hitler was Miss America five years running."

Durward smiled. "People get confused. They forget the simple truths. If everyone was kind, there wouldn't be any problems in the world."

"If everyone was smart, I wouldn't be standing here having this discussion."

"True," Star Raven said. "So why are you standing here?"

I worked my mouth once to make myself say something and heard, "Wanted to ask if you'd seen Florida."

"Why?" said Star Raven. "What do you want to yell at the poor kid about?"

"Forget it." I headed for the front door.

"Florida's around back," Star Raven said quietly. "Be nice to her, okay? I didn't have to tell you she was there."

I stopped where I stood, noting the "she," then said without looking back, "Okay."

When I turned down the dark alley beside Castle Pup, I heard a sound like a baseball being thrown against a board. When I came closer to the back of the building, I heard it again, louder.

A falling-in wooden fence defined Castle Pup's backyard. The gate had dropped from its hinges and been thrown into a clump of overgrown shrubs along the building. Flecks of white paint still clung to the gray wood. A flower garden had gone wild and the lawn had grown up, except for a wide circle where the turf had been stamped by people dancing or playing.

Florida wrenched the Bowie knife from the remains of

the wooden wall. I watched her, wondering why I hadn't realized before that she was female, then almost laughed, realizing that if Star Raven had said "he," I'd wonder why I hadn't seen *that* earlier. Florida hadn't changed when Star Raven told me her sex. I had.

The kid backed away about twenty feet, next to an elm tree, then lifted her knife to throw it again.

"Hey!" I called. "I surrender."

She glanced at me, then threw the knife. It hit close to where it'd hit before, in the middle of a poster of a man in a black costume and with high pointed ears: an old video superhero called Elfman or something.

"You still ticked?"

Florida wrenched the knife from Elfman's bizarrely muscled chest and stalked back to her place by the elm.

"I got mad. I took it out on you."

Florida threw the knife. I winced and hoped Elfman wore a steel cup.

"I brought a present." I fumbled in my bag, then lifted out the book.

Her pupils flicked to the corners of her eyes, stayed there, studying the book, then flicked away. The knife flew, catching Elfman in the middle of a gaudy yellow belt that he probably wore so motorists could see him pedaling his Elfcycle after dark.

"I could read it to you, if you'd like."

Florida marched up to the knife.

"Just nod or something, if you'd like that."

She yanked the knife free.

"Or not."

She stalked back to stand under the elm.

"Maybe I'll just sit over here." I sat on the back steps. "And read out loud."

Her next throw sealed Elfman's lips together.

"That a hint?"

Her shrug reminded me of Mooner, indifferent and bitter at once.

"I'm bad with hints." I opened up the book. "There's a picture here." I held up the book, though Florida, marching for the knife, didn't look. "Ah, well."

I began to read: " 'Squire Trelawney, Dr. Livesey, and the rest of these gentlemen having asked me to write down the whole particulars about Treasure Island, from the beginning to the end, keeping nothing back but the bearings of the island, and that only because there is still treasure not yet lifted . . .' "

I saw Florida's shadow at the edge of my vision. "It's about pirates. It was my favorite book when I was your age." I slid over on the step and flipped the page back to show the Wyeth illustration, then repeated, " '. . . that only because there is still treasure not yet lifted, I take up my pen . . .' "

Florida sat beside me.

I read two chapters, up to the captain going after Black Dog with a cutlass, before it was too dark to continue. I handed the book to Florida. "Here. It's yours. I'll read some more tomorrow night, if you want."

Florida's head bobbed once, quickly and decisively.

I laughed. "C'mon. Let's get some dinner." I started around the building, then noticed Florida still standing there, hugging the book in both arms. "Aren't you hungry?"

Florida ran back into a clump of overgrown bushes next to a vegetable garden. I was about to go on alone, when she returned without the book. As I started forward, she took my hand.

"Boy, will we look cute." She must not've heard what I meant. I shrugged and walked on.

The front steps were empty, which meant dinner had begun. I was hoping that some food would be left, so when Florida hesitated at the door, I said, "We don't hurry, we'll be lucky to get dog food."

Florida looked solemnly at me, then nodded once, and marched into the dark entry room.

CHAPTER TWELVE

DINNER
AND
DISCUSSION

I LED FLORIDA UP THE FRONT STAIRS. SHE STARED AT FESTUS. I said, "Gives me the creeps, too, but I'm sure not going to move it elsewhere."

Guitar chords, candlelight, and a smell of tomatoes, garlic, pepper, and oregano came from the common room. "Spaghetti," I said, sniffing loudly. "Maybe pizza. Durward's one prime wanker, but he cooks all right."

Florida dragged on my hand. When I glanced at her, her grip tightened and she marched ahead. I hesitated then, just outside the common room. Someone would laugh at me, either during dinner or afterward. Maybe I'd be teased about this for as long as I stayed in town. But I'd hurt Florida's feelings at the riverfront, and I didn't want to do that again. I drew myself up, smiled reassuringly at her, and headed in with her in tow.

Durward and two assistants were busy at one end of the

room, where ovens and washtubs and refrigerators had been brought in to create a makeshift kitchen. Forty or fifty elf and human kids filled the rest of the room. Maybe half sat around three long tables near the kitchen area. Others occupied the common room's mismatched sofas and armchairs. The rest sat cross-legged on the floor. They all talked while they ate with forks, chopsticks, and fingers from a miscellany of plastic plates, wooden trenchers, and chipped porcelain.

An elf with rainbow-colored dreadlocks was playing an eccentrically tuned guitar and singing in what could've been Elvish or Swahili for all I knew. Everyone ignored him. The cats and dogs poked at the diners and made noises to say that they'd gladly save anyone the trouble of carrying scraps to the garbage bin.

It sounded like any room where lots of people weren't worrying about being quiet for anyone else's sake. Florida and I waded into the noise. I focused on the spread in front of Durward—lasagna, garlic bread, spinach salad, cold herb tea—and wondered who'd inherited a lot of money.

Durward noticed us first, or at least he was the first one I noticed noticing us. He began his standard nod and smile of recognition. Then his eyes flickered. His smile grew wider. He nudged the woman beside him, and the elf next to her also looked our way.

The noise in the room diminished as if a sound engineer had faded the output from each group of diners. Faces rotated toward us, then away. I looked over my shoulder to see who was behind us, but no one was there.

"Hey, Florida," Sai called from a table where she sat with Mooner, Wiseguy, Strider, and Leda. "Hey, Ron."

Florida glanced at her and nodded shyly. I said, "Hi, guys."

The others smiled and said hello, except for Mooner, who nodded with his elven mask in place. A snatch of whispering circled through the room, then conversation resumed as though nothing odd had happened.

Thoroughly baffled, I walked up to the serving table. Ignoring me, Durward said, "H'lo, Florida. Help yourself to anything you like. I've got a bit of rice pudding tucked away, if you'd like that for dessert."

"Yeah." I remembered a taste of honey, walnuts, and raisins from two nights ago. "The rice pudding was great."

"Uh, there's just enough for our guest." Durward gave a glance at Florida that I was supposed to understand.

I looked at her, wondering what was going on. I almost said, "So what is she, the lost heir of Elflands?" Florida's grip on my hand had tightened, so I didn't. "Oh. Our guest. Well." I relaxed my hold. "Hungry?"

Florida nodded and let her hand fall to her side.

"Enough to eat a horse?"

Florida's eyes widened. She shook her head quickly, and I laughed.

"Here," said Durward. "I'll give you a little of everything. Don't finish anything you don't like."

I expected Florida to carry her plate to the corner where most of the little kids ate, but she stood beside me while I looked for a seat. Wiseguy didn't notice me, but Sai met my look, waved, and called, "Hey, guys, join us!"

I shrugged and walked over. Florida followed.

Mooner, with a tight smile, grabbed two empty chairs from the next table for us. "Glad you made it back from work in time." He looked at Florida, who seemed to be trying to figure out how to eat lasagna with a knife and fork.

"Me, too." I reached over and cut Florida's food into

113

cubes, the way Tony used to cut my French toast for me, the way Mom used to cut it before she got sick. "I'd hate to miss this feast."

Florida grinned happily at me, carefully speared a lasagna stack, and inserted it into her mouth with an immense smile.

"Wasn't referring to dinner," Mooner said. "It's a discussion night. Durward always outdoes himself whenever it's a discussion night."

I bit into the garlic bread, which was chewy and warm, proof of Mooner's statement. "What's to discuss?"

Wiseguy looked at me for the first time. "The future."

I had to look away from her eyes. My throat was suddenly dry, so I gulped half of my tea.

"Of Castle Pup," Sai added.

"The discussion's unnecessary," said Leda. "We know the future of Castle Pup. Nothing's changed."

"Depends," said Mooner. "This is a democracy, right?"

Wiseguy glanced at his grin, or maybe at his tone. "What're you planning, Mooner?"

He shrugged. "I want my side to win. What's odd about that?"

Strider shook his head and smiled. "Democracy makes no sense to me. 'People rule.' You might as well speak of ordered chaos."

Leda smiled. "And I thought you'd never been to one of our meetings."

Strider blinked. Everyone else laughed, and at last Strider said, "Well, we'll see. I hope the meeting's as amusing as your response promises."

"Oh, you'll be entertained," Mooner said. "Never fear."

Florida ignored the conversation and concentrated on

her food. I followed her example, since everyone else had finished eating.

Leda looked around the room. "Might as well start. Mooner?"

Mooner grinned and stepped on top of the table. With his fists on his hips, he announced, "You may wonder"—the room quieted—"why I called you together." He paused for five or ten seconds. "Okay, that's enough wondering."

Wiseguy rolled her eyes, but several people laughed.

"Castle Pup's bumbled along well enough for the past year," he continued. "But it's time to rethink what we should do. We've never really had a purpose, other than to live together and take in those who need a roof or a meal, and maybe set an example for the rest of Bordertown, to prove that elves and humans and halfies can live together in peace. Am I right?"

I heard a general murmur of assent. Gorty, the kid who'd paid for our pizza the night before, yelled, "Nah, we're here to show B-town how to party!" People near him laughed and agreed.

Mooner seemed to need his answer from Leda; he didn't smile until she shrugged and nodded. Wiseguy's eyes were dark slits as she watched her brother.

"It's hard to be an example," Mooner continued, "when no one knows about us. It's hard for us to grow when the Pack and the Rats and the Bloods and Dragonfire and all the littler gangs are out there grabbing the new kids. We can keep taking long shots that win us the occasional recruit, like cruising out to Stowaway's Bump to see if anyone's been tossed off the train. That's added, what, three people to our ranks?" He grinned at me.

"Besides, Castle Pup's got all the people it can comfortably handle. May have too many. Our jerry-rigged water system isn't really adequate for what's here. It gets harder every week to scrounge enough food for everyone."

"We get by," Leda said.

"Sure." Mooner's delight suggested that he'd hoped she would say something like that. "We get by. We've been getting by. But we've been operating like this for over a year. What about getting ahead?"

"Gee, Mooner," said Sai. "Don't tell me you're about to get to the point?"

Mooner bared his long white teeth in a challenging smile. "A point? Here it is. Bordertown's changing, and Soho's changing, too. A few years back there was no one here but squatters. Then someone turned an old building into a nightclub, and someone else started a general store. In fifteen years there'll be tourist buses rolling through the streets, and little open-air restaurants on every corner, and boutiques selling rich folks' versions of what the street kids wore the year before."

"That's the way of the world," said Leda. "Happened to Montmartre and Greenwich Village and Haight-Ashbury and Uptown. It'll happen to Bordertown. You think you can stop it?"

"Who said anything about stopping it? I think"— Mooner turned to let his gaze encompass everyone in the room—"we should anticipate it. We should turn Castle Pup into a music club. The first club that's explicitly for elves and halfies and humans." He beamed like the mask of comedy and basked in the stares of his stunned audience.

Wiseguy said, "Anyone who can pay the cover charge, eh?"

"Exactly, dear sister."

Mooner must've expected the surge of voices that his proposal brought. It seemed like everyone suddenly spoke, either to their neighbors or to Mooner. But he may not have expected what would end the babel.

Leda said, simply but quite loudly, "No."

Mooner shrugged. "Do we all decide, or do you?"

I saw the trap. I don't know if Leda did the best she could by ignoring it. "You're talking about turning Castle Pup into a parody of itself."

"I'm trying," he said patiently, "to save it."

"Ain't broke, don't fix it!" Sai yelled, which got a few cries of agreement.

Mooner shrugged. "If we were having a nice drive to the edge of a cliff, would you say we shouldn't turn the steering wheel until we'd gone over?"

Sai didn't answer that.

"Who," said Leda, "do you propose should manage this club?"

Mooner, with a graceful twist of his hand, indicated himself. "It'd be a lot of work, but it'd be worth it."

"A lot of glory," said Leda.

"A cheap coin," said Mooner. "I doubt there's much glory in taking the blame for everything that goes wrong." He turned his head to one side and looked at her. "Am I right?"

She sidestepped that by asking, "Who'd work in this new club?"

"All of us. As we currently do."

"Where'd you put the bands and the audience?"

Mooner opened both hands to indicate the area around us.

"Then we wouldn't have a common room."

"Not while the club was open."

"What about toilets?" said Durward.

"When we had some money, we could hire someone to fix the old plumbing. In the meantime there's the backyard for outhouses."

"What about the gardens there? What about Florida's shack?"

I glanced at Florida, who was studying Mooner.

"Still have the roof gardens. We can fix another place for Florida. With money and trade goods coming in, we won't need the back garden. Might not need the roof garden."

"So we quit being self-sufficient," said Leda.

"It's just a different kind of self-sufficiency."

Someone I didn't recognize said, "Things'll be pretty crowded with all of us and customers besides."

"True," said Mooner. "So we stop looking for new people, and we don't replace the ones who leave, until we have a core of people dedicated to the future of Castle Pup."

"Dedicated to Mooner's music club," said Leda.

"Castle Pup," repeated Mooner. "A place that'd be an example of everything you wanted us to be."

"And would turn a profit besides?" said Wiseguy. "What'd be done with that?"

"You can be rich and good," Mooner answered.

"Not according to Christ," said Durward. "Ever hear about rich people, camels, and the eyes of needles?"

"Fine," said Mooner. "I'll keep your share to make it easier for you to be good. Would that make me even better than you?"

A few people giggled; a few hissed.

"All right," said Mooner. "No jokes, then. Just the facts, ma'am. If we organize now, set up a business, and give ourselves stock, we could be rich in a few years. This is a great location and a great building for a club. People who wanted to use their money to help other people still could. No one's saying you have to buy toys for yourself. It'd be your decision. Each of you. Isn't that the way we do things here? If you didn't like the way things were going, you could sell your shares. What could be simpler?"

Leda stepped onto her seat and onto the table. "Damn you, Mooner, everything's fine already. Castle Pup belongs to the people who live in it. We're a family. You want to make us a business."

Mooner shook his head. "I'm telling my family we have to face facts."

"We don't!" Durward cried. The way everyone stared at him told me that he didn't usually act this way. "Not *your* facts! We have to have the courage to continue, to trust that we can do good things and endure bad things. We have to have faith in ourselves and our purpose." He extended his arm to point at Mooner. "We had that before you began to tempt us."

Mooner shook his head. "Oh, sit down, Durward."

"It's true," Durward said and sat.

"I think," said Leda, "we should vote."

Mooner looked around the room, then shook his head. "Tomorrow. When everyone's had time to think this over."

"It's going to be war," Leda said. "I'm not going to let you win easily."

Mooner grinned. "Oh, good."

CHAPTER THIRTEEN

SPARKS
IN THE
NIGHT

LEDA, WISEGUY, STRIDER, AND SAI LEFT THE TABLE.
Mooner watched them go. The meeting was breaking up;
maybe half of the household left, while the rest formed
little groups to argue.

"So what's the story on Florida?" I asked.

Mooner glanced at me and said, "Who knows? She
showed up one morning. We decided to keep her." He
smiled at the top of her head. "She's the hellhound of Castle
Pup. Keeps us all safe at night."

Florida gave a barking exhalation—her odd, delighted
laugh.

Mooner stood. "C'mon."

We strolled from group to group. Mooner told an elf I
didn't know that he hoped her band would play on opening
night when Castle Pup became a music club. She grinned

120

and immediately began planning the first set with some of the human kids.

He told Durward that he never would've suggested a music club if he hadn't hoped Durward would handle food and beverages—no one else could do half as well. Durward didn't answer, but he didn't say, "Get thee behind me, Satan," either.

Mooner didn't tell Sparks anything about the club. She headed away when he approached her in the crowd. When he called her name, she stopped but didn't look back. Catching up to her, he touched her arm and said, "It doesn't change things, kid. I still like you." He'd walked on when she whirled to stare at his back. She saw me watching, and there was something in her face that I couldn't answer. I hurried after Mooner.

He clapped King O'Beer's shoulder and asked him when Jeff would be moving into Castle Pup. He told some blond guy wearing purple snakeskin boots that he thought the boots were great. He listened to three pre-adolescents' totally unintelligible explanation of a game they'd been playing, and he nodded as though he found it interesting. He swung the little brown-haired girl through the air so she giggled, then passed her back to her mother, a Hispanic kid about my age. To my relief, he didn't kiss the baby. He asked several people what bands they'd like to hear at Club Strange Pupae, as though the vote were over and counted and won.

Wiseguy came up to him and said, "So—you planning to ruin Castle Pup, or steal it?" When Mooner lifted both hands in a silent "Who, me?" she said, "Or would either be fine by you?" He kept his mask of innocence until she snorted in disgust and left.

Strider and Mooner gave each other identical expressions of casual superiority. I hadn't noticed before that, at a glance, they were photo-negatives of each other. At a closer look, the differences didn't seem important: Strider stood a few inches taller, his hair was fine and very long; Mooner was stockier, his ears were smaller.

Mooner said, "I suppose your vote goes to the highest-ranking elf here, eh? Well, I hope you won't leave if a halfie happens to win."

A corner of Strider's mouth turned upward. "You misjudge me. I chose to leave Faerie. I do not expect to return. I'll vote with my heart." He smiled and said in a perfect Bordertown accent, " 'S cool?"

" 'S cool," Mooner agreed. He turned away and said, so only I could hear, "Like he has a heart."

Strider called, "And *I* hope you'll not leave should a halfie lose."

Mooner glanced back and showed a lot of teeth. *"Pas de problème, mon ami.* I never go till I've won."

Strider grinned. "Ah. You'll be around awhile, then."

Mooner lifted an eyebrow and walked on.

Sai appeared in the crowd, or maybe she was next on Mooner's circuit. He said, "Y'know, if the place becomes a club, we'll need a few good bouncers. Interested?"

Sai laughed. "Oh, Mooner."

"That's no answer."

She nodded, still amused. " 'Cause I'm female and less of a challenge to male idiots, or 'cause I'm a halfie and less of a challenge to pure-blood idiots of any race?"

" 'Cause you're bright enough to figure that out, and smart enough to use it without showing you're aware of it."

122

Sai's eyes narrowed. "I won't take crap from elves with their noses high so everyone can count their boogers."

Mooner laughed. "Toss out anyone you think needs tossing, elves definitely included. Heck, toss out anyone who offers you a booger count."

"Yeah?" Sai shook her head wistfully, as if princes of Faerie were already bouncing down Castle Pup's front steps. "If the vote goes for the club, do I get the job even if I vote against it?"

Mooner's ears shot high like a surprised cat's, then settled. He must've done it to amuse Sai, 'cause she laughed. "Deal," he said, and we wandered on.

He made a few more greetings and casual comments to people I didn't know, then said, "I've got to get things ready for tomorrow, Ronzoni. Be my eyes and ears here, okay?"

I shrugged. "Sure thing."

He put his palm on my shoulder and gave me the full Mooner charm: green eyes and wide mouth crinkled in pleasure at a secret knowledge that we shared. "It's good to know there's someone here I can trust." His lips twisted higher. "Y'know, I almost didn't head out to Stowaway's Bump the day you arrived, but one of Ms. Wu's fortune cookies suggested I should. Wiseguy and I made the ride into the Nevernever for kicks. I'm glad we did."

I smiled and tried not to blush. "Me, too. Would've been a long walk."

" 'S right. Later."

"Hey, what'd the cookie say?"

"Said, 'Wise folk and fools who think themselves clever Find what they seek, never-never.' "

I frowned at Mooner's back, not at him but at Ms. Wu's

fortune. Mooner's route brought him near Leda. He nodded. Leda held his gaze, then turned away, and Mooner passed from the room. I was still frowning.

"If one of 'em had left Castle Pup when they broke up, life'd be easier on everyone," King O'Beer said behind me. I turned so quickly that he laughed. "Sorry! Didn't mean to startle you."

"Mooner and Leda were a couple?"

"Sure. Back before Strider showed up. Till then, nobody thought it meant anything."

"Oh," I said softly, understanding several things at once.

"No," said the King, hearing that I'd misunderstood several things at once. "They didn't break up 'cause of Strider. They just broke up, and it seemed to be fine with all concerned. Then Strider and Leda hung out together for a couple of weeks, and Mooner didn't like it. He hasn't been too friendly to either of them since." Watching my face, he laughed again. "I keep thinking I should draw up a chart showing who's been involved with whom. You connect people through their lovers, and almost everyone in here's related. There are people already wondering where your name'll go on the chart."

I glanced across the room at Wiseguy. She and Leda and Sai sat together, talking intently.

The King followed my gaze, then shook his head. "You're hopeless, son."

"You gotta dream."

"*You* gotta dream." King O'Beer clenched my shoulder, then stepped away. "*I* gotta go see Jeff. The room's all yours tonight if Sparks doesn't come back."

I nodded.

He said, "I think we'll move him into Castle Pup tomorrow. He and I can clean up the storeroom at the end of the hall. Which means you can have my loft if you want it."

"Yeah?"

He laughed. "Sure. Wouldn't fit in the storeroom."

"Gee." I grinned. "That's great. I mean, not just for me. For you guys, too."

The King nodded. "Y'know, Jeff was around for a long time while I was nursing a crush on Mooner."

"Uh huh," I said. "Sparks isn't my type. Thank you, Miss Lonelyhearts."

The King laughed. "Okay, then. See you, Ron."

"Check." I watched him leave, then looked around. I saw people I'd met, but none of the groups were small enough that I felt comfortable crashing them. Florida had disappeared after Mooner's speech. Sparks and Star Raven were laughing with Gorty and Durward and some other kids. Strider was with Leda, Wiseguy, and Sai; I'd probably learn lots of interesting things for Mooner if I joined them.

I walked by. No one spoke to me. Wiseguy was saying something about "the stupidest idea he's had yet." I kept walking, got a drink of water, and sat alone at a table. I was about to leave when Sparks, Star Raven, and Gorty joined me.

They all grinned; Star Raven said, "Nice going!"

"Huh?"

"With Florida." She nodded like that explained it all.

Sparks said, "She never came inside before."

I frowned.

Sparks said, "Florida was all beaten and bloody when Mooner found her asleep in the backyard. He tamed her like you would a wild thing, setting out bowls of food and water until she trusted us. We built that shack out back for her."

"Is anything wrong with her? Physically?"

" 'Cause she won't speak?"

I nodded.

"Not that anyone knows."

"She's got a tongue," Gorty said, disgusted. "Points it at me all the time."

Star Raven said, "We wanted to take her to the Ho Street Clinic, but until tonight you couldn't get her inside anywhere. One of the doctors came out here, but she couldn't get Florida to go along with any tests."

"And she wanted Florida to be put up for adoption," said Gorty, wrinkling his face. "I ran away from five homes 'fore I got here." He stabbed a thick finger at the table. "*This* is our family."

I said, "Are the chairs your cousins?"

"Ha, ha," Gorty said, unimpressed by my wit.

"The doc didn't try to make us give Florida up," said Sparks. "She just pointed out that having a little kid in your backyard isn't the best thing in the world for the kid."

"Florida *wants* to be there." Gorty shrugged. "Mooner set up a watch, so someone keeps an eye on the backyard most of the time."

"Often it's Mooner," said Sparks. "He doesn't get near the sleep he should."

"The doc agreed Florida's improving. She's as safe as you can be anywhere in Soho. That's about all we can do."

We talked a little longer. When they left, I went to the roof and studied Bordertown in the dim light after sunset. Below me, Florida's shack was a black square hidden in blue-gray shadows cast by trees and Castle Pup. In the distance, parts of Ho Street glowed like a carnival from neon and faerie dust. Most of Soho's windows were dark, with occasional slivers of light from candles or oil lamps or magic lanterns. Beyond Soho, Dragon's Tooth Hill shimmered like an electric waterfall as rich people proved that they had all the illumination they wanted and more.

To the south I thought I saw the lights of the World. I looked east, then west. Something flickered over the woods of the Nevernever—fireflies, will-o'-the-wisps, marsh gas, or dragons, I couldn't say. I watched awhile, but I didn't see it again. Finally I squinted north, toward Faerie. Only a few stars above a hint of trees told me that I wasn't staring into a high dark wall.

In my room I read from a paperback of *Huckleberry Finn* that was on Sparks's bookshelf. When she showed up, she looked at me like she'd forgotten I lived there, then said, "You're still up."

"Down, actually." I meant more than the fact that I was lying on my mat, but I didn't want her to hear that. "Or should I say, yeah, thank God, here's hoping the third floor doesn't meet the first anytime tonight?"

She glanced back, then nodded tiredly. "I'm going to sleep. The light doesn't bother me."

"Who makes the candles?"

"We do. Now and then a bunch of us get together and do whatever needs doing. It's the Castle Pup experience." She put her hands on the buttons of her shirt. "Mind turning around?"

"If I did?"

She shrugged and began unbuttoning her shirt.

" 'S right." I turned on my side. I tried to keep from trying to identify each item of her clothing by the sound it made as she removed it, but Mark Twain wasn't quite as interesting as he'd been a few minutes before. He got better after I heard Sparks slide under her sheets.

I thought she'd fallen asleep, so her voice startled me. "Ron?"

"Yeah?" I turned.

Across the room, beyond my single candle, her face was a ghostly blur. "Does Mooner say anything about me?"

"No." Since she was curious, I said, "I could ask."

"God, no!"

"Okay."

In the middle of the next paragraph she said, "I guess that's good. I don't think I really want everyone to know how I rate."

I put the Twain aside. "The other night, when you and Star Raven had gone off, Gorty was asking Mooner about who he'd"—I hunted the right phrase—"been with. Mooner said giants don't brag about their height."

"Oh." After a moment, she added, "Thank you."

I shrugged. "It's what he said."

"I don't know what I expected. It's not like it was my first time."

I didn't know what to say to that, so I stayed quiet.

"Someone hurt him. I guess I thought I'd grab him on the rebound."

"That trick never works." I didn't speak from experience.

"No." And, again after I thought the conversation had ended, she said, "Does he mention anyone? In particular?"

"No. Why?"

"I'd like to know who's better than me. I mean, I know plenty of people who're better than me, but I'd like to know exactly who Mooner's big love is. Then I can tell myself it's okay, 'cause I'll know who I can never compete with. That make sense?"

"No."

"I think it's Sai."

"Why?"

"He had Leda."

"Oh."

"See, he couldn't love me, 'cause he knew he could have me anytime. And he had Leda already. So it must be Sai or someone I never met."

Since she seemed to be waiting for an answer, I said, "Okay."

"Sai's so strong," Sparks said. "She doesn't need anyone. No wonder he wants her."

"She's a little heavy for my taste."

"Mooner's not obsessed with appearances."

"Gee, sorry," I said, pretending to be hurt so she wouldn't notice that I was.

Sparks said, "I didn't mean that like a comparison. He just isn't. And she is pretty."

Sparks would never be pretty. In her voice I heard an acceptance of this that made me angry and sad. "That's a fringe benefit for someone who isn't obsessed with appearances?"

"Maybe. Maybe it's not important, but it's nice to be with people you like to look at."

"People like to look at people they like." I just said it to try to make her feel better. I guess it worked.

She smiled. "Y'know, you're not as dumb as you look."

"Everyone says that."

"I'd been wondering if you wore that watchband to tell your right hand from your left."

I nodded. "Yep. If I could just remember which wrist it's on . . ."

She laughed. "You're a good person to talk to, Ron. You know, one on one."

I thought of other things that could be nice, one on one. I said, "No prob."

"G'night, Ron."

"Good night, Sparks."

I blew the candle out and lay there, listening to the wind. I didn't fall asleep for a long, long time.

CHAPTER FOURTEEN

THE PLAN

I WOKE EARLY THE NEXT MORNING. THE ONLY PERSON IN THE common room was the elf with rainbow dreadlocks. He sat in a stuffed chair by a window, staring into the empty street.

"Anything for breakfast?"

He turned a bleary look toward me that said he hadn't slept in a long time. "Food. Yeah."

"Food would be good," I agreed, amused.

"Food!" He ran into the cooking area.

I chased him, afraid he'd hurt himself or break something. He yanked open an antique refrigerator that had a spellbox wired to its top. "Food!" He grabbed a handful of cold lasagna from a baking pan and held it out to me.

"I can help myself, thanks." I thought about leaving, but there was nothing threatening about him, only something earnest, and maybe something blissfully mad.

"Food is sleep is energy is power is peace is magic is God."

I nodded. "You took the words right out of my mouth."

He bit at my face like a snapping turtle or a creature from a straight-to-video horror flick. I jumped back, and he giggled. Then I realized that he'd mimed catching my words in his mouth and swallowing them.

"Anyone watching over you while you're in Never-never Land?" I asked.

"I take care of myself." He walked haughtily away, nibbling on his handful of lasagna.

"Okay," I told his back.

I found a clean plate and a spoon, scooped up some cold lasagna, poured a glass of room-temp tea, and sat at one of the tables to eat. Rainbow Dreads was back in his chair, watching the street, so I watched him. I couldn't decide if our entire encounter had been a game, or if he might hurl himself through the window at any moment.

The bald elf who'd washed with me the other morning leaned into the room, holding out a milk bottle half-full of something too thick to be milk. "Manna from Mooner," she crooned.

"Peca-peca-peca-peca!" cried Rainbow Dreads, reaching his hand toward her. "More!"

"What's that?"

The bald elf turned toward me, so lazily catlike that I must've surprised her by being there. "Ah. The pretty boy."

I didn't need sarcasm. "Screw you."

She grinned. "The well-spoken pretty boy with great expectations." She waved the bottle. "This is Dragon's Milk, called *abed peca'aryn* in the true tongue. Will you suckle at the dragon's teat?"

A dark hand clapped her shoulder, and Mooner swept into the room. "Waste it on round-ears? Don't be silly." He gave her a loud kiss and saluted me with the glass jar in his other hand. It was a quarter full of something that wasn't flat cherry soda. "H'lo, the Ron! Ignore Janelle; peca only makes humans puke. If they're lucky. Don't you want to stay straight? Gonna be a big day." I heard a reminder that the elves surely missed. "If not, you're welcome to some raw happiness." He held out his glass of Mad River water.

The idea of doing the day in a cheerier frame of mind was tempting. But I didn't trust myself to act properly straight; I'd be a fool to try to get by in an altered state. "No, you're right."

"Good." Mooner released Janelle's waist and poured Dragon's Milk into his glass, making something that looked like strawberry yogurt. He sat at my table. Janelle and Rainbow Dreads took deep drinks of the Dragon's Milk, then licked each other's liquid mustache with re- markably long tongues.

Mooner said, "Y'know what I like about elves on peca? They're like cats on catnip. Sai wouldn't have any problem with elves if she got 'em all dosed."

"I s'pose." I didn't like the idea of anyone dosing any- one else. "Sai's working out her problem with elves."

Mooner glanced at me, then grinned coldly.

I took another bite of cold lasagna while Mooner sipped his River Dragon Delight. He made a sound like a growl and shook himself, then laughed. I said, "Listen, is every- thing okay?"

Mooner nodded. Before he could speak, the door opened. Two bare-chested male elves in jeans and sandals staggered through. I recognized the two I'd seen in the hall sleeping with the fat kid Mooner called Strawberry. They might've been twins; maybe they were just elves with shoulder-length blond hair hanging in their faces.

"Ah!" cried one. " 'Tis Mooner, Prince of Sleep! For like the moon he—" He glanced at the other.

"Hides half his face, Ace?" said someone in the hall. I'd begun to recognize the voice when the door opened. Barefoot in jeans and a blue Hawaiian shirt, her dandelion hair matted, her eyes half-lidded in sleeplessness or skepticism, Leda swaggered in. The taller elves stepped back to make room for her. Mooner raised his glass in salute.

"No, no, no, no," said the second of the hallway twins. "Frightens sheep."

The first said, "The moon doesn't frighten sheep."

The second stared at him. "Gods, a critic. What other secret sins will I learn this morning?"

"Well," said Janelle, smiling, "with practice—"

"Peca!" Leda grabbed the bottle from Rainbow Dreads, then saw me as she brought it to her lips. "Hey, what's'is? Ron."

I nodded.

"You don't want any. Makes humans sick. Some die."

"So I hear."

"Good." She took a long drink. "More for us, Gus."

"Sai said that stuff's addictive for elves."

She closed her eyes and shook her head. "Don't get superior, Ron. It's so tiresome." She laughed suddenly. "Let's have music!"

"I could play." Rainbow Dreads reached for his guitar.

"An acceptable substitute." Leda took another drink, then said, " 'Dance and sing, we are eternal; Let us still be mad with drinking: 'Tis a madness less infernal Than the madness caused by thinking.' "

Janelle said, "I'll drink to that."

Leda smiled morosely. "John Davidson. Nothing like a minor poet for major melodrama. That what you say, Ray?"

I shrugged.

Rainbow Dreads began an odd, almost familiar tune. Leda and the other elves were slipping into private worlds. Mooner looked at them, then at me. "See?" He smiled and sipped from his glass of blood-pink cream. I didn't know what I was supposed to see, so I nodded and headed upstairs.

Sai's tour of Castle Pup had included a room at the back of the third floor that she called the studio. I opened it and was met with smells of paint, turpentine, and damp, rotting cloth. A stocky Middle Eastern woman with a long ponytail was working on a scene that I didn't recognize: elves in medieval clothing rode down a road at night, and a pale figure crouched nearby as if about to attack them.

"Help you?" She glanced at me and continued to paint. Riding among the elves was a human who looked like Mooner.

"Maybe. I need some paint."

"How much?"

"I dunno. A quart?"

"Matter what color?"

"Something light would be nice."

"Anything to trade?"

"Uh." I pulled out the can of lentil soup from my pack. "This?"

She grinned. "Grand! I'm stocking up for a trip into the Nevernever." She pointed at a clutter of cans and bottles against one wall. "Take the tin of yellow-gray. I mixed it up for an abstract that was too boring to finish. If you need a brush, take the stiff one over there, but bring it back, okay? You're not planning any particularly fine work, are you?"

"No. I'll bring it back. Thanks."

I spent the rest of the morning wandering around B-town with my paint and brush. Much of Soho is Graffiti City. I added my bit on almost every block: TONY—LOOK ELSEWHERE. THE KID. If he'd been in Soho for any length of time, he would've found Elsewhere.

I got into work around noon. I didn't want to. I didn't want to come at all. A door banged in back as Goldy entered with a box of books. I twitched, but the only person who noticed was some rich elf down from Dragon's Tooth Hill.

I couldn't quite read his expression. Maybe it was disgust, maybe it was pity. Whatever it was, I didn't like it, or maybe I didn't like his green velvet blazer and the mirrored Nightpeepers over his eyes. I said, "Preppie elves. Frightening."

He glanced at me like he'd like to play lacrosse with a stick made of my bones and my head for the ball. Then he smiled, took a coin from his pocket, and held it out. "Here. Go, before the clerks note a beggar in the store." His accent was like Strider's and the elves who'd harassed Florida two mornings back.

I looked at the coin, and I looked at the elf. Then I saw Mickey approaching. I said, "Thanks, tips aren't necessary. We're here to make your day a little brighter." I glanced at Mickey. "Right, boss?"

She pursed her lips and asked the elf, "You are pleased with the service?"

He glanced at me, then laughed. "Of course." The coin disappeared from his hand. I couldn't tell if the magic was real or stage. He wandered toward the back of the store. "I'll browse, thanks."

Mickey said, "Something happen?"

"Only my mouth. Sorry. I'll watch it, honest."

She gave me a look that I couldn't read, then said, "There're oatmeal-raisin cookies in back, if you want one." She headed toward her desk. I followed, got my oatmeal-raisin cookie—enhanced with almonds and chocolate chips, proving Goldy cooked as well as he dressed—and began taking inventory.

So much for starting work inconspicuously. I wanted the day over. I wanted Mooner to get whatever was his so he could be done with Elsewhere and I could quit playing spy. I didn't like keeping secrets and playing roles. If I did, I'd still be back home playing the loser who could never replace his older brother.

The front-door bells tinkled. I looked up quickly, but that was being attentive to business, right? Then I gaped, which wasn't suspicious at all. Two more of Castle Pup's inhabitants had come to call.

Sai and Strider stood inside the door. They had their arms around each other's waist and were looking toward the back of the store rather than toward me. I ducked down, ostensibly continuing the inventory, and wondered if their arrival meant something had changed Mooner's plans.

I heard Goldy cry, "Yo, Sai! Looking for your job back?"

She laughed. "Just popped in to say hello. And introduce you to someone."

"The fellow attached to your side?"

"Isn't he grand? I can wear him with anything. Goldy, Strider. Strider, Goldy."

Goldy said, "So Leda's no longer the only elf exempted from your prejudices?"

"Course not. Leda's a friend. This is a specimen of an old and corrupt race that I'll use for exhaustive experiments."

All three laughed. Goldy said, "Exhaustive. Hope you survive it, man."

Strider said, "Anything for science."

Sai cried, "Mickey!" as if she were suddenly ten years younger. Mickey cried, "Sai!" in the same way. Mickey's feet made a rapid drumbeat on the iron stairs. When I stood, Sai had her arms around Mickey's torso and Mickey was bashing her forehead against Sai like a cat, which appeared to be an old joke, 'cause they both laughed.

"This," Sai announced, taking Strider's arm and yanking him near her, "is Strider. You should like that name; Leda gave it to him from some book. He even read it. Strider, this is Mickey. She's all right, even if she thinks book dust is better for you than sunshine."

Strider bowed, which should've looked silly given his torn jeans and his long-sleeved black T-shirt. It didn't, maybe because he did it as though it were the natural way to greet someone you respected who wouldn't or couldn't take your hand. Mickey laughed and curtsied, without Strider's practice but with much of his grace.

"You did good, kid," Mickey said. "You noticed, though, that he's an elf?"

"Say what?" Sai spun to stare at Strider.

"The ears give it away," Mickey said, as if the height and the skin and the eyes didn't. Strider, without smiling, waggled one ear, then the other.

"Darn," said Sai. "If I'd kept the receipt, I could exchange him for something good."

"A motorcycle in excellent repair," Strider suggested.

"A skateboard with three wheels left, anyway."

Strider and Sai looked at each other. Then Sai said, "Not even for the Harley 750 with the midnight-blue finish that's in the window of Ashtoreth's Bike Repairs."

Strider met her gaze. "Nor for the cold, cold crown of Faerie."

"It come with a midnight-blue Harley?"

Strider shook his head and gave a tight, perhaps wistful, smile.

Sai nodded. "Then not even for that."

"Good God," said Goldy. "I think it's love."

"It may," Mickey said quietly, "have been a marriage."

"In Faerie," said Strider, "it would've been. But both parties must know what they've pledged. In my heart—" He glanced at her, almost shyly. Shyness was not something I expected of Strider.

Sai took his hand. "Ditto."

"So I was the best man and didn't even know it?" Goldy shook his head in disgust. "I would've dressed." No one pointed out that, in a red boat-neck shirt and gray trousers, he was the best-dressed person there.

"Uh, Goldy." Mickey turned away. "I think I've got something in my eye. In both of them."

As Goldy patted Mickey's eyes with a clean handkerchief, I stepped out from the racks. "Hi, guys. I was the best eavesdropper, I guess. Congrats."

Sai looked at me and smiled. "Ron. Thanks."

"He may've been the best," said the elf in the Night-peepers, coming from behind another stack, "but he was not the only—" He stared at Strider, then dropped to one knee and said, "Your high—"

"Don't!" Strider leaped to grab the elf's shoulder and yanked him erect. "I'm Strider, here. No one bows to me out of duty, habit, or fear."

"Or love?" the elf asked.

Strider smiled at that. "To those, I bow as low." He returned the rich elf's bow, and the rich elf looked away.

"You mock me."

"Yes. Out of love."

The rich elf's head turned toward Strider, but the Nightpeepers hid his expression. "Thank you."

"The rules of Bordertown are different," Strider told him. "I learn them slowly, perhaps because they change as I begin to grasp them. I'm not who I was. I'm becoming Strider. And you?"

"Here, I am Leander."

"These are my friends." The sweep of Strider's hand brought us back into the story. I suppose we all closed our mouths and tried to look like this sort of thing happened every day before teatime. "Mickey, Goldy, Ron." A tiny pause said as much, in Bordertown, as an hour's speech might've in the Elflands. "Sai."

"I'm honored." Perhaps he was. When elves and halfies relax, you can read them like a billboard. When they're being formal, it's easier to second-guess a shopping cart. Leander asked Strider, "May we speak privately?"

Strider glanced at Sai, who nodded. Mickey said, "You can use the living room. Upstairs."

"Thank you." Leander drew Strider toward the circular stairs.

"So," Sai asked, "how do you like your job?"

I nodded. " 'S okay."

"The kid's a good worker," Goldy said.

"For a white boy," I reminded him.

"A credit to his race." Goldy nodded. "A strong back is a terrible thing to waste."

"How's Leda doing?" asked Mickey.

Sai shook her head. "Hard to say. She was back into the peca a few days ago. Wiseguy thinks Mooner gave it to her."

"Mooner." Mickey nodded. "He could be something if he wasn't so bitter."

"He's not bitter," said Sai. "He just doesn't care for anyone besides himself."

"I don't think that's true," said Mickey. "He just doesn't know how to show he cares."

Sai laughed harshly. "That's for sure."

"He's afraid he's not as good as he wants to think he is," said Goldy. "That's reasonable. Who is?" He drew himself up and looked around quickly. " 'Sides me, of course."

"Of course." Mickey bumped him with her shoulder.

"Mooner's been good to me," I said.

All three glanced my way. My tone surprised me, too, but that didn't make me want to change it.

"Didn't say he's the Antichrist," said Goldy.

"He's been good to a lot of people," said Sai.

"Okay, then."

"He's got a temper," said Sai. "You don't want to be his enemy if you don't have to."

"Or his friend," said Goldy.

I looked at him.

"Sorry," said Goldy. "You like the Mooner, fine. Your business. I better bring up the next box of books." He nodded to Sai. "Glad you stopped by." He headed for the back of the shop and the basement stairs.

"Goldy had to throw Mooner out of the store," said Mickey quietly. "He hit me."

Sai stared. So did I.

"More of a slap, I guess. Knocked me down, anyway. It didn't hurt so much as shock me. I think it shocked him, too. Goldy had him out of here before anyone had time to think."

"The bastard." Sai put her hand on Mickey's shoulder.

"He's got a lot of anger," Mickey said. "It isn't easy growing up a halfie in Bordertown."

"Tell me about it. But that isn't an excuse. There aren't excuses for things like that."

"Mooner's working on it. What he's doing at Castle Pup will make it easier for the next generation of halfies in B-town."

"Still doesn't excuse hurting you," said Sai.

"It's over now." Mickey glanced at me. "Listen, if Mooner's your friend, don't let what we've said change anything. He needs friends. Okay?"

"He just hauled off and hit you?" I said.

Mickey frowned. Sai said, "Some people do, y'know. My aunt used to whack my cousins whenever she had a rough day. Oldest cousin still has scars on his back from her belt."

Mickey said, "It wasn't the sort of thing that's likely to happen again, okay?"

"Okay." I looked away. I'd heard what they said, but I put the pieces together differently:

Mooner had brought me to Castle Pup when Wiseguy had left me. He liked having me around. People either looked up to him or were afraid of him, and he wasn't afraid of anyone.

But people didn't stand by him. Strider was taking his place everywhere, first with Leda, then with Sai. His own sister preferred Strider's company.

If I'd been there for Tony when he needed me, I'd never have had to come to Bordertown.

"Don't worry. I'll stand by him."

"Good," said Mickey.

"The bastard," said Sai.

"Let it go." Mickey bumped Sai's shoulder to get her attention. "I did."

"You forgive him after that?"

Mickey nodded.

I wanted to ask, "If you're such a saint, what'd you steal from him?"

Sai said, "I'd kick him in the balls, then spit in his face while he writhed on the floor."

"Yeah," said Mickey. "I keep forgetting you're a pacifist."

They both giggled. I shrugged and turned away. "I better get back to work." I headed for Mickey's desk to get another pen.

While I hunted for one, I overheard a bit of conversation from upstairs. Strider was saying, "—abandon your quest, then?"

"No. I can't return without the heir."

"It'll be a long wait."

"Soho may not charm me, but Dragon's Tooth Hill does. There's something of a society there, among the exiles and the merchants and the more successful artists. I hope you'll visit."

"As Strider?" He laughed.

"Even as Strider. Those of the Hill speak slightingly of Soho to hide their envy from themselves. A visitor from Soho could make me in Bordertown society."

I found a pen and headed toward a shelf labeled: Accounting, Espionage, and Other Arts of Deception. I couldn't concentrate on my work. Fortunately, it wasn't work that needed much concentration.

Leander left with a Graham Greene novel and a copy of *Miss Manners' Guide to Excruciatingly Correct Behavior*. Sai and Strider went ten or twenty minutes later. Sai didn't get anything, but Strider bought a copy of Kerouac's *On the Road* and Chandler's *The Big Sleep*. Mickey told him, "If this is research, you'll be a monster when you're done."

During the tea break I asked Mickey what she knew about the lost heir of Elflands.

"Not much," she said. "I'm not even sure who Faerie's rulers are. Some say they're two elves named Oberon and Titania, but that sounds like an elven joke to me. They have lots of princes and princesses, and some sort of parliament, or at least that's the most popular rumor. But until a human crosses the Border, we'll never know for sure."

"I didn't think there *was* a lost heir," Goldy said. "It's just one of those Bordertown sayings."

I nodded. "If there was a lost heir, how'd you know him if you saw him?"

"Probably have pointy ears."

"Oh, thanks heaps."

Mickey cocked her head to one side. "About a year ago there were posters all over town promising gold for news about an elf with three moles forming a triangle on one shoulder. Why?"

"Just curious." I refilled my tea, added lemon and honey, and tried to sound casual. "What about, uh, ghosts?"

Goldy laughed. "Friend of mine swears he saw James Dean cruising with Jimi and Elvis and Norma Jean. Man thinks I'll believe anything."

Mickey said, "If ghosts are real anywhere, it'd be here. But I stay skeptical."

"You ever hear a wailing late at night?"

"Hear lots of things late at night," said Goldy. "Don't have to believe in ghosts to account for 'em."

"Why?" asked Mickey.

"Just curious." I sipped my tea. "If there were ghosts, what'd account for them? Like, why would they haunt a particular place or person?"

Goldy looked like he was going to laugh, but Mickey gave him a glance, and he didn't. She said, "In most traditions I know of, ghosts hang around because they've got unfinished business. Usually it's a murder to avenge or a secret to tell, but I suppose there's all kinds of unfinished business. Is that what you mean?"

"Maybe. Why would one person see 'em and someone else not?"

"Some people are supposed to be closer to the spirit world. Usually people who've had an illness or an accident that almost killed them. Or people who're obsessed with death."

Goldy, passing behind me toward the tray of almond cookies, said, "Or people that a ghost wants to get."

I said, "If—"

Something grabbed my shoulder. I gasped and looked up at Goldy, who, smiling, said softly, "Boo."

"Very funny." I whirled to face him. As I did, I looked toward the front of the store.

For most of the day I'd been checking the window almost every twenty seconds. It figures that the Packers would show up at the one time I was distracted.

"Packers!" I yelled. "They're back!" Eight or nine of them were already crossing the street, led by the long-haired kid with sideburns. They ran easily, eager without hurrying.

"*Merde,*" said Goldy.

All I could think was that I hadn't paid attention, I'd screwed up again, the Packers were too close and this time they'd work us all over and trash the store, too.

Mickey whispered, "*Guard-spell-now!*"

The lead Packer slammed his shoulder into the front door and swore. The door might as well have been a steel wall. The guy gave the handle a wrench, but it didn't turn, or even rattle. The Packers shouted at us, but their hearts weren't in it, and after a bit they left.

"What a way to end the day," said Mickey.

Goldy frowned. "They're hardly the best and brightest of the Pack, but I don't see why they came back. Couldn't be for the sake of their wounded honor; you made it clear yesterday that they couldn't get that back by attacking you. And if they wanted me, they'd wait till I was alone some-where."

"Can't guess gang logic," said Mickey.

"Sometimes you can," said Goldy. "I ran with the Pack for a while. A classier chapter than the one we've seen, mind you."

"Of course." Mickey smiled.

"Maybe they were bored," I said. When they both looked at me, I regretted having spoken.

"Maybe," Goldy agreed.

"Well, they're gone." I pointed. "And we've got a customer."

An elf kid I didn't know stood outside, trying the door and waving at us. The moment of truth had arrived.

Mickey sighed. "Open Channel D."

The handle gave way, and the elf half fell through the door.

Goldy said, "It's probably too late to get Magic Freddy over to change the password."

Mickey glanced at me. "Oh, it can wait till morning."

She didn't need to say that I was the only one who could give away the secret, so they'd know who to blame if anything happened. But all Mooner and I were going to do was take back something that belonged to him anyway. Once he had it, whatever it was, he'd be proud of me and forget about Mickey. What I was doing was best for everyone.

It felt great to have everything go right for a change.

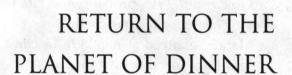

CHAPTER FIFTEEN

RETURN TO THE PLANET OF DINNER AND DISCUSSION

S TRIDER AND SAI WERE SITTING ON THE FRONT STEPS, WATCHing the sun set. I said, "Hey, Strider. Something crawled up your sleeve."

"Oh?" He tugged up the right sleeve. No birthmark.

"Uh, I think it was the other one."

He looked at me and smiled. "Right. Finish your prank on some more trusting knave."

"What's the punch line?" Sai asked.

"No, really, I thought—"

Strider laughed and, hugging Sai, said, "Off with you, trickster. We're Cupid's willing victims; we needn't be yours."

I shrugged and headed around back to read another chapter to Florida.

Forty minutes later, rushing in late to dinner, I noticed that something had changed in Castle Pup. Maybe I noticed it 'cause Florida did. She skidded to a halt just inside the common room, and I stopped so I wouldn't bump into her.

There wasn't any music. I looked and didn't see Rainbow Dreads. There wasn't any smell of food. I saw a pot of pale orange macaroni and a tub of small red apples, but whatever odor they had was lost in the usual smells of Castle Pup, smells of people and smoke. The room was full of elves and humans and halfies, forty or fifty of them, and they ate and they talked, but something had changed— something more than the absence of music or the smell of food.

Gorty gave one of his loud, self-absorbed laughs, probably at something Mooner had said, and I saw more of what was missing. There wasn't any conversation. People said things, but they didn't discuss and argue and inform and entertain. There wasn't any happy laughter, just an occasional mocking or challenging pretense of amusement; even people's humor had become serious. Then I saw why.

War had been declared. I knew just enough about the inhabitants of Castle Pup to identify the armies.

Mooner had seized the middle ground, taking the nearest of the three long tables and much of the lounging area for his party. King O'Beer, Jeff, and Gorty sat among them, along with the artist I'd gotten paint from, and, a little to my surprise, Sparks.

Leda's command staff occupied the far table, by the kitchen area. Leda herself was conspicuously absent. At the head of the table Wiseguy sat with Sai and Strider on one side and Durward and Star Raven on the other.

I didn't know enough to tell whose people held the center table or the couches by the windows. A few faces there were particularly familiar: the girl with the brown-haired baby, an elf who'd sat near me during my first dinner in Castle Pup, and Strawberry.

I looked for Janelle, didn't see her, and realized what else had changed. At least a quarter of Castle Pup's elven population was absent. Three or four elves sat near Wiseguy, and one or two sat near Mooner. So far as I could tell, the rest hadn't chosen sides.

"C'mon," I told Florida. We went to get our macaroni, apples, and tea.

The elf behind the serving table didn't react to Florida's presence. Maybe people were already used to her coming inside. Maybe anticipation of the vote made everything else insignificant.

Mooner called, "Ron-ton-ton! Got a seat with your name on it!"

My gaze met Wiseguy's. She watched from the next table, her feelings behind the same mask that Mooner so often wore. If she'd said anything, or even smiled, I might've joined her table and her party and her life.

The name carved into the chair that Mooner held was Ambrose. I didn't quibble. Mooner grabbed a high stool for Florida. She sat, pushed her hair away from her face, took a big bite of macaroni, then stopped to smile at me and rub her hand in a circle over her stomach.

"Yeah. It's good. Maybe we'll be lucky and have Spam tomorrow night." I looked at the macaroni and hoped that the orange stuff was made from real cheese. Otherwise, dinner'd taste like warm bland goo, at best.

"There's lots of pepper," Mooner said.

"Thank God." I shook pepper until the top of my dinner was more gray than yellow, then took a bite. It tasted like warm bland goo with lots of pepper.

"We eat worse some nights. We don't eat at all some

nights." Mooner shrugged. "Almost makes me wish I'd let the vote happen yesterday."

"Why didn't you?"

He smiled and said nothing.

Jeff and King O'Beer grinned at me. The King said, "Jeff and I're pretty much moved in. Wait'll you see what we did with the room."

"Can't wait." I glanced at Sparks and wondered what she thought of having me as her only roommate. Her face was covered by a lock of blue hair and an apple that she was biting into.

"How was work?" Jeff asked.

"Good." I gave a quick look to Mooner, who nodded.

"Must be heaven," said Jeff. "Working in a bookstore. If you decide to quit, let me know."

"Books." A frown creased Gorty's Play-Doh features. "Only one kind of book I've got any use for."

"Did you know," said King O'Beer, "that collectors' books often come with the pages uncut? So they're already stuck together. That'd save you time and effort."

Jeff said, "Some people take the idea of a love affair with literature a bit far."

Mooner said, "So, Gorty, do you take your books out for dinner and dancing first?"

Gorty nodded at Sparks. "D'you guys mind? There's ladies present."

Sparks laughed. "C'mon, Gorty. I'm not embarrassed."

Gorty grimaced. "Yeah, but *I* am."

Everyone laughed. I felt the tension ease. I was stupid enough to bring it back by asking, "So why don't you get the vote over with?"

"Not till 7:30." Mooner seemed to be the calmest person in the room. He drank from a coffee cup, then set it down.

Earlier I couldn't see what was in it. Now I was relieved to see that it only held coffee.

I glanced at the strap on my wrist. King O'Beer smiled and pulled out a gold windup pocket watch. "Two minutes to go. That's according to the clock on the west face of the Mock Avenue Church tower. Time can be tricky to measure close to the Border."

"Doesn't matter exactly," Mooner told me. "Just so everyone's eaten. Maybe the only smart decision this group made was that all decisions should be made on a full stomach." He poked at his half-eaten dinner. "Too bad we never said what the stomach should be full of."

Florida held out a hand toward Mooner's plate. Her own was so clean that a cat might've licked it.

"You want more?"

She nodded.

"Eat, with my blessings," he said. She grinned and began gobbling up Mooner's bland goo; I had to look away. Mooner said, "And people worried that her mind had been hurt. Clearly, the only lasting damage is to her taste buds."

Florida shook her head and kept eating.

I said, "You're going to explode."

She grinned and nodded.

"Almost time," said Mooner. He waved at Wiseguy, who looked away. Strider smiled coolly at him, and Sai rolled her eyes. I wished that there was some way to avoid choosing sides.

"Where's Leda?" I asked.

Mooner's smile seemed to creep out against his will. "Am I her keeper?"

"Hope she's not back on the peca," said Sparks. "She keeps trying to quit, then she keeps getting more somewhere."

I glanced at Mooner.

"All she has to do," he said, "is say no."

"Yeah, sure," said King O'Beer.

"There was a real sense of mission when I first came here," Sparks said. "It got lost about the time Leda started in on the peca. Wish I knew what was cause and what was effect."

Mooner frowned. "Is it time?"

The King pulled out his watch. "According to the west clock. According to the others, it's six and a half hours early, two and a quarter hours late, and 11:59 forever."

Mooner smiled thinly. "Thank you, King of Beers."

From the far table Wiseguy called, "Time to vote!"

Mooner smiled. "You're sure? I don't want to rush you."

"It's time," Wiseguy said. "Everyone's here that's going to be here."

"You want to vote without Leda?"

"She's sleeping off a Dragon Milk jag. As you know. Along with Janelle, Dark Mark, Riff, Raff, Danger Woman, and half a dozen other elves and halfies who would've voted against you."

"Really? That seems awfully irresponsible."

"Yes," said Wiseguy. "It does. Imagine that."

Mooner shrugged. "Well, if it doesn't matter that much to them—"

"Right." Wiseguy turned away. The cold war between the siblings had reached subzero temperatures.

"You'll speak for Her Majesty?" said Mooner.

"I'll speak for Leda," Wiseguy said.

"Then I'll speak for Her Majesty's Loyal Opposition. Unless there's a third proposal before the floor?"

In the crowded common room the only sounds came

from a few babies, who were quieted by the nearest adults.

"Very well." Mooner stood, smiling yet serious. His voice, calm and deep and reasonable, filled the room. "I've nothing new to add. I say Castle Pup must change or die. It's very comforting to pretend that isn't so, but I love this place and what we wanted it to be too much to let Castle Pup die in its sleep."

"So you want us to commit suicide!" someone shouted.

"No," said Mooner quietly. "I'd have us dare to succeed." He sat.

A halfie at the far end of our table grinned and showed Mooner his thumb, pointing up from his fist. Mooner smiled.

"Well," said Wiseguy, studying all the faces. "I wish I could simply say, 'I'd have us dare to continue,' but I won't. This isn't a decision to be made after a few appeals to your courage.

"We're all brave here. If we weren't, most of us'd be huddling with the strongest gangs of our own kind, humans with the Pack and elves with the Bloods. The halfies who could pass for one race or the other would do so. A few of the rest of us would make alliances with whatever gang would tolerate us, as members or, more likely, as mascots or clowns. The majority of us would simply live as we had before Leda opened Castle Pup to anyone.

"We've built a good place here, all of us together, elves and humans and halfies. This is a noble experiment, and we can be proud, 'cause it's succeeding. Sure, we're going through a tough time. This vote is proof of that. But I believe it's worth it. It's worth fighting harder. It's worth looking for less drastic solutions.

"If Castle Pup is full, let's not change and reduce it. Let's improve it and expand it, fix up the first floor, maybe.

Or let's find a building that no one else wants 'cause it's in horrible shape and turn it into Castle Pup, Number Two. I don't know what the solutions are, but I know they're out there if we keep hunting for them." She looked around. "I guess that's it."

"Where'll you get money?" Mooner called. "You can't fix up this building or any other without money."

"We can all work together—"

"That's your labor costs. What about tools and supplies? Where do you get paint and lumber and plaster and roofing paper? Where do you find people with the skills to do good work? How do you keep people working, day after day, on something that big, without pay?"

"People who believe in the project will keep working. Supplies will come from somewhere. You've got to have faith."

"We've had faith for two years. Where's it gotten us? The music club solves its own problems. It makes money so we can fix the place up."

"As a music club!"

Mooner nodded. "And when there's more money, we can fix up another building to be the new, improved Castle Pup."

"Several years down the line. If the club succeeds. If you don't get sidetracked by running a club and forget why you started one. And in the meantime you abandon the kids of Bordertown to the Bloods and the Rats and the Pack."

"No," said Mooner. "We seduce the Bloods and the Pack to our side with the best club anyone's ever seen."

"A fine example," Wiseguy sneered. "Halfies as servants and entertainers."

"No!" Mooner hit the table with his fist, and Florida,

gasping, jumped away. I put a hand on her shoulder. Mooner didn't notice. He said, "Can't you see? We got to show 'em we can do anything they can, and better. We got to rub their faces in the fact that they screwed up royally. We got to make them seek us out and beg to be in our company. We want 'em lining up in front of Castle Pup, hoping they're cool enough to get inside. We want 'em imitating *us*, 'cause then we'll know we've won!"

Wiseguy began to shake her head while Mooner shouted, "Yes, damn it, people respect power! None of us will get anywhere until we have some."

"There are many kinds of power," Durward said.

"Yeah," sneered Mooner. "Turn this cheek. Turn that cheek." He slapped his butt. "I turn this cheek." He shook himself, then held out his hands like he needed to snatch something from the air that he couldn't see. His voice grew calmer, and he looked over our heads as though there were another audience there, far larger than the one in this room. "We can do it. Everything we need is here. It's here, and we can matter in Soho!"

"I think," Wiseguy said slowly, "we should let other people speak."

Mooner stared at her, then nodded and sat.

Sparks stood. "I— I just wanted to say that I hope this doesn't destroy us. I want the nightclub. I think it's a good idea. But for it to work, we need the people who hate the idea, so we won't forget what we're working for. So I hope we can all stay friends. That's all." She sat down quickly. Several people nodded and smiled, and a few applauded.

An elf I didn't recognize stood up. "And I hate the idea. If I wanted to work in a nightclub, I'd have a lobotomy, then apply for a position at The Lightworks." She sat down to applause, too.

156

Durward stood. "Maybe I'm a little simple—"

Gorty yelled, "Say it isn't so, Durward!"

Durward ignored him. "But I believe if you stop doing what's important to you so you can do something you don't want to do in the hope that you'll be able to do what you originally wanted to do, only better, you'll lose track of what you wanted to do in the first place."

"Say that again, slower!" Gorty yelled. He might've added more if Mooner hadn't given him a glance.

"We're succeeding, slowly but surely." Durward nodded at me. "The presence of John there is the latest proof. And don't I see a new face among the people who say we're failing?" He sat.

Mooner said, "Jeff's moving in has more to do with King Obie's charms than with Castle Pup's."

One of the kids who'd been telling Mooner about her game the other night stood up. "Having a nightclub here could be lots of fun. People and bands and stuff happening. It'd be grand! And people would be passing through all the time, seeing how great we get along with each other."

"Like now," Wiseguy said. There was a ripple of laughter in both camps.

"I think it's the best idea I've heard in a long time." The kid sat down.

A brown-haired halfie stood. "Not only do I not want to work in a nightclub, I especially don't want to live in one. I have enough trouble putting up with the occasional party night, with strangers wandering everywhere and trash all over the place and so much noise you can't get to sleep until dawn. You want that every night? We'd go mad!"

Someone called, "But we *are* mad!"

Wiseguy looked around the room. "Does anyone else

have anything useful to add?" When no one offered anything, she nodded. "All in favor of turning Castle Pup into a nightclub?"

Twenty-seven hands went up. Gorty had raised both of his, so the count was twenty-six.

"All opposed?"

Thirty-two hands went up. No one raised both hands.

I looked at Mooner. The mask had settled into place.

Wiseguy said, "Do we need to count those abstaining?"

Mooner shook his head.

"Well!" She smiled for the first time that evening. "Since we're all here, is there any other business?"

Strawberry stood up. "Someone doesn't raise the outhouse seat when he uses it. It isn't funny."

A pale halfie stood up. "Did we spend any money on the macaroni mix?"

Wiseguy glanced at Durward, who shook his head.

The halfie asked, "Did anyone pay us to take it?"

"I'll note," Wiseguy said, "that you're less than satisfied with dinner."

While this sort of thing continued, Mooner sat in his seat and watched the conversation. He still wore the impervious mask, so he may not have heard any of it.

At last Wiseguy said, "All right, that's enough. Get out of here, you bums." She smiled, pleased either for her sake or for Leda's that Mooner had failed.

Leaving, Strider passed by Mooner's chair. "Nice try. If you'd just drugged seven more elves—"

Mooner launched himself at Strider. Strider stepped back, bumping into Sai. Mooner's fist missed him, but his forward kick caught Strider in the stomach.

Wiseguy yelled, "Mooner! No!" Sai might've, too.

Mooner stepped in, snapping several punches at

Strider. Strider brought his arms together in front of him to take the worst of Mooner's blows. Before he could do anything more, he fell backward. For a second I thought Mooner had done something that I couldn't see.

Mooner had done nothing; Sai had yanked Strider back. She stood there in a fighting stance, fists in front of her, body turned to one side, feet slightly apart. "C'mon, Mooner," she said. "You looking for fun?"

"My fight," Strider gasped, out of breath. "I smarted off when I didn't have to."

"Mooner," Sparks said, reaching for his shoulder.

"No!" He slapped her hand away, hard enough that Sparks winced.

"Mooner," Wiseguy said. "Don't do this."

Strider stepped forward. "Or do this. Anticipation—"

Mooner snapped a side-kick at Strider's chest. Stepping aside, Strider caught Mooner's foot and yanked. Mooner, in midair, tried to kick Strider with his other foot, but Strider leaned his head back while pushing Mooner forward, dropping him on his back onto the floor.

Mooner landed rolling away from Strider and came up against a chair that toppled onto him. He caught it and threw it at Strider, who batted it aside with a sweep of his forearm.

Sai said, "Stop it, Mooner. You don't want to do this."

Mooner staggered to his feet. "The hell I don't."

Wiseguy said, "Okay, you don't want to be nice. Be smart. You're outnumbered, Mooner. No one wants to hurt you."

Mooner looked around, and the mask broke. Something desperate showed in his face as he studied each of us. Like the others, I stared in horror and disbelief and fascination. I didn't realize until too late what he was looking for.

"All right, then. You can all rot here! I'm—" He stopped and stared beside me. Florida stood there, half-hidden by my leg. "Florida?" Mooner stepped closer to us.

Florida began to gasp repeatedly. She moved behind me. I turned enough to put my hand on her shoulder. I said, "It's okay, Florida. He's not mad at—"

"Even you," Mooner whispered, staring at Florida.

"You scared her," I began.

"And you!" he shouted at me. Before I could answer, he whirled and stabbed his finger at Sparks, who'd begun to cry. "And you!" And at Gorty, who stared, perplexed. "And you!" And at a halfie I didn't know. "And you!" And then, in almost a conversational voice, he pointed at Wiseguy and said, "And you."

"Mooner, just 'cause we voted—"

"All of you!" Mooner flailed his arms as if summoning thunderstorms. "You're—" His arms shook with fury. "You don't—" He flung his arms downward in disgust. "Forget it." He stalked toward the door, pushing people out of his path. "I'm out of here." He began to run. "Bastards!" On the last word he might've begun to cry.

I started after him. Wiseguy caught my arm and shook her head. "Let him go." She said it as if she'd seen this before, or had expected it for too long.

"Let him go," my father had said, and I'd watched Tony walk from the house, and he never came back.

I twisted free of Wiseguy's grip. For a long second we stared into each other's eyes. God knows what she saw in mine. I saw pain and fear and a plea for something I didn't understand. I ran after Mooner. Florida might've made a grunting sound as I left, but she didn't follow.

CHAPTER SIXTEEN

HOT
TIMES

I YELLED MOONER'S NAME AS I STUMBLED DOWN THE DARK stairs to the first floor, though I knew I was too late. I was good at being too late. I expected to hear his bike engine, but I didn't. Even if I had, I wouldn't've done anything differently. Running through the entry room, kicking up leaves, paper, and dust, I called, "Mooner, wait up!"

I burst through the front door and put all my strength into a last, desperate shout. "Mooner!" The word reverberated in the still street.

At the bottom of the steps, straddling his bike in the twilight, Mooner said, "Trying to wake the dead?"

"It's all right." I walked toward him, doing my best to hide my embarrassment. "We're with you, Mooner. There's a lot of us with you. We can try again . . ."

He looked over my shoulder. I turned and saw the quiet doorway to Castle Pup, then understood. I turned back.

161

"They don't want to bug you while you're mad."

"But you do?"

"Hey, I understand. I mean I don't, I can't. But I thought maybe . . ." I shrugged, not having the slightest idea how to end that sentence.

"You get the password?"

"Huh? Oh. Yeah."

We were the only people on the street within sight of Castle Pup. In the distance a seedybox blasted the chorus of "Magyar Soldiers."

Mooner said, "I'm waiting."

"What's it matter now?"

"I thought you were with me."

"I am."

"What's the password?"

The logic was simple: If A, then B. So I answered 22. "I want to come along."

"That's the password?" He didn't smile.

"I'll tell you there. Just let me come along."

I waited for the backward snap of his wrist, the thunder of his bike. At last he said, very, very quietly, "Why?"

"You'll need somebody. To watch. To help carry. I dunno. I can help."

"What's the password?"

I inhaled, exhaled, and sacrificed Mickey. " 'Open Channel D.' "

Mooner nodded. "Okay."

"Okay?"

"Okay!" he snarled. "Get on or get gone."

I got on. The bike leaped screaming into the night. Mooner took corners fast and low. I held on to his waist and tried not to think about what must happen next.

To my confusion and relief, we headed toward Ho Street rather than Elsewhere. He stopped at a place on the corner of Market and Love that was identified by a sign in the window reading: BAR. I followed him in. Maybe he just wanted to get drunk. I decided that could be a good idea, to keep him from doing something stupid. It made sense at the time.

For two hours we drank and didn't talk much. I tried to convince him to wait another night or two, but Mooner held on to one point: Mickey would change the password the next morning.

When we left, I'd had three beers and Mooner had drunk four. They didn't appear to have affected him. I felt like I was just watching the world, no longer a part of it. My feet seemed to know what to do, so I didn't worry about that. I worried about getting safely in and out of Elsewhere.

The streets were slick from a rain that I hadn't noticed in the bar. The night was as dark as Mooner could wish. A cloudy sky hid the stars and the moon.

Mooner drove slowly on the wet pavement. Whether that was for our safety, to delay our arrival at Elsewhere by a few more minutes, or to savor finally getting what he wanted from Mickey, I was sober enough to be grateful.

The bike's headlight carved out little scenes of Bordertown at night. A group of Packers laughed together under a burned-out streetlamp. A lone elf walked quickly along Mock Avenue. Two kids ran toward Ho Street with a big bass balalaika and a huge handmade drum. Someone in a drab raincoat slept on the steps of a boarded-up church. Dogs ate from the garbage in an alley. We passed a few other bikes, a purple pickup truck, and a patrol car with its occupants hidden behind mud-spattered silver windows.

Mooner killed the engine noise and the bike lights about a block from Elsewhere. The bike was slowing, so I may not've worried as much as I could've when he did that. It did occur to me that if something hit us, I wouldn't have to care what Mooner wanted from Mickey.

We coasted into the alley behind the bookstore. No vans were making midnight deliveries to Wu's Worldly Emporium or the Mock Avenue Gallery. No one had left a dumpster in the alley to be picked up the next morning. No one had passed out for the night in places where vehicles rarely traveled. Mooner didn't even hit a pothole or an empty bottle. Maybe halfie eyes are better in the dark than human. Maybe Mooner's crazy luck protected us both.

The bike stopped.

"Off," Mooner said.

I stepped onto gravel and mud. Something touched my leg, but it was just a tall weed and Mooner didn't hear my gasp. The buildings around us added their shadows to the night. Two lamps burned on the floor above the bookstore, one in the office, one in one of the bedrooms.

I breathed deeply, catching wood smoke, spilled oil, and the burnt-leaves scent of Mooner's exhaust. The sky over Faerie was clear. Stars always seemed brightest over Faerie.

As my eyes adjusted to the dark, I recognized shapes in Elsewhere's back lot: four battered garbage cans, a wire cage for burning paper and leaves, a heap of broken office machinery topped by a bicycle without wheels, a rusted-out station wagon on concrete blocks, a wire dressmaker's dummy that stood in the middle of Goldy's little garden as the world's most ineffectual scarecrow. Sparrows had built a nest in the dummy's guts, and Goldy didn't have the heart to chase them out.

The first light went out fifteen minutes later, the second one about half an hour after that. A quick burst of rain drove us into the back doorway of an abandoned building across the alley. When the rain slackened, Mooner stepped over by his bike and whispered, "Open Channel D."

I looked at the back of Elsewhere. The ivy crawling up its bricks rippled under the raindrops. I couldn't remember if the ivy had been still before, and I didn't know whether a guard spell would've blocked the rain.

Nothing else had changed. There were no flashes of lightning, no explosions, no yells in the dark, no lights suddenly turning off within Elsewhere, no demons emerging from the shadows, no innocent-appearing things like the wheelless bicycle or Goldy's scarecrow lurching into life to pursue us.

Mooner nodded and strode up to Elsewhere's back door. I glanced both ways, maybe 'cause I'd said I'd be the lookout, then followed him. He put his hand on the door, turned the handle with complete confidence that it would open, and stepped inside.

If Mickey had been suspicious, she would've bolted the back door. She trusted me.

I hurried after Mooner and closed the door. I couldn't see a thing. Taking three steps, I put my hand to my right to check where I was, and almost screamed. I'd touched a wool jacket that hung from a hook near the basement steps. A sound came from below, something anyone else would've credited to the noises that old buildings make. I hurried after Mooner.

Stepping over the second step, the squeaky one, I tiptoed down, keeping my feet as close to the center of the steps as I could. Sometimes Goldy left books piled on one side of a step, meaning to carry them up or down the next day. I'd forgotten to warn Mooner that Vado or Topé might be napping on the stairs, but apparently the cats spent their evenings elsewhere in Elsewhere.

Halfway down, I heard a click, then a dim light let me walk more confidently. Mooner stood in the basement with his cigarette lighter at arm's length in front of him.

"Where is it?" I whispered, meaning the thing that Mickey had stolen.

Mooner put a finger to his lips for silence. He brought a candle stub from his jacket pocket, lit it, pocketed his lighter, and set the candle on top of a water heater. When he turned to me, the candle was behind him, hidden by his shoulder. The tips of his hair seemed to glow, and one rough cheek shone in the darkness. He smiled.

Fire gods tend to be dark people because they work in mines with coal. Now, when I remember Mooner's smile, I think of Hephaestus and Lucifer. Then, I simply smiled back, pleased that I'd done the right thing by helping him.

He turned slowly, surveying the room. Several wooden beams supported the floor above us. The walls were covered with crumbling oak paneling. Books, newspapers, and magazines had been stacked everywhere, things that Mickey thought were worthless but hated to throw out because they were old and irreplaceable, and she might be wrong, and someone had cared enough to publish them.

An ancient safe, like something in a cowboy movie, sat to one side of the room. Mooner didn't try its handle. He pointed at some stacks of coverless skin magazines and wagged his finger, gesturing toward the center of the room.

I shrugged, figuring that whatever he wanted must be hidden behind those heaps of old-men's fantasies, and brought over a stack. The top photo showed a very clean kid who looked funny in an ancient hairstyle and nothing else.

When I stood to get a second pile, I saw Mooner had gone to the opposite side of the room and picked up a bundle of newspapers. Maybe I'd misunderstood him, so I waited. He stepped beside me, grinned, and threw the newspapers into the air.

I snorted a small laugh. The papers fluttered like giant origami bats. As they settled over ancient paperbacks and tired textbooks, Mooner picked up two handfuls of skin mags and whirled them outward.

I didn't laugh again. I thought of Mickey and Goldy having to clean up the mess, and I frowned: we had come to get something and leave, not to play like three-year-olds.

Mooner scattered another handful of skin mags, surrounding us with pictures of undressed people in silly bits of clothing in silly locations, cowgirls in Cadillacs and telephone repairmen on swimming pool decks. I suppose it would've been hilarious if I hadn't been wondering whether the people upstairs could hear a *Penthouse* land on a section of *The Weekly World News*.

"We should get going," I whispered.

"Sure." Mooner picked up the candle and motioned with his chin for me to start up the stairs.

"Isn't what you want here?"

"Oh, yes." He went into the far corner and bent down. I wanted to yell, "Careful with the candle!" But I knew he knew that, and I didn't dare disturb Mickey or Goldy, and I could see from the way he handled it that Mooner was as aware of the lit candle as I was.

He watched, and I watched, and the candle came down.

I suppose I thought he was setting it on a table or a ledge that was hidden from me by newspapers. I didn't suspect what was happening until the candle tipped forward. And then I didn't understand it, didn't believe it, and only watched stupidly as he brought the flame to the corner of a yellow sheet of newsprint.

"But—!" I called, a loud whisper.

Mooner picked up the burning sheet and threw it farther back into the room.

"No!" I called again, a louder, harsher whisper. I leaped across the room to beat at the newspaper with my bare hands. The sheet broke into scraps, and the flame died under my palms.

Mooner touched the candle to another sheet. As I ran to pound out that fire, I whispered, "Mooner! Don't!"

He smiled and lit a third sheet.

The first two newspaper pages were still smoldering, but I abandoned them to break up the third one. "C'mon, Mooner, stop it! Why're you doing this?"

"For fun." He touched a fourth sheet and held it in front of me.

I grabbed the sheet from him before it had really begun to burn, threw it onto the floor, and stomped on it. I wanted to get the candle from him, then get us both outside and safely away, but he kept the candle carefully out of my reach, cupping its flame with his free hand.

"Get what Mickey stole, and let's go!" I hissed. "You said you'd only take what was yours!"

He held the candle under his chin like a kid playing on Halloween and grinned, the very cheapest stage Mephistopheles. "She stole my heart."

I lunged for the candle. He stepped back. "She did,

y'know. Stupid armless bitch. Said I was a child when I told her I . . .'' He looked at me, then nodded at the mess around us. "The only thing she loves is this shop."

"C'mon, Mooner. Don't do this. *Please.*"

"Get upstairs."

"Somebody will get hurt. It isn't worth it."

"They'll have time to get out." He jerked his chin at the stairs. "Go on."

"Moon—" I began. I stopped when he tapped his lips with his finger. I looked up, thinking we'd been overheard. Mooner began to light scraps of newspaper, one after another with the quiet efficiency of a production-line worker in Hell. I stepped toward him.

Something hit me in the stomach. I doubled over and stared at Mooner. He threw a flaming scrap of paper far back into the basement.

I said, "Don't d—"

He kicked me again, almost lazily. The papers in the back of the room began to flare up.

"Oh, God," I whispered, and tried to stand. "Don't—" It was too late now for me to do anything by myself. "Fire!" I gasped, as loudly as I could. "Fire!"

"Yes," Mooner agreed, pleased with his handiwork. He tossed the candle into the only dark corner of the room, grabbed me under one shoulder, and pulled me to my feet. "C'mon."

"Fire!" I yelled, looking for anything to help me smother the flames—a heavy blanket, buckets of water or sand—while fire raced across the scattered newsprint.

I wrenched off Tony's jacket to pound the burning papers with it. Mooner yanked the jacket away and, continuing the same motion, tossed it into the flames. I went at him with both fists, swinging madly, but he caught my arms and pulled me into a bear hug.

"C'mon! Want 'em to catch you?" He dragged me half-way up the stairs. I still struggled. At the landing I broke loose. Flames from below cast wild shadows on his face. "Okay," he said, and turned to go without me.

A cold wind rushed by as if someone had opened the back door onto a blizzard. The wind plunged into the basement. I heard a sound below us like a muffled explosion, and Mooner and I stood in darkness.

He mumbled something short and fierce that I couldn't make out, then hurried up the stairs. I scrambled after him, trying to understand what'd happened.

Magic. Magic had put out the fire. Who knew what it could do next? Brooms might fly up and beat us, stairs might open beneath our feet, ghosts might block our way wherever we turned.

The back door slammed. A flashlight from inside Else-where blinded me. I threw up an arm to shield my face as Mickey said, "Just Ron?"

"Somebody with 'im." Goldy's broad shadow entered the flashlight beam, and his feet drummed on the bookstore floor as he sprinted toward me.

I spun about, yanked open the back door, and ran into the night, screaming, "Wait up! Wait up, damn you!"

The backyard was bathed with light from an overhead lamp. I felt like the escapee in the prison yard when the spotlights come on and the dogs are released and the guards begin to swivel their machine guns.

Beyond the light, Mooner, the anonymous shadow of a midnight biker, lifted his middle finger toward Mickey or Goldy or me and raced silently away.

"Come back!" I ran after him. "Come back, you—!" I

couldn't stop to throw rocks or scream curses. Goldy followed close behind. I ran into the alley, knowing I couldn't escape yet having to try. When all you can do is hope for miracles, you hope for miracles.

Maybe one came. After a hundred yards or so, I realized that I was alone, that Mickey had been calling Goldy's name and he'd turned back, that I was crying, that I didn't know where to go or what to do, that my lungs hurt and my feet hurt and my stomach hurt, that there was nothing for me to do now but keep running, that if I stopped running, the events of the night and the events of my life would rush over me and drown me.

So I ran. I ran toward Ho Street because it was bright and crowded and noisy. If I could find Tony anywhere, surely I'd find him there. I ran up the middle of Mock Avenue and ignored the shouts of annoyed and amused bikers. My breathing steadied. My various pains grew numb, a little like my mind.

To-*ny*. To-*ny*. I silently called as I ran, pacing the syllables to my running. Left foot, *To!* Right foot, *Ny!* Left foot, *To!* Right foot, *Ny!* I'm *here*, Tony! I *came to Border-town*, I'm *here*, Tony, I'm *here*.

People muttered things as I passed, words that had no meaning to me. I entered Ho Street and turned down it.

I'm *here*. I'm *here*. Electric lights and faerie dust cast strange hues onto the street and the people, onto the air itself.

I'm *here*. Bits of music, rock and world-beat and Celtadelic and jazz fusion and jazz fission, swirled by from nightclub doors and seedyboxes.

I'm *here*. Faces, elf and human, swam past. I couldn't see Tony in any of them. I could see Tony in all of them.

I'm *here*, Tony! I'm *here!*

I was running toward the Mad River, though I didn't think about my destination.

Someone said, "What's that?" clearly not meaning me.

Someone said, "Dunno."

Someone pointed, away from the street.

I stumbled to a stop.

To the south, a piece of the sky glowed.

"Something's burning," someone said.

"Castle Pup," someone whispered. And I realized that the someone was me.

CHAPTER SEVENTEEN

SON OF
HOT TIMES

I WASN'T ALONE IN MY RACE TO CASTLE PUP. THE PEOPLE I bumped aside probably thought I was just another gawker or ghoul hurrying to get in everyone's way. Bikes passed me, as well as faster runners. A drop of something cool and damp fell on my face. After that happened a few times, I figured out that it'd begun to drizzle.

When I turned onto Market Street, I saw that the flames centered on the back of Castle Pup's third floor. So much for Durward's gardens, I thought. At the same time I thought: It's not too bad. The lower stories look fine. Everyone must've had time to get out. Everyone must be out, and the rain'll put out the fire.

The back of the third floor was the art studio. Surely, paint fumes would've kept anyone from sleeping in the art studio. I couldn't remember who had the room next to it. Halfway down the hall were Sai's room and the storeroom that Jeff and the King were fixing up. The room I shared with Sparks was near the front steps. Someone would notice a fire in the art studio. Everyone would have time to get out.

Then I saw flames in a window on the second floor. Only a miracle would put out *that* fire.

A van from the Soho Free Clinic squealed to a stop half a block from Castle Pup. A black woman in a long coat got out with a bullhorn and shouted at the crowd, "Please, everyone get back from the building! For your safety and for the safety of those still inside, please get back from the building!"

A guy and an elf woman got out of the other side. The guy snagged my arm and said, "We need help clearing the area."

I jerked my arm loose, yelled, "I live in there!" and kept on, elbowing through the ring of gawkers. Most of the inhabitants of Castle Pup stood around looking numb or confused or defeated. I recognized a few faces: Strawberry, the Hispanic girl with her two-year-old, and Gorty. Seven or eight people were stretched on the street on blankets or wadded-up coats. I spotted the girl from the art studio giving mouth-to-mouth resuscitation to a boy of ten or so and started toward them.

Someone called something from far away. I couldn't make out the words or recognize the voice, but I stopped in the crowd because someone was calling to me.

The wind whispered urgently, "Help me, help me, help me . . ."

In the alley beside Castle Pup a pale woman in long white robes reached out, beckoning for aid. Her lips moved desperately, not quite in sync with the cry for help. Her eyes focused on me, as if I were the only person in the street. Maybe for her I was. Everyone else ran by as though she wasn't there.

I don't know why I wasn't scared of her this time. Maybe it was because I'd seen her before, or maybe I had too many other things to be scared of, or maybe I didn't see her as some weird thing but as someone in need. Or maybe it was because her appearance made me afraid for Florida, so I didn't have time to be afraid for myself.

The White Lady drifted back into the shadows when I ran toward her. I stumbled over something in the dark alley, discarded lumber or the broken fence gate, and kept on, shouting, "Kid! Where are you, kid?"

I had light in the back that I didn't want. Castle Pup's rooftop outhouse had fallen down, burning, onto Florida's shack. The shack leaned in on itself, and one wall smoldered. Fire rippled among the weeds of the abandoned garden.

"Florida!" I yelled.

Something scurried within the shack like a trapped squirrel.

I grabbed the wooden door handle and yanked twice. The first time it didn't budge. The second time it came off in my hand. I threw it aside, yelled, "Stand back!" and threw myself against the jammed door. It buckled under my shoulder, and I staggered into the tiny room.

Someone yelled, "Uh!" and hurtled into my arms.

"Florida," I said, and hugged her close as I staggered out. "You okay?"

"Uh, uh!" she said, nodding against my chest.

"Good." I carried her through the alley. She held something hard that poked me. When I set her down at the edge of the ring of gawkers, I recognized the copy of *Treasure Island*. "Keep back from the building," I said. "If we get separated, look for me at Elsewhere, okay?"

She nodded, and I ran back toward Castle Pup.

Sai came down the smoky front steps with a baby in one arm and an upset cat in the other. A small boy took the cat as I approached, and ran back into the crowd. Star Raven followed Sai, her arm around a dazed human girl wrapped in a blanket.

Gorty took the baby from Sai and, whispering, "It's all right now, you're both safe," led the human girl away.

"Is everyone out?" said the elf from the clinic.

"Don't know." Sai coughed. "We need to do a head count. Anyone seen Strider?"

"No," I said.

"I think Mooner's still in there," gasped Star Raven.

"Mooner," I repeated. I bent over and breathed deeply, trying not to feel sick.

"C'mon." The guy from the clinic, an older man with a cigarette-stained mustache, took Star Raven's arm. "Let's move."

"Mooner spotted the fire," said Star Raven. "If he hadn't . . ."

"I'm sure," I said.

Durward met us with the head count. "Ten missing that I know about." He ticked them off on his fingers. "Leda, Wiseguy, Mooner, Jimmyjack, Thornton, Strider, Marvin Gardens, Sparks, King O'Beer, Stetson."

Sai made a tiny sound at Strider's name. I said, "Jeff was s'posed to move in tonight."

Durward winced. "Eleven."

I heard sirens. Help was coming, but not quickly enough.

The elf from the clinic looked back at Castle Pup and gave a small smile. "Eight."

Strider, bare-chested and barefoot in baggy black trousers, emerged from the doorway with an unconscious elf under each arm. One was Leda, and the other was a guy that I didn't know. Strider staggered as Sai and two others ran up to help him.

The rain fell harder. Several Native American kids and a couple of elves in jeans and beaded denim jackets were dancing in the street. Near them, an Oriental man and woman in yellow robes sat chanting something I couldn't hear. An elf in black leather stood with his arms raised, gesturing at Castle Pup and the sky. Two white women and two black women held hands and sang while another woman drew patterns in the mud with a double-edged knife. I couldn't tell if this was magic or street theater.

The two people from the clinic were beginning to put on gas masks. "Let me come," I heard myself say.

"Forget it," said the elf.

"I know the best places to check."

The elf began again. "For—"

"Kid's right," the mustached guy said, handing me his mask. "Don't do anything stupid." He removed his long canvas coat. Jerking his head at the street show, he said, "Don't know how long the Bordertown Irregulars can slow the blaze."

"Why you?" Durward asked with a cough. The side of his face was smudged with ash.

It was a good question. I couldn't tell him I felt responsible since I didn't know why I did. I shrugged. "I haven't been in the smoke yet. Why should you guys get all the fun?" I pulled on the mask and began buttoning the coat.

The mustached guy gave me a flashlight and tapped the

breast pocket of my borrowed coat. "There's a fire charm in there. If the magic holds, it'll help you a little. Can't count on it, of course. Good luck."

Sai saw what I was doing and yelled, "I should go!"

"Me!" gasped Strider. Someone had lent him a green nylon rain poncho, but he began to yank it off.

"Heroes," the elf from the clinic muttered, then yelled, "No time to fight for the clothes!"

Her companion said, "We're risking one of you kids. That's already too many."

"Good luck!" Sai called.

"Stay close," the elf told me, heading up the front steps. "We go in fast, we get out fast. If your friends aren't where you think they are, we don't have time to search the building. Understood?"

"Sure."

The entry room wasn't too bad, but the smoke thickened as we climbed. I'd heard that more people died from breathing smoke than from fire, and I wondered if that was true. If it was, what were the odds of finding anyone alive? I was sweating, but I didn't know if that was from the heat of the fire, the heat of the mask and the coat, or only the effect of my fear.

The elf yelled, "Anything explosive in here?"

I might've told her it was a little late to be asking now, or I might've told her, "Yeah, Mooner." I yelled, "Old building. Who knows?"

"Put on your gloves."

A leather gauntlet was stuffed into each pocket of my coat, so I pulled them on.

Two goggle-eyed monsters bearing victims met us on the second floor. The monsters wore torn jeans and black leather jackets. It wasn't until I recognized Wiseguy's red boots and Mooner's black ones that I realized they'd found old military gas masks. Their victims were unconscious elves, undoubtedly more of the kids from Mooner's peca party. Wiseguy carried Janelle. Mooner carried Rainbow Dreads.

I pointed upstairs. "Sparks an' Jeff an' the King are missing!"

I could barely see Mooner's eyes through the smoke and the foggy glass of his mask, but they opened wide, maybe at my voice, maybe at my news.

Wiseguy yelled, "Marvin Gardens is in the second room on the left!"

"C'mon," said the elf from the clinic. "Get the one we know about first."

"I'll check upstairs! I'll be careful!"

The elf mumbled something suspiciously like swearing, but she headed into the second-floor hall as I climbed on.

Someone was coming up from the ground floor in a coat and a gas mask like the ones I wore. The clinic guy might've had another set of fire gear in the car, or one of his partners might've followed us, or Sai or Strider might've forced someone to let them come after us. I didn't dare take the time to find out. I continued into the swirling clouds that hid the third floor.

I knew that I felt the fire now, or maybe I was just more frightened than I'd ever been. Though I'd climbed these stairs often in the past four days, in daylight and in darkness, the smoke made the route strange, as if it'd lead me somewhere I'd never been. When I thought I was near the top, I glanced down, turning my flashlight beam that way without thinking. Mooner had passed Rainbow Dreads to the newcomer and was starting after me.

I hurried on. Through my mask I heard the hungry roar

of the fire. I wondered how quickly it was eating its way toward me. The outer walls were stone, and storm rains were falling on the roof, but I doubted either was significant. The building was full of fuel: oak and maple and mahogany in the floors and the paneling and the bookshelves.

By the time I headed down the third-floor hall, I was sweating as if I'd been running through a sauna in a parka. My eyes watered. The lenses of my mask were gray with soot and dust. My throat felt ludicrously dry, considering that under the coat my body was soaked. The flashlight beam didn't penetrate far. For all that I could see, I might as well have been walking on the bottom of the ocean.

I threw open the door to the room I'd shared with King O'Beer and Sparks. The first thing my flashlight showed was the shirt the King had lent me for my first day at Elsewhere. It was neatly folded over a rung of the ladder to the loft. The second thing was a sheet of lined notebook paper tacked beside the shirt.

Since it might be a clue, I grabbed it. It said: RON— ALONG WITH THE LOFT, I'M LEAVING SOME CLOTHES AND A BLANKET THAT JEFF AND I WON'T NEED. HOPE THEY'RE OF USE. At the bottom, in place of a signature, was a little drawing of a crown.

The goggle-eyed monster stood in the doorway. Mooner said, "We have to get out!"

"You bastard!" I hit his shoulder, pushing him back. In the hall the heat was worse than before. Toward the back of Castle Pup I saw flames within the smoke. The ceiling over our heads crackled, and a bit of burning wood fell on Mooner's gas mask. He twisted suddenly, and it bounced, still burning, on the floor.

"I warned everyone!" He grabbed the sleeve of my coat,

pulling me toward the stairs. "C'mon! I pounded on this door. If they're not here, they're okay."

"Jeff and the King moved into the storeroom!"

The goggle-eyed monster snapped its head back to look down the burning hall.

"Sparks is missing, too."

"But I knocked . . ." He looked again at the burning hall. The smoke seemed eerily light. In spite of the rain and the magic of the Irregulars, the fire was coming closer. I think we were both thinking the same thing: Sparks must've gone back to check on Jeff and King O'Beer, only to be overcome by the smoke or trapped somehow with them.

Above the roar of the fire came the sound of a beam breaking or a floor falling in: some wooden thing creaked and screamed, snapped loudly, then crashed. Ignoring the sound or prompted by it, Mooner ran toward the store-room and disappeared into the smoke, a shadow charging into the bright, chaotic haze.

I didn't wonder what drove him, guilt or egotism or madness or self-sacrifice or a quiet certainty that his luck would get him through, as it always had. I gaped in fear and awe.

He couldn't carry Sparks and Jeff and King O'Beer by himself. I touched my breast pocket, noted that there was something hard like a gem in it, hoped the fire charm's magic would hold, and took a step to follow.

The ceiling groaned agonizingly. I stopped, and the roof fell in before me. A long shard of something ripped my borrowed coat. A wall of rubble hid the fire, and the dust cloud was too thick for my flashlight.

"Mooner!" I screamed. "Mooner!"

The way before me grew lighter as the fire crept into the debris, then surged for the dark sky. Heat rolled over me like a wall of force, like being slapped by God, driving me back.

"Mooner!" I shouted as I backed away. "Mooner!" And then I turned and ran for the stairs, screaming, "Tony, you bastard, damn you, you bastard!"

More of the roof fell in as I reached the second floor. The shock waves, or maybe the surprise, threw me forward. Festus's bottle rocked in my flashlight beam, then toppled from the rail it had balanced on. The fire was too loud for me to hear the bottle hit and break.

Somehow I made it out, scrambling down the last flight of stairs. A cloud of smoke and dust preceded me into the street.

Someone took my gas mask; maybe I dropped it. A heavy rain was falling, and I looked up, welcoming the raindrops on my eyes and tongue. Someone asked about Mooner. Someone took me to the back of an ambulance and wanted me to lie down. Instead, I stalked over to where people lay on stretchers. Two had blankets covering their faces.

"Who?" I asked Durward. He was huddling nearby with an arm around Star Raven.

"Marvin G.," he said. "And Jimmyjack."

A strand of matted rainbow-colored hair hung down from under one blanket.

"Smoke inhalation," Durward said, without my asking. "Janelle and Tiptoes are at the hospital, along with Max Minimum. Smoke might get Janelle and Tiptoes yet. Something in the fumes from the art room. Max fell from the second floor during the panic. Might've damaged his spine. It's such a stupid damn thing."

He didn't ask me about Mooner. I nodded and walked on.

The street hid itself under puddles and mud. Silver Suits kept the gawkers back and directed traffic while firefighters ran around us.

I don't know how long it took me to realize that no one was trying to save Castle Pup. The firefighters were concentrating their efforts on the nearest buildings to keep the blaze from spreading. The street magicians worked to help them. Castle Pup burned freely, and the rain continued to fall.

Three or four people in Free Clinic coats hustled back and forth among the fire's victims. Wiseguy, Strider, and Sai stood nearby, watching them. I went to Wiseguy and said, "There's something I've got to tell you."

She looked at me, very tired and very beautiful, then said, "It's not your fault."

"I—"

She put her arm on my shoulder, and I saw that she was crying. "Mooner did what he had to. He always did."

"But—" I staggered back from her. "But Sparks and the King and—"

She blinked. "What about them?"

"They'd be alive if . . ."

"If?" She stared at me, then pointed.

I turned slowly.

Across the way Sparks and Jeff and King O'Beer stood together, watching Castle Pup burn.

"If?" Wiseguy repeated.

I shook my head and stumbled across the street, avoiding people in long coats who ran purposefully to and fro.

King O'Beer saw me first. "Ron!"

The others turned. Sparks said, "We heard about Mooner."

Jeff said, "We'd gone to my old place to get another load

183

of stuff. And when we got here—" He shrugged and grimaced. "I'm sorry."

A tug on my shoulder brought me around to face Wiseguy. "What did you mean, they'd be alive *if?*"

"I don't—"

"What!"

"If—" I stared at Jeff and the King and Sparks, and I remembered Mooner running into the bright cloud of smoke. "If. I don't know. If there hadn't been a fire. If." I had to look away.

Goldy was walking through the crowd toward me. Firelight glinted on his metallic hair and the lenses of his glasses. His face was grim.

"So, Ron," he said. "Happy now? Couldn't get a fire going at Elsewhere, so you got a good one going here."

"I didn't," I said.

"Ah." Goldy nodded. "Your evil twin."

"Mooner's dead," I said, hoping he'd understand what that meant.

"And a couple others as well, I hear. You plan on that?"

"I didn't do it! I was trying to stop it. At Elsewhere and here."

Goldy nodded again. "Did a little better at Elsewhere."

"What's this?" Wiseguy asked.

Goldy indicated me with a lift of his chin. "Kid was playing with matches in our basement tonight. He didn't know Mickey bought fire insurance from Magic Freddy."

"I wasn't!" I looked from Goldy to Wiseguy to Sparks to Jeff to King O'Beer. "I wasn't!"

"Right," said Goldy. "Your evil twin learned the password to get by Mickey's guard spell. That must've been who I chased away."

"No," I said, "That was me, but—"

184

"But?" said Goldy.

The others watched. I couldn't read anyone's emotion. "Mooner did it. I tried to stop him, but he—"

Wiseguy hit me. Not a slap. A punch to the face that knocked me back, splitting my lower lip and loosening a tooth.

"I didn't!"

No one smiled. No one spoke.

Wiseguy turned and walked away.

"I didn't! You've got to believe me!"

"Right." Goldy turned to follow Wiseguy, then looked back. "Live with it. You'll suffer more, that way."

"I didn't do it," I said quietly.

Sparks said, "You'd better go away, Ron. No one's in any shape to deal with this tonight."

"But—" I looked at King O'Beer.

The King and Jeff glanced at each other. The King said, "Sparks is right. I'm sorry."

Jeff said, "There are people who'll hurt you when they hear."

"But I didn't do it!"

"You think it matters?" He shook his head. "I'm sorry. You'd better go, whether you did it or not."

"You don't believe me."

"I don't know what to believe," King O'Beer said. "But if you need—"

I turned and walked away.

"Ron!" Sparks called. "You don't have to—"

I didn't look back. Maybe they'd all toast marshmallows over the embers of Castle Pup and tell happy stories to each other. I didn't know or care. I walked away from the flickering light of the fire, away from the lights of Soho. I walked into the darkness.

I filled my mind with *Tony, I'll find you, Tony, I'll find you, Tony, I'll find—* and *It's not too late, I can fix it, it's not too late, I can fix it, it's not—*

At the river I had a choice again. The sun had begun to rise. I looked across the bridge toward the woods of the Nevernever and thought about going off to live alone. Then I looked down at the Mad River and thought about swimming into it until I could swim no more. Then I looked nearer, at the abandoned warehouses and factories along the river's edge, and I yelled, "Specs! Specs! I'm back!"

After a minute or two a kid half my size and age in a pair of dirty brown hiking shorts came out of a building, rubbing his eyes with his fists. "This is Wharf Rat territory."

"This Specs's territory?"

The boy nodded. "He's asleep."

"Yeah?" I yelled again, "Specs! Wake up, Specs!"

The wiry girl, Doritos, came out, and there was nothing dreamlike about the way she stalked toward me. "Whathfuyouwan!"

"Specs."

"He want you?"

I laughed. "He better. He's got me."

She closed her eyes and shook her head. "C'mon."

The boy darted into the building. We followed.

Eight or ten people slept on the floor in one room. Doritos led me through them to another room. Specs sat on the edge of a bed in black boxer shorts and a baggy green T-shirt. He wiped his wire-rims with the hem of his shirt, put them on, and blinked at me.

"Ron. I'm beginning to think less of your style."

"Gee, I'm crying inside."

"Okay. Maybe it's your timing that could use some improvement."

"The girlfriends don't complain."

Specs glanced at Doritos, who said, "I 'spect they stand in line for this one."

Specs said, "This is not a social call?"

"No."

He waited.

I swallowed once. "I'm thirsty, Specs." I stopped because I knew I couldn't say another word.

He smiled and reached toward a scarred nightstand by the bed. On it sat a smudged carafe half-full of red liquid. "Well, then, Ron, you came to the right place." He lifted the carafe and held it out. "Don't worry. Be happy."

"Yeah," I said. "Oh, God, yeah."

I held the carafe up and thought: *Cheers, Mooner. Cheers, Tony.* And I drank.

CHAPTER EIGHTEEN

OZONE
EXPLORER

I DON'T REMEMBER MUCH ABOUT THE NEXT MONTHS. WHAT I do remember feels as if it happened in a dream or a movie to someone other than me.

Which makes sense. Rococo, a Chinese kid who always seemed to be wearing fifteen necklaces and twenty earrings, gave me a new name early in my stay with Specs's Rats: Gone. She said, "That Ron. He's usually around, but he's always gone."

It's funny that for all the River I drank, I can't remember its taste.

I remember general things about Gone's life. I slept in a corner of the main room of Specs's hold, except when it was hot and I slept on the roof. If I went away for some reason, I slept where I could, on the street, in an alley, under a bridge.

I hardly remember anything about food. Eating's a lot

less interesting when you're drinking River. I remember a feast when someone had stolen a case of canned stew and a carton of Oreos, but we gorged for the novelty, not for the food, enjoying the brownness of the stew and the smoothness of the cookie centers more than the taste.

I can't even tell you about the people I lived with. They came and went. For all I know, they were sold into slavery, but I doubt anything sinister happened in Specs's gang while I was with them. Sinister calls for planning. Gone, the only Rat I know well, was too interested in the river's dreams to plan anything involving a world that no longer was real.

Sometimes, when we were hungry or bored, we'd steal things. I remember the Great Bicycle Chase, when we snatched some bikes parked outside a house and people yelled at us as we pedaled away. I remember stuffing zucchinis and green beans into my pockets while someone distracted a greengrocer. I remember a clerk hitting me on the head with a loaf of French bread and calling me a thief while I laughed.

We didn't steal often. We didn't need to. Soho gave us a shelter, even if the roof of our building leaked and the windows were broken. The river gave us water and happiness. All we lacked was a steady source of food. Sometimes some kids would take slingshots and hunt squirrels and raccoons and rats of the four-legged sort. Often the river gave us ways to buy what we needed.

Useful things floated onto the banks or drifted near enough to snag. When someone spotted something farther out, Specs would order kids into a leaky duckboat for a salvage mission. I remember crewing on trips that won us a lot of scrap lumber, a bale of hemp that probably fell off a dock, a new life jacket that still makes me wonder if it'd been knocked overboard or thrown to someone who never caught it, three plastic flamingos tied together with yellow rope, and a drowned elf whose bloated body we stripped of Faerie clothes and jewelry, then returned to the river.

After the drowned elf I swore I wouldn't drink River again. The vow lasted for most of a day. After that I quit pretending I could quit when I wanted to. In some ways it was a relief to believe that I'd sunk as low as I could.

I remember two scenes well from my time as a Rat.

The earlier one occurred a day or two after I'd arrived, before Rococo gave me my Rat name:

"Well, then, my Ron," Specs said. "I hear Castle Pup burned the other night. Same night you came calling. Any connection?"

"To what?"

Specs pulled a mouthwash bottle full of River away from me. "Any connection between Castle Pup burning and you coming here?"

I blinked at him. "Everything's connected, Specs. Clever fellow like you can see that." I giggled.

Specs nodded. "Thank you, Ron. Don't get any hot ideas around here, understand?"

I rolled my eyes and reached for the bottle.

"They're having a funeral for the kids who died. Doubt it'll be open-coffin for the guy they hauled from the ashes."

I went outside and threw up.

Specs called, "I take it you won't be attending the services?" He must've been right. Surely, I'd remember if I had.

The second scene comes with more detail:

Someone had the bright idea of throwing a concert in one of the old parks by the river. Lots of bands were advertised, and most of them showed up. I remember Cats

Laughing's guitarist making a face as he broke a string, and the dancers all applauding.

I don't remember much about the riot at the end of the night, when Packers and Bloods decided they'd had enough of coexistence. I know that my side hurt for days when I was a Rat; maybe I got a cracked rib during the excitement. Maybe the two incidents weren't connected.

The clearest part of the memory begins with a voice. Someone called, "Ron?" I'd been Gone long enough that I wouldn't have noticed, if the voice hadn't been familiar.

I was passing the stage, ignoring some folksinger who thought a song's message was more important than its lyrics or its tune. The sun had set, but the sky was still pale at the horizon. Portable lights were strung around the field, and I was walking under one on my way somewhere, maybe to look for people from Specs's gang.

A thin kid in baggy trousers and a black turtleneck strode toward me. As she came near, the overhead bulb picked out blue tints in the spikes of her hair.

"Sparks," I said, pleased with myself for remembering her name.

She smiled. "How've you been? You look grand."

"Yeah, well." I'd washed myself and my clothes for the concert with the vague idea of picking up women. I'd even cut my hair, trimming the left side by a few inches and deciding that looked good enough.

"We wondered what happened to you."

I shrugged again. "Moved in with some people I met."

"Like it?"

The idea of liking Specs's place amused me. I grinned. "It's a place."

"I've hardly seen anyone since . . ." She gave me a quick look from the corners of her eyes. "You know."

I nodded, seeing she expected that, while I sifted stale memories.

"King O'Beer and Jeff are in Jeff's old place. It's crowded, but they're happy."

She said this as if it was good news, so I nodded again. Then I frowned, finally finding all of the pieces of an earlier life. "You decided I didn't do it?"

"I didn't . . ." She looked away, gnawed her lower lip, then looked back. "I never decided you *did* do it. We just didn't know that night, y'know. When I thought about it, it made sense. Mooner had a thing about fire."

"Ah."

"I talked to some of the others. That guy from the bookstore . . ."

"Goldy."

"Goldy. He said maybe you didn't set either fire, but you sure handed Mooner the matches. Something about a password?"

"Doesn't matter now."

"You couldn't've known." Sparks put her hand on my wrist. "If you talked to them, if you explained, they might—"

I had a swallow of River left in a medicine bottle in my coat, but I felt embarrassed about drinking it in front of her. "What's to explain? I didn't do it."

She squeezed my wrist and shook it a little. "C'mon. I mean, from their point of view—"

"They've got theirs. I've got mine."

"Okay." She released my wrist. "You here alone?"

I'd come with a few Rats, but I hadn't seen them for hours. "Ummmmm. Yeah. Effectively."

She laughed as if my slow thoughts were an act for her

benefit. "Me, too. I came with Durward and Star Raven. They're having another argument about spiritual responsibilities versus social ones. Excuse me, a discussion. I told 'em I was going for a walk." She glanced at me again. "And not to wait up."

"Oh." I nodded. "A walk could be nice. I was just"—I gestured vaguely—"walking."

"Great! Mystical Undertones won't be up for two more sets. We could probably go to the bridge and back by then."

Heading through the crowd toward the river, she asked, "Who've you heard from?"

"No one."

"Really?"

I nodded.

"Well. Let's see. The woman at the bookstore fixed up part of her basement for Florida."

I almost said I guessed I'd done them both a favor then, but I didn't.

"And nobody's seen Leda since she got out of the hospital. Somebody said her dad came and got her. Sai and Strider are bouncers at Danceland; can you believe it? Durward's got a position in Reverend Bob's Bordertown Ministry. But he isn't a jerk about it. He just helps people. Star Raven's doing pen-and-ink illos for *Surplus Art* that're really pretty good. She says she's a socialist now. And she introduces herself as Rave and wants her old friends to call her that. What else? Gorty joined the Pack. I ran into him at Danceland, and he's become a complete ass. It's too bad. He used to be sweet sometimes. Who'm I forgetting?"

I shrugged and didn't say that I'd forgotten them all. Then, to prove that I hadn't, I said, "Wiseguy."

"Oh, yeah. She and Leda broke up. And she's pregnant.

The father's some elf, nobody we know. Somebody she met after Castle Pup burned. They're supposed to be getting married. Or maybe they already did."

I said something between an "ah" of understanding and an "uh" of pain. I wanted a drink of River very, very badly.

She glanced at me. "King Obie said you had a crush on her."

"Yeah. I was such a dink."

"*I* thought you were nice."

"Eh," I said, but I grinned.

We followed an overgrown path along the riverbank. I'd walked it before, and my night vision was better than hers. When she stumbled, I took her hand to guide her.

A few of the park lamps had been lit again, but they were far apart, serving as beacons more than illumination. Sparks didn't release my hand when we passed through a circle of light. The path was busy enough with other strollers that I didn't worry about getting jumped, yet the darkness and the distant sounds of the concert provided a semblance of isolation.

After a few minutes Sparks said, "So. What's your story?"

"Huh?"

"You didn't spring from the brow of Jove as a full-grown dink, did you?"

I smiled 'cause she laughed and squeezed my hand. "I achieved dinkdom. I attended Dink U. I was valedinktorian."

She smiled. "Dink you." After a moment she said, "I grew up in Bordertown."

A park light illuminated a slice of the river. Something shapeless, maybe a clump of moss, floated by.

"Nice place," I said.

"We call it home. Why're you here?"

"Philosophers have been asking that—"

She squeezed my hand. "*Bzzt!* Try again."

"It matter?"

"Who knows?"

"You care?"

She smiled again. "Who knows?"

I sidestepped the question. "Okay. I'm here 'cause Castle Pup didn't work out."

She glanced at me but only said, "Yeah. Elves and humans and halfies living together. Maybe it was doomed all along."

"Might've worked."

"I wish. Maybe you can only trust your own."

"And who's your own?"

"There's the rub. No one is."

I nodded. "We come from the same family."

"No family," Sparks said firmly. "My grandparents died childless. My great-grandparents never met. The mammals from which I'm descended were caught swiping triceratops eggs and mashed flatter'n amoebas before they could mate."

I laughed. "Tony—my brother—and I came in boxes. Children, male, guaranteed for fourteen years each. Notice how everything falls apart right after the warranty's up?"

"Where's your brother?"

"Headed for Faerie."

"Humans can't get in."

"Didn't say he made it."

She blinked. "Bordertown's as close as we can get."

I shrugged and looked away. "Okay. He's back in a box, waiting for repairs."

"Oh." Sparks squeezed my hand again. "Sorry."

"Eh. It was over a year ago."

"What happened?"

"Warranty ran out."

"You don't have to talk about it."

"Good."

"We could sit by the river."

"Fine."

We found a place hidden from the path by a clump of brush. I watched the river, tempted to drink but not needing to. Sparks sat beside me, her hip by mine. I remembered her undressing in our room in Castle Pup, and I remembered that we'd talked about important things one night, though I couldn't remember what they were.

"It's beautiful," she whispered.

I looked to see what she meant, and saw that she meant everything: the dark river, the silvered, star-flecked outlines of clouds, the far silhouette of the woods of the Nevernever, the sounds of crickets and bullfrogs, the smells of the earth and the river.

"Yeah," I whispered. My voice shook.

"What?"

"Tony—" I knew I'd have to say it quickly, or I wouldn't be able to say it at all. "He was going to run away. To Bordertown. He went swimming instead."

"Oh."

"Off the highest bridge around. I always thought he was afraid of heights."

"Sounds like he had good cause."

I stared at her, then laughed like it was the funniest thing I'd ever heard. Maybe it was the funniest thing I'd ever heard. "Oh, yeah. He had good cause."

"Maybe he wanted to prove he wasn't afraid."

I stopped laughing, fast. "Yeah? He was afraid to run

away, and he was afraid to stay home. Only thing he wasn't afraid to do was make us responsible for his own decision. Bastard. Bastard, bastard, bas—"

"Hey, ease on." She gripped my shoulder. I shook my head, but she didn't let her hand drop.

"Know why I came to B-town?"

" 'Cause he didn't?"

" 'Cause this is where magic works, sometimes. 'Cause this is the place he dreamed about. I thought if there was anyplace where people could come back . . ."

"He'd come here?"

I nodded and couldn't stop myself from shaking.

"Hey, it's okay."

I jerked my head from side to side. "Pretty stupid, huh?"

"Not really." She moved her hand from my shoulder to my neck. "Sometimes, when it hurts, you have to let it. You have to work through—"

"Bastard." I meant Tony.

"Shh." She put her arms around me.

"He didn't—"

"Yes?"

"He didn't care." I heard myself getting louder, but that didn't matter. "He didn't *care*. About anybody." I wanted to hit something, the ground, a tree, something that couldn't feel anything. "He went away and, and—"

"Say it."

"And he left a note saying he hoped I'd have a good life, a good damn life! And he, and he—"

"Yes?"

"He killed himself," I finished, very quietly. We sat there for a minute or two, not speaking. Her arms were warm and comforting, and several different needs fought inside me. At last, needing to speak, I said, "I don't know why it's a big deal. I knew that."

"Sometimes you have to say it."

"I've said it. Not here. But I've said it."

"Sometimes you have to believe it."

"I don't. Want. To believe it."

"You have to. You can't—"

"I can! You know what believing it means? I wake up in the middle of the night and wonder if maybe I hadn't torn the covers off his comic books when I was four—"

She smiled. "That must've been it."

I stared at her, and I felt exhausted. "Forget it." I didn't care what she or anyone thought. I yanked the bottle of River from my pocket, pulled the cork, and drank the last swallow.

"It occur to you that Tony— What's that?" she asked, her voice guarded.

"An empty bottle, now. Don't worry. There's plenty where that came from." I jumped down to the river's edge, sinking in to my ankles, reached as far as I could to hold the bottle under, then climbed back up the grassy bank.

"You're not going to drink that?"

"Why not?" I took a gulp. Something brushed against my teeth, but I flicked it away with a fingertip. "Ten zillion fish can't be wrong." I held the bottle out to her.

She shook her head.

"C'mon. Make you feel better."

"No, thank you."

I drank again. "Ol' Tony sure wasted an opportunity, huh?"

"Looks like he's not the only one."

"Ooh. This disgust you?"

"Makes me sad."

"Poor you."

"I thought we—"

"Sure." I grabbed her around the waist and pulled her to me.

"Don't."

"C'mon. I thought you wanted—"

"Not like this." Her body tensed, maybe to push me away, maybe to knee me.

"Make up your mind." I let her go.

She stepped back, saying, "I did. Things changed. You . . ." She shook her head.

"Sure."

"Good-bye, Ron."

I glanced from the river to her.

She stopped by a clump of brush and looked at me. "There *are* ghosts in Bordertown. But you won't find any this way."

"So what?"

"Yeah," she said. "So what?" And she shook her head, and she left.

I was very much alone in the dark. But after I'd drunk a little more River, Mooner came and told me that I was quite the kid, and Tony said I'd become the guy he'd always wanted to be.

CHAPTER NINETEEN

THE MOUTH
THAT
ROARED

MY LAST HOUR AS A WHARF RAT BEGAN LATE ONE DAY IN early fall. The leaves were turning rich reds and yellows, so the trees looked like fireworks made solid. Six or eight of us walked up Zelazny Street by the old graveyard. The wind rustled litter around toppled tombstones and leaning statues of angels and babies and wistful Jesi with wide-spread arms.

We were moving fast 'cause the day was cool, not 'cause we had anyplace in particular to get to. Marvelous Martha was telling about giving River to a stupid runaway who didn't know what he was drinking, and everyone laughed.

When a rumble of motorcycle engines came near, we all looked up. Ten or twelve Dragon's Tooth Hill elves were riding toward us. They were proud, clean, gorgeous, and, by elven standards, young. They wore blood-red leathers and rode new bikes that'd been customized for the Border-lands with silver and rosewood spellboxes.

Two or three were bareheaded. The rest wore helmets painted like their bikes with elaborate Celtic designs and creatures that might exist in the Elflands: basilisks and sea serpents and beasts so strange that I couldn't guess their names.

The Rats walked warily, closer to each other, shoulders stiff. I stooped and picked up a handful of mud. Doritos, beside me, grinned her tight, dangerous smile. Specs glanced back, said, "There's more of them." I didn't look at him.

The nearest biker began to swerve to give the Rats plenty of room. At my side, muck dripped between my fingers.

The biker passed beside me.

I began to lift the muck to fling it. Then I froze.

One of the approaching Dragon's Tooth Hill elves, even seated, looked smaller than the others. She wore a black leather jacket with a high, dragon-winged collar, loose wine-red sleeves, and black cuffs. One leg of her jeans had been embroidered with a lightning bolt. Her boots were stitched from many strips of leather, most of them red and brown, a few black and purple. Her hair, the color of the sun reflected on water, was cut in an elaborate wave that displayed her pointed ears.

She wore the latest rich-kid fad: tiny humanoid crea-tures dangled by their ankles from earcuffs, singing so softly that only their wearers could hear them. They were expensive because they didn't live long in captivity. Two hung from one ear.

She passed by, and I continued staring, recognizing

her profile and still unwilling to believe that this was Leda.

She didn't look at us. I watched her ride away. Her companions passed, too. Like her, they never acknowledged our presence.

I opened my hand and let the muck fall, then wiped my palm on my pants leg. Specs said, "I don't believe it. You're getting smarter in your old age."

I said, "C'mon!" and turned to run after the elves. I didn't expect the Rats to follow, but they did.

After a block or two I lost the elves, but I thought I knew where they were going. A little farther on I saw a gaggle of new bikes parked in front of Under the Hill, an elf club on Rymer, and I knew I was right.

Doritos caught up to me. "So," she said. "How *do* you pour sand into a magical gas tank?"

"C'mon. Let's integrate an elf joint."

"Oh, my." She smiled. "You're so socially responsible."

"Hmm." Specs sauntered up to us, looked at the bikes, then looked at Under the Hill. "One of these days, Gone, one of your entertainments will go too—"

An elf with a long mohawk stepped outside the door, crossed his arms, and leaned against the wall. He wore a steel chain through the loops of his jeans and, cocked back on his head, a feed cap that read: SHIT HAPPENS. He didn't say anything, probably 'cause he didn't need to.

"I suppose," Specs said, "we could improve the tone of this place."

"Sure couldn't hurt it," another Rat said, a little guy called Beasley.

I started for the door. The elf moved to block me, but Doritos made a whistling sound, then blew across her knuckles. She wore a lot of big rings with sharp projections. I smiled, and the elf stepped aside. As I entered

Under the Hill, I nodded to him and said, "Nice evening, Mr. Happens."

The main room was large and dark and crowded with heavy wooden tables and chairs. I couldn't see it well; a haze diffused the light from the candles at the occupied tables. The place smelled of beer, roasted meat, burnt peppers, fresh-baked bread, and smoke from cigarettes and the open hearth where several logs blazed.

Two humans—the only ones there besides us—and a halfie were playing a jazzed version of an English folk tune on a stand-up bass, a guitar, and congas. By Soho standards this was a nice place: unbleached cotton tablecloths covered the tables, and the floor was cleaner than some dishes I'd eaten from.

Under the Hill was half-full of elves, mostly Bordertown types. I noted three or four Bloods at one booth, too few to jump us unless other customers joined in. I didn't know the house policy on fighting, or whether the Bloods would care if they'd be welcome back, or whether Mr. Happens could call in reinforcements.

We must've made a fine sight. We didn't look exactly alike, but we looked similar, so I'll use me as an example. My hair hadn't been washed in a *long* time. My clothes were rags that might've brought a couple pence if I'd lucked out selling 'em: a big brown overcoat, gray jeans, green fingerless gloves, one lace-up white tennis shoe and one red deck shoe. A battered black derby sat near my ears 'cause it was a size too large for me. The only material tie between this Wharf Rat and the kid who'd come to Bordertown was the watchless studded band on my wrist.

An elf in a black frock coat over a red leotard gave us an I-wish-there-weren't-people-around-so-I-could-vomit look and said, "Do you have reservations?"

203

"Yeah," I said, heading toward an empty table that was near Leda's group. "We'll order something anyway."

"Without a reser—"

"We'll just sit here till the folks who have this table show up. 'Cause we don't want to be any trouble."

"No, ma'am," said Doritos. "We be so quiet."

"Yeah!" Marvelous Martha put her fingers to her lips and made a hushing sound so loud that people across the room looked up. "We're slumming. Don't want anyone to think we don't belong, uh uh uh."

The elf in the coat looked at Mr. Happens, who'd followed us in. He shrugged, and she shook her head. The bartender, a shorter elf with wiry black hair, looked at them both, and I got bored following the silent conversation. I put my feet on the table and said, "You fairies have a nice place here."

"Take your shoes off the table," the elf in the coat said.

"Oh?" I looked at my feet, then began to unlace the tennis shoe.

"And your feet."

"Oh. Gee. Sorry." I managed to knock a bit of muck from one shoe to the tablecloth as I put my feet down.

"This isn't a good place for trouble," Mr. Happens said.

"Or much else," said Doritos.

I pulled out every coin I'd managed to save and spilled them onto the table. I picked out the largest, the only really valuable one, a dirty Krugerrand, and flipped it to Mr. Happens. "Get us a bottle of the house swill, boy-o."

He let the coin fall and stared at me.

"Or maybe you'd rather we told some friends in the Pack that you wouldn't serve us 'cause we're human."

"I'm not sure you are," said Mr. Happens, but he bent over, picked up the coin, and nodded at the bartender.

204

As he walked away, Doritos said, "So, how long have you had friends in the Pack?"

I grinned and shrugged.

Most of the elves were pretending space warped around our table. Leda sat with her silver-haired companions about fifteen feet away, drinking something red from a jeweled bottle and laughing now and then in a lazy, haughty way.

I had trouble imagining that Dragon's Tooth Hill princess under a dandelion cloud of hair, dressed in biker boots, old jeans, and a beat-up jacket. The cheapest thing she was wearing now would've cost me five years' indenture to a Bordertown merchant lord. I studied her to be sure I knew her. When I found myself thinking she was attractive, I sneered and looked away.

"Your drink, ladies and gentlemen." The elf from behind the bar set a carafe and a tray of glasses on our table and left as quickly as he could without running.

"All right." I splashed some wine into each glass, then drank from the carafe. Specs rolled his eyes, but I didn't care. My performance wasn't for him. I stood, took another drink, then sauntered toward Leda's table. "So, y'all slummin', too? These poor Soho elves're pretty funny, eh?"

Leda glanced at me, looked into her cup, and sipped from it.

"It must be difficult," said a handsome elf who gave Leda a knowing grin, "to acquire wisdom in a human's short lifespan."

"From the evidence," said an elf wearing something like golden barbwire around her head and neck, "it must be impossible."

Most of them laughed. Leda only smiled and sipped her drink again. I grinned at the elf in barbwire.

Something in her expression or her tone or her accent helped me recognize her. Her hair had been dyed an icy metallic silver, but her pupils were still a reflectionless black. The handsome elf beside her had hair the pale blue of a shadow on snow on a sunny day. It was no longer the color of fire.

They both had an accent that I hadn't been able to identify when I'd first met them. Then I couldn't hear the differences between Leda's Dragon's Tooth Hill accent and the Elflands accent shared by Strider, his visitor at Elsewhere, and this pair.

I laughed. "Snatch any babies lately?"

Matte Black and Firehair glanced at each other. The rest of the elves watched with something like amused bafflement.

Matte Black said, "If you think there are changelings in your family, the answer more likely lies with your mother's morals than with Faerie's intervention."

Firehair and a few of the others snickered. Leda smiled.

"I'm not talking about changelings," I said, seeing that I had hold of a secret. "I'm talking about grabbing little kids—"

"What *did* this human's mother lie with?" Firehair asked loudly. "An ape would account for his looks; an ass, his manner."

"Hey, screw you, fairy."

Firehair winced. Behind me a couple of the Rats applauded. Firehair pushed his chair back, but Leda shook her head and told him, "Why bruise your beautiful hand?" She looked at me and smiled, and I thought she'd finally recognized me under my dirt and my hair. She said, "Doesn't his bark reveal his nature?"

I sneered and said, "Yeah, yap, yap, yap, you Elflands bitch."

Most of the Wharf Rats laughed. Out of the corner of my eye I saw Mr. Happens start toward me.

Leda said, "Well, if you're that interested in bitches . . ." Her next words were Elvish. Her friends began to snigger, and Matte Black might've nodded to Firehair, but I wasn't paying close attention to them.

"Yeah, f—" The words rasped within my throat like shards of metal. I tried to bring my arm up to slosh wine on the elves. My arm wouldn't obey. The carafe fell and shattered. I opened my mouth, maybe to scream, and couldn't utter a sound.

I looked at my fellow Rats. Doritos gawked. Specs began to laugh, and the others joined him, even Doritos.

My body hurt, inside and out, so suddenly that at first I didn't understand that what I felt was pain. I doubled over, bringing my hands up to my face. Something was wrong with my eyes. Colors were fading, and, impossibly, my hands were elongating. Ruddy fur sprouted from my fingers, from my face, from my body. My flesh and bones twisted in excruciating—

Hey, it wasn't a thrill. Leave it at that.

I howled, as much from fear as pain. Sneering, Mr. Happens reached for my shoulder. I shoved him aside with a push from one hairy hand and loped out of Under the Hill. Laughter followed me into the night.

CHAPTER TWENTY

A BIG
HAIRY
DEAL

I NTO THE MOONLIGHT, ENDLESSLY ACHING.

Low in the skies, bright in my eyes: full moon, ice moon, merciless, unwinking, all-seeing, all-revealing moon. Wolf moon.

Too many smells. Of territory. Of food. Of death. Of fear. Of pain.

Too many sounds. Metal singing: sirens, whistles, rolling wheels, closing doors. Dogs barking: jealousy, hatred, cowardice, suspicion, recognition. Bikes braking: curiosity, fear, revulsion, amusement, rejection. People yapping: Whazzit? Clown? Creep? Funnyface. Leave'm'lone.

Too many sights. Motion screaming, *Here!* Cars, bikes racing by, a challenge, a threat, a broken promise of prey. Things watching in shadows, grays within grays, browns within browns, lush textures, not color. Owls flying above city lights, meat seeking meat, beyond reach. Cats leaping in alleys, leaping again, gone.

One taste: sour pain.

Everywhere an itching. Everywhere a hurting. Clothes taut, stretching, ripping. One shoe lost. Something thick between the bare foot and the ground, a moccasin or a wool sock or bandages or caked mud or . . .

A swipe at feet with clumsy fingers: thick nails shredding shoelaces and tennis shoe, doing nothing to the tangled pelt over both feet, nothing to the leathery pads beneath them.

Howling, endlessly howling, I ran through the night.

In darkness (an alley? an abandoned building?) dogs surrounded me, called by my pain or my cries. The leader, a vizsla with gray in his muzzle, nuzzled me. I leaped up and roared. The vizsla backed away, his growls growing quieter.

I sensed his confusion. Was I a human to fear or a dog to fight? I walked on two legs, yet I smelled like a challenge to his leadership. His uncertainty increased as I advanced. At last he rolled onto his back, baring his stomach.

I pounced: relieving my hunger might relieve my pain. My teeth closed around the vizsla's throat. The vizsla stayed still. The pack, eight or ten mongrels and purebreds gone wild, circled, wary, confused. My mouth hurt, with too many teeth and a thick tongue. My stomach burned, but I knew I could eat. At that moment I knew nothing else.

All I needed to do was snap my jaws. I wanted to. I wanted to make something else hurt like I hurt. I wanted to eat without being aware of anything besides eating. I shook the vizsla by his throat and growled, preparing to bite at the height of my rage.

I couldn't. I released the vizsla and backed off, whimpering my frustration. The vizsla had surrendered. Dog law demanded that I let him live. Dog law said that I was now alpha wolf, leader of the pack. The vizsla had recognized that.

Pain ruled me, but out of the pain crept the knowledge that I wasn't like the vizsla or his pack. I didn't need to obey their law.

I started forward again. The vizsla looked up: damp dark eyes, lean long face, throat and belly still offered to my jaws.

I wasn't like the vizsla or his pack. I turned and ran. Dog law said they could chase me, and they did, but I outran them with ease.

All I wanted was a hole or a home, a hiding and a huddling place. I lifted my nose to sniff for a safe or a comforting scent, and knew I was alone: unique, unwanted, abhorred.

Sometime in the night I came to Specs's place. If the door had been locked or if the latch had caught, I might not've gotten in. My hands might as well have been trapped in heavy mittens. I fumbled with the door, then fell against it, and it swung wide.

I staggered into the front hall. I wanted to creep into a corner, turn my back to the world, and lie still until morning, until this strange illness left. When I bumped into something—a chair or a table—voices came from the main room:

"Whozere?"

"Specsback?"

"Idawannalook. Yulook."

"Whyzitaweezme? Whyntchu—?"

The door opened. I turned my head toward the wall and shaped an answer in my mind: It's me! Gone! What came out was a growl: "I' 'e! 'Arh!"

Something blinded me: a flash of fire from a cigarette lighter. The spot of fire dropped a foot or two and died in midair. Something small hit the floor just as Rococo slammed the door between us.

In the sleeping room the conversation grew louder:

"Itzomthinoutathewoods! Itzagodamonster!"

"Nah!"

"Yeh!"

"Lemesee!"

I yelled, "I' 'e!"

"Donopenthedoor!"

"I' 'e! I' 'e!"

"Git!" someone yelled. "Gidoutahere!"

"G'on!" Rococo yelled.

I thought I'd been recognized at last. I could've cried in gratitude as I pushed against the living room door to stumble in. Two candles showed a crowded room with a dozen half-dressed kids leaping out from their blankets and sleeping bags.

"Ohfuh!"

"Itzere!"

"Geddit! Jeezisgeddit!"

Something hit me in the face, a rock or a bookend, something heavy and hard. I groaned and reeled backward.

"Hitit! Drivitoutahere!"

Something struck my shoulder and broke on the floor, sounding like a bottle or a china figurine. "I' 'e!" I screamed desperately. "I' 'e!"

"Killit! Killitnow!"

Three or four people jumped on me, hitting and kicking me, ripping at my clothes and my fur. Rococo danced around us with an iron fireplace poker and clubbed me whenever she saw a patch of fur.

" 'O!" I yelled. " 'O!" I shook the Rats off and ran.

They followed me into the front yard. Sticks, rocks, bottles, and bricks showered down. The Rats shouted names I couldn't hear well enough to understand, but I understood their meaning. Despite the pain from Leda's spell, I could still feel other, subtler pains.

You can't trust Bordertown's streets. I ran for the Nevernever time after time, yet I kept finding myself looping through Soho. Finally, exhausted, gasping for air, I fell to my knees in the middle of a field of ashes, burnt timbers, and sooty broken walls. I panted, trying to catch my breath. I might've curled up to sleep there, but when I looked around, I saw I was in the ruins of Castle Pup.

Maybe my instincts had brought me to the last place where I'd felt safe. Maybe it was coincidence. Maybe it was some cruel, subtle magic of the Borderlands.

I raked the charred ground with my claws and roared. I beat my fists against the ground until tears ran down my nose. Wiping them away, I felt my face, strange and inhuman, under the fur. My jaw was thrust forward. My nose was thick and cool and damp. My teeth were small bone knives.

I couldn't curse God or Leda, because I couldn't speak. I howled again and ran.

I don't know how long I ran, or how fast, or how far. Somewhere on Ho Street a car ran into me. Feeling like I'd been hit by cold wind rather than steel, I fell in the street.

As I tried to stand, the car's occupants got out. One, a pudgy, middle-aged guy in a white tasseled suit, was humming something under his breath. I caught a half-sung snatch of song: "You ain't nothin' but a—" He stopped, held out his hand. "Y'okay, son?"

"Rrawr?" I answered. Hearing my voice, I staggered back and tried again. "Hrrarr! Grraw!"

"Can't help you, brother," said a thin black guy with a bandit's mustache and a wild globe of wiry hair. "But somebody's needing to talk with you, if you're ready to hear."

"Grrr-ow?"

"Good," said a homely white woman with a gravelly voice and a pleasant grin. She reached for the back door of the car, a limousine that seemed to contain the night sky within its paint job.

When she opened the door, Tony got out.

"Rrrr!" In terror I backed up, looking from side to side for escape, ready to attack anyone who got in my way, even—or maybe especially—Tony.

"This is the only chance I've got," Tony said. "It may be the only chance you've got, too, Ronnie."

"Rrrr?"

He nodded.

I narrowed my eyes, then lifted a fur-covered hand and tapped over my heart.

Tony winced and looked down, then looked at me. "I hurt you, kid. I'm sorry. That's half the reason I'm here."

I cocked my head to one side.

"I didn't mean to. Hurt you, that is. But you've paid me back, Ronnie, whether you wanted to or not."

"Wrraw?"

"You're holding me here."

"Rrow?"

The homely woman said, "Might be worse places to be held."

The black guy shrugged. "Might be better places to go."

The pudgy guy scratched his head. "Can't find a decent peanut butter 'n' banana sandwich nowheres 'round this town."

The homely woman sighed. "Maybe we should let 'em have their conversation alone."

I ignored them and shook my head to answer Tony. His companions left, returning to the limo.

Tony nodded. "I had my reasons for doing what I did. Good or bad, they're mine. You can't know them, and you can't take credit or blame for them. That's just how it works."

"Rrah!"

"Neither of us can change things. You've grieved, Ronnie. Now it's time to let me go."

I extended a furry middle finger.

"Not for my sake. For yours."

I stared.

He nodded. "New things are waiting for you if you let th—"

I turned and ran. A block away I glanced back. The night-colored limousine had disappeared without a sound.

Near dawn, weary and dazed, I found myself scratching at a door in a dark alley.

The door opened. Light spilled out. I leaped away and brought up both arms to hide my face. Crouched in the dirt, I whimpered once, pleading for something without knowing what it could be.

214

"My—!" I heard, not addressed to me. "Close the door before—"

Goldy, wearing nothing but a pair of pin-striped trousers, stood in the doorway, peering into the twilight as if he didn't believe what he saw. Mickey stood beside him in a black kimono and beaded moccasins. She stared into the night as if too sure of what she saw. Peeking around her was Florida, hair cut close to her skull, ears like bat wings. She wore red plastic flipflops and a big yellow T-shirt that read: I THINK, THEREFORE I THWIM.

"Er?" Florida tugged on a sleeve of Mickey's kimono.

Goldy began to pull the door closed.

"Er!" yelled Florida, lunging forward. Mickey shifted to block Florida with her leg, but Florida moved too quickly. She grabbed Goldy's arm and hung from it, her flipflops dangling several inches above the floor. "Er!"

I couldn't understand anything beyond the obvious: I'd upset and frightened them and failed again to find a place that would take me in. I stumbled back, deeper into the shadows. But the shadows had grown lighter; the night was withdrawing my only cover.

"Er!" Florida ducked under Goldy's arm and darted through the door.

"Careful!" Goldy followed Florida and caught her by the waist. "That thing could—"

That thing wanted nothing but to escape, but *that thing* couldn't think of a way to show it except by doing it. *That thing* knew it should never have come here, of all places, even if it had no place else to go. I lifted both hands in a gesture of peace and harmlessness and kept backing away.

"Er!" Florida yelled, hitting Goldy with both hands. "Er!"

"Shh!" Goldy held her in one arm and let her hit him. "It's all right, Flor—"

"Er-ra!" Florida screamed. "Er-ra!"

Mickey ran up beside them, saying, "Florida? What's—"

"Er-ra!" The kid pointed at me.

"Let her go," Mickey told Goldy.

I started running.

"But—" Goldy began.

"Er-on!" Florida cried.

The sun had begun to rise. The streets of Bordertown could not trick me any longer. I would find my way to the woods of the Nevernever and live there forever, like any wild thing.

"Er-on!" Florida had wriggled away from Goldy, or maybe Goldy had set her down. I heard pursuit, the thwap-thwap of feet in plastic sandals, but I knew I could escape with ease.

"Ron!" Florida called, and I stopped in the middle of the alley.

"Ron?" whispered Goldy, close behind her. "Not—?" As I turned, Mickey caught up to Goldy and nodded at him.

Florida stopped two feet in front of me and held out her arm. "Ron?"

I nodded.

"Ron." She reached toward my wrist, touching my father's watchband lightly, then took my shaggy fingers in her small hand. "It's—" She grimaced and licked her lips and began again. "It's o—" She squeezed my fingers. "Okay. Ron. Don't be . . . scared, Ron. It's okay."

I shook my head and tried not to feel anything at all, but I couldn't.

Florida turned toward Goldy and Mickey. Their eyes flicked from her to me and back again. Goldy said, "My God—" and Mickey called softly, "Florida? Honey?"

I hesitated. Florida yanked on my arm, and I followed, letting her drag me.

Florida stopped in front of Goldy and Mickey. "This is . . . my friend. He's Ron."

Goldy whistled, shook his head, and said, "Oh, boy."

Mickey studied us. Her gaze lingered on Florida, then on me. "I think," she finally said, "we could all use some breakfast. Do werewolves eat pancakes?"

I gave a small nod.

Florida tugged on my hand. As we headed toward Elsewhere, she told Mickey, "Woofs like pancakes an' chocolate milk."

No one spoke as we went in the back door. I wanted to walk through the store, to run my finger along the spines of a shelf of hardcover books, to see the morning light slanting through the dusty window by the basement stairs, to smell the bookstore smells and know that I was welcome again in Elsewhere.

Florida hurried ahead, dragging me up to the second floor. Vado looked up from where he lay in a pool of sun on the kitchen counter, saw me, and raced for the safety of the back bedrooms. I stopped and stared at my hands. Then Topé sauntered in to twine around my ankles as he looked for the thing that had frightened Vado.

While Goldy mixed pancake batter, Florida drank chocolate milk and watched me from the far side of the linoleum-topped table. When her glass was empty, she set it down with both hands, lifted one finger to tell me to stay, and went downstairs.

"Found your jacket," Mickey said. She sat nearby with

her feet up on a chair where Topé lay. "After the fire. We threw it out. It was pretty badly charred."

I shrugged.

"Seemed odd that you'd burn a jacket that you liked so much."

I shrugged again.

Goldy, at the stove, said, "People do odd things. Even if the wolfboy wasn't our firebug, he opened the door for one."

I stared at Goldy's back, then looked out the window. Sunlight was bright on the roofs of Bordertown. Pancake batter sizzled as it hit the griddle.

"Right?"

The smell of breakfast made me think of Mom and Dad, and of Tony as he used to be. I'd have to send the folks a picture of their younger son, the thing from the pit.

I looked at Mickey and Goldy and nodded.

Mickey said, "Why?"

Bright plastic letters and numbers on magnets decorated their large industrial icebox. Some of them had been used to write: LIBERTY MEANS RESPONSIBILITY. THAT IS WHY MOST MEN DREAD IT.—GEORGE BERNARD SHAW. I pushed the letters aside, then picked out: SAID HE HAD TO GET BACK SOMETHING OF HIS.

Mickey lifted an eyebrow and gave a small smile. "His self-respect?"

I shrugged.

Mickey looked away. "Poor Mooner."

Goldy, flipping pancakes, glanced over from the stove. "I liked the Shaw better. So, Wolfboy, what's the story?"

"Arrh!" I barked at him as I began to say something like "Gee, can I tell it in words of one syllable?" By the time

I'd reached for the plastic letters, I found myself writing: MAGIC. LIKE THE NEW LOOK?

"Not bad." Goldy filled a plate with pecan pancakes and put it before me with a bottle of pure maple syrup. "You want to be careful who you surprise at night. But with a bath and clean clothes, you'll break hearts left and right when you stroll down Ho Street."

Mickey said, "Too bad about your voice."

I shrugged and swallowed a huge bite of my breakfast. PRICE OF VANITY, I wrote, and left the room.

In Elsewhere's bathroom two candles and a cracked mirror showed the teen wolf in all his glory: golden eyes, long snout, tufted ears, reddish brown fur. I turned my head from side to side, trying to study my profile, then splashed cold water on my face and combed my fur with my claws. There's something very strange about combing your cheeks.

I'd always wanted people to see me and know I was special. You do have to be careful what you wish for.

Florida was back in her seat when I returned to the kitchen. She slid a book over to me: a battered copy of *Treasure Island*. I grinned and ate two plates of pancakes. Between the first and the second, Florida touched the fur on my hand. "Pretty, Ron."

After breakfast Goldy went to work in the store, 'cause I'd indicated that I'd wash dishes. Florida went out after Mickey told her that I'd be there when she came back. I gave her Dad's wristband, which made her grin. She wrapped it twice around her arm to keep it on.

While I washed, Mickey filled me in on changes in the bookstore and the neighborhood. Wolves, I found, could yawn recognizably; Mickey offered me a cot in a room they used for storage. I put the last dish in the wooden rack to dry and was so tired that I didn't stop to write THANKS on the refrigerator.

I woke on a cot in a room full of books. Someone had slid hairy monster gloves over my hands as a joke . . .

I sat up and gasped for breath, then forced myself to breathe slowly. This was Bordertown. The magic would go away. I'd be Ron again . . .

I ran into the washroom and studied myself, hunting for some sign that the magic had lessened. I saw none. If anything, my body was accepting its new form: my fingers no longer felt clumsy, my vision no longer seemed blurred, and I couldn't remember when I'd quit hurting. I winced in disgust and scared myself when the mirror-monster bared its fangs.

That amused me. I threw back my shoulders and admired my grin. I imagined new names for myself: El Lobo. Alf A. Wolf. Lone Wolf. The Werewolf Kid. Jack Fangs.

There could be worse fates. If I stayed a teen wolf, I'd never have to worry about zits.

I returned to the dark storeroom and lay on the cot, telling myself how great it'd be to stay a monster for the rest of my life.

If there'd been River nearby, I would've drunk. I thought that, then blinked, seeing another effect of the spell. Gone needed River. El Lobo didn't have any addictions yet.

Maybe this new identity wasn't so bad. At least, I thought, I'll be treated with some respect.

"Hey, Wolfboy!" Goldy called up the stairs. "You sleeping the day away?" Before I could decide how to answer, he added, "Mickey and I scavenged some clothes for you! They're on the couch in the living room!"

Mickey yelled, "The hot water's working! There's a towel for you in the bathroom!"

I padded into the living room to scoop Vado off a neatly folded long-sleeved black shirt and a pair of gray jeans. As I was about to toss the cat aside, he purred. So I stood in the living room for a couple of minutes, petting him and looking at the clothes set out for me. Next to the shirt and jeans were a pair of black sneakers like I'd worn when I worked here as the new kid from the World.

At last, realizing that I'd feel stupid if anyone walked in and wondered what was so great about some second-hand clothes, I set the cat down and went to take my bath.

CHAPTER TWENTY-ONE

THE
BLANK
FORTUNE

C LEAN, DRESSED, BRUSHED FROM HEAD TO TOE, SMELLING OF
peppermint soap and cinnamon toothpaste, definitely not
feeling human but feeling something like good, I tried to
sneak out of Elsewhere. Mickey met me on the back stairs.
"Lookin' pretty sharp."

I gave her a thumbs-up and moved to pass. She didn't
step aside.

"I never heard Florida talk before. If you run off, I may
never hear her again."

"Rrr."

"She's got a nice voice. Shame to let it go to waste."

How much can you say with a shrug? I turned and
crooked a finger for her to follow. The magnetic letters let
me spell things out for both of us: I'M TIRED OF RUNNING.
That looked way too melodramatic, so I immediately
shuffled the letters.

222

Mickey grinned with so much delight that I blushed under my fur. "Good."

I waved good-bye. Mickey said, "You'll be back for dinner?"

My turn to study her. She smiled, so I nodded and wrote: WHY'RE YOU BEING NICE?

"Does it matter?"

I nodded.

She laughed. "It bother you?"

I nodded.

"Good. Suffer. But don't suffer so much that you're late for dinner."

I nodded and started down the stairs.

"Oh, Ron?"

I glanced up.

"When people stare, or pretend they aren't staring . . ."

"Rrr?"

"It doesn't mean anything. If you saw you on the street, you'd look, too. It doesn't mean anything about who you are. Okay?"

Something in her voice made it hard to meet her eyes, but I did, and nodded, and understood a little of why she was being nice.

She laughed. "Good. Give 'em hell, Wolfboy."

I grinned as I left.

Goldy was right; people reacted differently in daylight. They stared, but they looked away quickly, either out of consideration for my feelings or 'cause they didn't want to appear too uncool. I swear I overheard one tell a friend, "What, the coyote kid? Hey, you should've seen the people I went to school with. *They* were strange."

When I walked minding my own affairs like any other

B-towner, no one freaked. Once I darted across a street to beat some unusually heavy traffic. A poor kid on the other side screamed and ran like—well, like a hellhound was on his trail. I didn't laugh, for fear I'd cry.

I took care to walk the rest of the way.

A sign in the window twitched and shimmered with faerie dust lettering: MIDNIGHT MADNESS SALE! 30% OFF ALL GEASES! TALISMANS, HALF-PRICE! DON'T PAY ELFLANDS PRICES FOR ELFLANDS QUALITY MAGIC! COME TO MAGIC FREDDY'S! WE TURN THE COMPETITION TO TOADS!

The inside was brightly lit and painted glossy white. Metal racks held ripped-open cardboard boxes full of arcane things like crystal balls, Ouija boards, electronic equipment, plastic mice, and stuffed toads (the competition?) posed on tiny skateboards. A sign on the far wall said: MAGIC IS A STATE OF MIND.

The only person in the place was a pale kid with indoor skin who wore a white lab coat. He glanced at me. "Hey, great mas— Oh." He frowned, and I began to leave. As he waved his hands a little while mumbling something, my fur tingled. He beamed in delight. "Whoa, cool spell!"

I squinted at him.

"Don't see much magic that stable, 'specially in the Borderlands. You could keep that shape forever if you wanted." He grinned. "So, looking for anything special?"

A large blackboard at the back of the store had notices chalked on it, like No RABBITS' FEET—WHAT'S THE MATTER, DON'T YOU *LIKE* BUNNIES?" and "HALF-PRICE ON NOVELTY CANDLES. IMAGINE THE LAUGHS WHEN, IN THE MIDDLE OF A DEMON-BANISHING SPELL, YOUR FRIENDS BLOW OUT A CANDLE . . . AND IT RELIGHTS!

I took a piece of chalk to write: SUPPOSE I DIDN'T WANT
TO STAY LIKE THIS?

He blinked. "It's a curse?"

I nodded.

"Bummer."

I sighed. It sounded like a warning growl, but the guy
didn't notice that.

"There're supposed to be some major spellbreakers in
the Elflands. But you have to be elven to cross the border,
and then who knows what you'd find. I don't suppose
you're el—"

I shook my head.

"Hmm. Only sure thing's to have it undone by the
wizard who did it." He waved his hands again, and I felt
as if I had fleas. "If I was you, I'd stay in the Borderlands
till then. There's something shaky at the heart of this spell.
If you crossed into Faerie or the World, you might become
human. Or the change might become permanent so no one
could ever change you back. Or things might get way, way
weird, and you'd end up a poodle or a dachshund."

I thought about spending the rest of my life as whatever
Leda had meant me to be, a mutt that'd find dead things in
the road and roll in them, happily thinking it doesn't get
better than this.

The clerk scratched his head and looked up to the left,
as if the answer were hiding among the ceiling ducts. "You
know, you could try a short-term fix, like an illusion to look
like your old self. Or Humphrey Bogart or whoever you
wanted."

I glanced at him with a flicker of hope just as he shook
his head. "Nah. That might do for a few hours or days.
Then you'd hit a place where magic didn't work right, and

the illusion'd either fail or it'd strobe off and on, human, wolfguy, human, wolfguy. Be a great effect. But I don't think it's what you want."

I shook my head.

" 'Sides, illusions are easy for a decent magician to see through. Now—" He squinted, then said cheerfully, "If the fur's only on your hands and face, you could have a magician move it onto your chest or wherever. That'd be so subtle hardly any magician'd notice it, and in a spot of weird magic, the fur might crawl around your body some, but it wouldn't necessarily go back to your hands and face. Yeah! That's—"

I shook my head.

"Whole body?"

I nodded.

"Ah, well. You'll be warm in winter, at least."

I glanced at him.

"And a spell like that would be mighty expensive."

I wrote: WHAT WOULD IT COST TO TRY TO BREAK THE CURSE? I DON'T HAVE MONEY NOW. I COULD SAVE UP SOME IF—

He interrupted. "It isn't that I don't want your money. I just hate to see you waste it. The best wizards in town'll say the same. Seriously. Ask Milo Chevrolet or Ms. Wu or that elf on Avalon if— I said something?"

I scrawled: THANKS! and ran out. When someone pointed at me, I remembered to slow down. I waved and grinned at the pointer and walked undisturbed to Wu's Worldly Emporium.

Ms. Wu had customers, an East Indian family and a lone elf in red leather. I think they all checked for a back door as I sauntered in the front. The store hadn't changed that I could see, but its smells were even more intriguing now. I especially noticed almond cookies, coconuts, and baked noodles among the scents of pine, dried seaweed, ginger, sandalwood, and roses.

Ms. Wu wore old jeans and a man's white silk dress shirt. She saw me, saw her customers' uneasiness, and smiled broadly. "Ah, the wolfboy! I'll be with you in a minute."

One Indian kid whispered to another. I caught "Wolfboy" in the sentence. They stared in awe until their mother tugged their shoulders and told them not to bother people they hadn't met. I couldn't tell her they weren't bothering me, and I couldn't thank her for referring to me as people.

After the others left, Ms. Wu turned to me. "Yes?"

I made a scribbling motion with one hand. She handed me a pen and a pad of paper, and I wrote: WHY DIDN'T YOU WARN ME THAT THIS WOULD HAPPEN?

She glanced at the paper, shook her head, and smiled. "I'm afraid I didn't know. Sorry."

I wrote: THE FORTUNE COOKIE. BARK AND BITE.

She laughed. "Ah! Then I did warn you!"

I twirled one finger slowly in the air: *Big deal.*

She turned her head to one side. "I can't know who'll take a particular cookie. I rarely want to know. Even if I knew which fortune you'd received, I couldn't guess what it meant."

WHY DO YOU DO IT, THEN?

She frowned at the paper. "Why do I give out the fortunes?"

I nodded.

"Because I can. Because they entertain people. Because it pleases me to do them. Because they harm no one, and perhaps I might write something that will help someone, somewhere, in some small way. Should I stop?"

I shook my head and wrote: I WANT TO BE HUMAN AGAIN.

She said gently, "You are human."

I took the paper back, crossed out "be," and wrote "look."

She shrugged, still smiling. "Do you know who did this?"

I nodded and almost growled.

"Find that person." She reached into a bag on the counter and pulled out a fortune cookie. "Magic, like most things, is easier done than undone." She offered the cookie to me. "I'll understand if you refuse this."

I wanted to knock it from her hand to the floor. Instead, I took it, snapped it open very carefully, and unfolded a blank slip of paper.

I held it out. Ms. Wu glanced at it, then laughed and pointed at the pen in my hand. "Congratulations. Few have the opportunity to write their own fortunes."

I set the paper down and moved the pen tip toward it, ready to write my opinion of her fortunes for her.

"Or perhaps we write our fortunes each day, and the cookie is reminding you of that. Whatever the truth, you might consider the future you'd like before committing yourself to one."

I started to speak and couldn't, of course. By then it occurred to me that she might have a point. I nodded, tucked the blank sheet into my shirt pocket, and left.

Coming out of Ms. Wu's, I saw an elf leaving Elsewhere with a bundle of books under one arm. His back was to me, but his posture or his green velvet blazer made me wonder where I'd seen him before. The answer didn't come immediately, so I walked on.

Find Leda? I had no idea where she might be. Convince her to take back her curse? I had no idea why she should. Could she take it back? In the Borderlands no magic was certain. She hadn't been able to undo her spell on the gingerbread men at Castle Pup.

I walked without a destination. When a cute elf looked at me and shuddered, I realized I wasn't ready to face people. I wasn't sure I ever would be. That's when I knew where I wanted to go.

None of the Rats showed themselves as I approached the Mad River. Maybe they had other things to do. Maybe they saw me on their turf and decided to sleep late. I didn't mind not meeting them. There were things I would've liked to say to Doritos, and even to Specs, but I didn't think they would've understood, no matter how clearly I'd have spoken.

The wind whipped at me as I made my way across the bridge. In the distance the Nevernever waited. I could spend a lifetime exploring it, and I thought that I'd like to. I hadn't solved my problems by running away from the World. Perhaps I could solve them by running away from Bordertown.

The wind whispered, "Come back!" so softly that I thought I was hearing my imagination or my conscience. I almost laughed. Then I remembered when the wind had spoken to me before. Afraid to look and afraid not to, I spun about.

I was alone on the bridge. There was no hazy shape of a woman floating above the water, no night-black limousine creeping through the rubble.

Standing there, watching sun specks dance on the river and the woods and the city, I thought about ghosts and people and responsibility to the living and the dead. At last I took out the slip of paper from Ms. Wu's cookie, set it on the bridge's rusty railing, and scribbled four words.

Florida was waiting on one of the barricades at the entrance to the bridge. As I approached, she hopped down and said, "Okay?" I wanted to tell her she shouldn't have followed me, that she might've gotten hurt. After a second I nodded.

"Good," she said. "Let's—"

"Hey, look!" someone shouted in the distance. "Visitors!"

Someone else said, "Maybe the little elf's—"

I turned. Four Rats were running toward us with rocks and sticks in their hands. When they saw my face, they skidded to a halt. The nearest one said, "Yo, uh, welcome. Nice day, eh?"

I nodded. I didn't recognize them, but Gone might've shared River with them sometime.

"Well, uh, we got things to do, y'know. Busy, busy, busy. 'Bye."

They left as quickly as they'd come. Florida grinned up at me. I rumpled her hair, and for a moment I saw myself looking up at Tony.

"We go home now?"

I blinked, then nodded.

"Good." She marched a step or two ahead of me for most of the way back to Elsewhere, only stopping now and then to identify things that interested her: "Squirrel." "Music. I love music." "Mmm! Smell bread? Good!"

I nodded or grinned when I was supposed to, and she seemed content. As we came closer to Elsewhere, the streets became more crowded. I watched Florida. Whenever expensively dressed elves appeared, her face would become wary and her hand would fall near the sheath of her Bowie knife.

I squatted and tapped my shoulder. She blinked and said, "Ride?" When I nodded, she grinned and clambered on. I stood, surprised by how light she was, then realized that I must've gotten two or three times stronger when I became the Hound King.

On my back Florida laughed. I didn't feel her tense up, not even when a couple of rich young elves approached. They only grinned at us, and one gave us a thumbs-up that Florida and I both returned.

Carrying her toward Elsewhere, I remembered the story of how Mooner had found her, alone and abused, and then I thought about Matte Black and her friends hunting elf kids in Bordertown. And I saw that I'd have to make at least two visits before dinner, one back to Ms. Wu, and then one to Danceland.

CHAPTER TWENTY-TWO

I FOUND
MY THRILL ON
DRAGON'S TOOTH HILL

DANCELAND IS AS DARK ON THE INSIDE AS ON THE OUTSIDE: cinder block walls painted black, relieved only by bits of chalk art by Bordertown's best sidewalk cartoonists. The place was almost empty when I arrived, because people rarely showed up before the bands began.

Sai, wearing baggy striped trousers and a green Danceland T-shirt with the sleeves rolled up, was across the cavernous room at a pool table. She gave me a look, then a second one, decided I was harmless, or at least hadn't given her an excuse to throw me out, and sunk her shot.

Strider came through another door, lugging a rack of clean glass mugs. He'd ripped the sleeves off his Danceland shirt, which was black, like his jeans and his engineer boots. His long white hair seemed to glow in Danceland's dim atmosphere. I waited by the door until he delivered the mugs, even though I doubted Strider was the sort to see me and drop things.

When he stepped out from the bar, I gave him a note: GOLDY AND MICKEY CALL ME WOLFBOY. I'M STAYING AT ELSEWHERE NOW. AT CASTLE PUP I WAS RON, THE NEW KID.

"Yeah." He nodded, then smiled, and I felt a lot better about admitting who I'd been. "I heard you'd taken up with some Wharf Rats. You look more like a real Strange Pup." He spoke with a Bordertown accent, and a dragon like something out of a medieval Bible had been tattooed on his left shoulder. No one would mistake him for a prince of Faerie now.

I wrote: I'M NOT A RAT ANYMORE. AND I'M SORRY ABOUT CASTLE PUP.

Strider nodded. "Likewise."

ARE THE PUPS STILL AROUND? IN ANY FORM?

He shrugged. "Guess we're all in grad school now."

ANYONE SEEN LEDA?

He shrugged again. "Prob'ly why the Pups are history. She kept us together."

IT'S IMPORTANT.

He looked askance at me, pale elven irises sliding to the corners of his eyes, then away. "The loss of Castle Pup hit her hard. As you might've guessed."

I wondered if she'd known who she was cursing at Under the Hill, and wrote: WOULD ANYONE KNOW HOW TO FIND HER?

He handed the paper back. "Want something to drink? O.j.? Beer?"

I didn't want anything to make me stupider just then. I lifted an imaginary teacup to my lips.

233

Strider called, "Val! Two coffees, please!" Which was close enough; I didn't correct him.

He indicated a small round table and took a stool. I sat across from him.

"Look," he began. "Becoming Wolfboy was prob'ly a good idea. There'll be ex-Pups who'll always blame Ron." I started to scribble something, but he caught my wrist. "Not all of us. But Wiseguy thinks Mooner died a hero. No one wants to tell her otherwise."

I began to pull my wrist free, then realized there'd be nothing to be won in a contest of strength. I looked at his hand, and he let go.

I placed a claw on the earlier question on my notepad: ANYONE SEEN LEDA?

He smiled. "I'm trying to tell you I've got nothing against you, Ron. I wouldn't keep anything from you."

I wrote: UNLESS IT WAS IMPORTANT.

He nodded. "Unless it was important. But it isn't, in this case. Someone saw her on Dragon's Tooth Hill once, but that doesn't mean she's there now. Her father wanted her to spend a few years in Faerie. That was one of the reasons she ran away. If she's back with her family, she's prob'ly doing what they want."

A gray-haired woman put two cups of coffee and a plate with little bowls of cream, sugar, and honey before us. Strider said, "Ah, Valda. Did I ask you to marry me today?"

The woman set her hand on his head. "Ah, Strider. Did I remind you to mop the men's room today?"

He grinned. I sipped my coffee and scribbled my next note. As Valda left, Strider read: YOU'RE NOT THE LOST HEIR.

He blinked twice, which for Strider was a complete loss

of composure, then laughed. "Gods, no! One of the un-countable and insufferable princelings of Faerie, yes, though I'll deny it if you ask again. You thought I—?"

I nodded, then wrote and underlined twice: FLORIDA.

He studied me. Sai must've noticed something, because she came over and said, "Is everything—?" She still held a pool cue.

"Fine," Strider said immediately, then said, "No, my heart, I've lied, though I didn't intend it. This is Wolfboy, who was Ron, who knows Florida's secret."

She glanced at me. "We could kill him."

For a long second I didn't realize that was a joke. Then Sai said, "Why're you here? You could've found one of the Elflands' ambassadors and sold your story—"

Strider said, "That's why I haven't killed him." It took another long second to realize that was a joke, too.

I handed Sai the slip of paper from Ms. Wu's fortune cookie.

She looked at it, then gave it to Strider, who frowned as he read it. " 'You will be happy'?"

I nodded. Then I wrote on my notepad: IT'S HARD TO BE HAPPY WITHOUT HELPING PEOPLE.

"Florida doesn't need help," Sai said.

YEAH? I wrote. HOW LONG CAN SHE HIDE FROM THE ELF-LANDS TYPES THAT'RE HUNTING HER? WHAT'LL THEY DO WHEN THEY FIND HER?

Strider looked at Sai. "You can watch the place?"
She nodded.

"C'mon," Strider told me.

I glanced at Sai, who said, "Go on. If anything scary was going to happen, I wouldn't let Strider leave without me."

Strider gave her a kiss. "Don't harass any elves while I'm gone. Not unless they really misbehave."

"Heh," said Sai. "What's the point of having power if you can't abuse it?"

A couple of little kids followed us for a few blocks along Ho. I turned and growled, and they ran away giggling. Strider headed north toward Dragon's Tooth Hill. I walked beside him, watching for Leda and Matte Black and the elf who'd been in Elsewhere looking for Faerie's heir.

The houses became cleaner and larger and better cared for as we climbed Dragon's Tooth Hill. Trees on the hill were groomed into spreading archetypal trees, and bushes were clipped into squat idealized bushes, and gardens were well-weeded model gardens, and lawns were probably cut every five days. I didn't like it. I kept expecting people dressed all in white to leap out from a hedge and trim my hair and mend my clothes.

Strider led me to a tidy little house on a tidy little street. I expected a tidy little person to answer the door, but I didn't expect that person to be Wiseguy.

"Strider!" She gave him a hug, leaning a bit because she was either shoplifting a watermelon or pregnant. I stared. She wore a brown wool smock over a salmon-colored blouse, and Russian-inspired boots that a real cossack could have sold to buy a small herd of horses. Her hair was cut in something like a flapper's bob.

"This is Wolfboy," Strider said. "Wolfboy, meet Wiseguy."

She smiled. Whatever else had changed, she could still make my mind go blank and my heart spasm. She offered her hand. "Welcome to our home. Wiseguy's an old name, though I don't mind it from old friends. I'm Lucia Uriel-

Green; I hope you'll be a new friend. Please call me Lucy."

Her hand was warm and strong, and she didn't hesitate to offer it to the monster. I was glad for the first time that I couldn't speak. We stepped into a front room with dark cherry woodwork, pin-striped green wallpaper, and brightly polished brass fixtures. We might've just stepped into the nineteenth century if there hadn't been two motorcycle helmets hanging from the coatrack, next to a green velvet blazer.

A man came down the hall toward us, calling, "Is it company, my Light?" When he stepped into the front hall, I recognized the elf who'd come to Elsewhere in search of the lost heir. "Strider, welcome! By my faith, welcome!" He wore slippers and a gray cardigan, and I thought he'd read too much about the way humans lived.

After he and Strider had hugged, Strider nodded at me. "Wolfboy, Leander Uriel-Green. And vice versa."

"I'm always honored to meet a friend of Strider's." Leander's handshake was firm and friendly. "Treat my house as your own."

I made a note on the pad that Ms. Wu had let me keep: DON'T SWEAT. I'M HOUSEBROKEN.

He laughed. "If you accompany Strider, I don't even ask that of you. But I am grateful."

"Come in." Wiseguy glanced at Leander. "Shall we sit in the parlor? I'll get tea if—"

He kissed her forehead. "No, no, I will. You should sit—"

"Actually," Strider said, a little patiently and a little amused, "we're only here to clear up one thing."

"Oh?" said Wiseguy.

"He knows about Florida."

"Oh," said Leander, very quietly.

237

"We could kill him," said Wiseguy.

Strider snorted a laugh. "You and Sai."

"What should we do?" said Leander, eyeing me calmly, and I suspected that for him, the idea of killing me was merely an unpleasant option.

"We should tell him what we're doing. He seems to think that you're hunting for her and that I've managed to put you off her trail so far."

"Ah." Leander looked at me. "I'm playing a dangerous game, Wolfboy. Let me tell you a few things that you may know, in order to tell you a few things that you may not:

"For the lords of Faerie, the Border is an inconvenient necessity. It permits trade, and it keeps out humans, and it allows elves to pass through at only a few locations. All of these things are seen as desirable.

"But there are those who think Faerie and the World should have greater knowledge of each other." He glanced at Wiseguy and smiled. "Strider and I are of that party.

"Power shifts constantly among the factions in Faerie, and the struggles sometimes grow fierce. A few years ago the heir was brought to Bordertown for her safety. Her parents thought no one would think to seek her outside Faerie, but they were wrong. Because they were wrong, they died. The heir escaped, alone, and the task of finding her fell to me."

Strider smiled. "How hard did you have to work to be standing where it fell?"

Leander looked embarrassed. "Well. Be that as it may. I've reported that I've found her, and that she's safe, and that it would be extremely awkward to extract her just now. Faerie's current rulers would not care to explain that they misplaced the heir, so they're willing to wait to have her returned with as little fuss as possible."

I stared at him.

He smiled. "Faerie has always been more patient than the World. It's believed that the heir's being cared for by extremely wealthy and influential humans. If I play the game properly, she could reach adulthood in Bordertown."

I continued to stare.

"Ten years in the World can be a few days in Faerie," Strider said. "By the time they think to check on Leander's story, Florida will be fully grown and ready to decide her future for herself. We may succeed."

"Even if we keep her safe," Leander said, "we may fail. It's easy for elves to learn to hate humans here. But she's fallen in with the best company, I think. What better school for the heir of Faerie than a bookstore in Bordertown?"

Wiseguy laughed. "You say that with a straight face."

He nodded. "When I consider giving her to those who would shape her into what they wish her to be, I feel ill."

I wrote: YOU'RE TALKING ABOUT A LITTLE KID WHO SUFFERED SOMETHING SO TERRIBLE SHE WOULDN'T TALK AND WOULDN'T GO INDOORS.

They all read it. Wiseguy said, "She's seeing a counselor at the Free Clinic. The counselor agrees that she's getting better."

WITH FAERIE'S MONEY, SHE COULD—

Strider, watching me write, interrupted. "We know one of the things that happened to her. She saw her parents die. The killer came from Faerie. You think it'd be better to send her back?"

SHE NEEDS HELP.

Leander said, "She needs to be in the company of those she loves and trusts." He gave a slightly embarrassed smile. "Which seems to include you. I talked to Mickey this afternoon while you were out."

DOESN'T THE KILLER KNOW SHE'S IN BORDERTOWN?

"The assassin's dead," Leander said. "It seems her father was struck from behind and died instantly. Her mother managed to kill the assassin before she died. Our opponents may suspect the heir's here, but they can't know it. They have all of Faerie, the World, and the Borderlands to search."

Strider added, "We can guard her better here than in Faerie or the World. Almost everyone in Soho knows her, even if they don't know who she is. An entire community watches over her, just as it watches over any kid there."

Leander said, "When she goes back to Faerie, she can learn whatever she needs to be the heir. But until then she can learn whatever she needs to be Florida."

I wrote: WHAT DOES SHE WANT?

Wiseguy said, "I asked her if she'd like to go back to Faerie. Her eyes made like saucers, and she shook her head, and she didn't smile for the rest of the day. What do you think?"

Leander said, "We'll continue to ask her. When she wants to go, we won't stop her."

Strider said, "So you approve?"

I looked at each of them and nodded.

Wiseguy said, "Gee, I guess we won't have to kill him after all."

"Yes," Leander agreed. "Thank the gods."

I wrote: YOU SHOULD PROBABLY SPREAD THE WORD THAT

240

THERE'S NO LONGER A REWARD BEING OFFERED FOR THE ELF WITH THE BIRTHMARKS.

Leander said, "I did that the day Strider told me Florida was at Castle Pup."

OH? SOME RATS APPROACHED US THIS AFTERNOON, AND THEY SEEMED ESPECIALLY INTERESTED IN FLORIDA. MAYBE IT WAS JUST 'CAUSE SHE'S SMALL.

He looked at that and shrugged. "Perhaps."

I thought I'd done as much as I could for Florida's future, so I decided to do something about mine. If I could find Matte Black, I might be able to find Leda, so I wrote: DOES YOUR PARTNER COME BY ELSEWHERE TO CHECK ON FLORIDA, TOO?

Leander blinked. "Partner?" Wiseguy and Strider looked at the sheet in some alarm.

I wrote: YOU KNOW. THE LEADER OF THE GANG THAT WAS SNATCHING LITTLE ELF KIDS IN SOHO IN ORDER TO FIND THE HEIR.

Leander said, "The only people who know both who and where Florida is are the people in this room, and Sai. I came to Bordertown alone."

"Mickey and Goldy know," Strider said. "They saw the moles in a triangle on her shoulder. But they wouldn't tell anyone."

"Describe the elf-snatchers," Wiseguy said.

I began: THERE ARE ONLY FOUR THAT I'VE SEEN. THE LEADER'S—

In the street Florida screamed, "Ron!"

I leaped for the door. Because I slowed down to open it, Leander caught up to me and set a hand on my shoulder. "Wait." He glanced through a small window in the door, so I did, too.

Four familiar-looking elves rode their bikes in tight circles around Florida. She had her Bowie knife out, and one elf, shaking blood from his fingers, appeared to be swearing.

Strider, catching up to us, said, "What—?"

Leander undoubtedly watched the same elf I did, the one I thought of as Matte Black. "Crystaviel." For me, he added, "Of the other side. You thought *her* my partner?"

I nodded.

Strider yanked on the door. "Bugger this. We've got—"

Leander put his hand against it. "If she recognizes us, it's all over. They'll know—"

"What is it if we let them have Florida?"

"She might get away."

In the street Florida leaped from side to side, seeking an escape. The four riders stayed close to her. One had picked up a stick and was about to knock the knife from her hand.

I pushed Leander aside and went through the door. Wiseguy followed, saying, "They don't know me."

Matte Black—Leander's Crystaviel—saw us and shouted, "Stay back! This Soho filth has stolen something of ours."

"Didn't!" Florida yelled, and at that moment the elf with the stick batted away the Bowie knife.

"I know her family," Wiseguy said. "Let's take her to them, and if—"

The elf with the stick was the fellow who'd had flame-colored hair. He caught Florida and, grinning, lifted her.

"Don't hurt her!" Wiseguy yelled.

Firehair's hold pinned Florida's arms to her side. But it didn't stop her from twisting enough to sink her teeth into the lobe of one of his ears. He screamed and dropped her, and the next thing I knew, I was standing in the middle of the street holding Florida, who seemed to be fine.

A middle-aged human woman had appeared on one of the lawns. She called, "Lucia! Is everything all right? Should I call the Silver Suits?"

Crystaviel smiled delightedly. "Why, yes. Perhaps that *would* be the best solution."

Wiseguy winced, then yelled, "I don't think that'll be necessary."

"If you're sure." The neighbor, looking doubtful, returned to her house.

Crystaviel said, "It's possible that we made a mistake."

Her three companions looked at her in amazement. Firehair said, "What the—?"

"The thief," Crystaviel announced, "had three marks on the left shoulder in the shape of a triangle. I saw that clearly."

"Ah," said Firehair, grinning.

Wiseguy looked at me. I wished I could've said something then to comfort her, but all I did was walk toward Crystaviel.

Wiseguy shouted, "Wolfboy, wait—!" as I put my hand on the left sleeve of Florida's baggy T-shirt. Florida's eyes grew wide. I nodded to her and tugged up the sleeve.

Crystaviel leaned forward on her bike like the wolf being presented with Little Red Riding Hood. Then her dark eyes blinked twice, and she looked from Florida to me and back at Florida's shoulder. She muttered something. My fur tingled, but when she looked again at Florida's shoulder, she only frowned.

At last she announced to the air, "We were mistaken." Without a backward glance she gunned her bike and left.

Firehair looked at me and shrugged. "Yow," he said, touching his ear. The elf with the sliced hand smiled at us, saying, "That's some kid, you bet."

Florida turned in my arms and hid her face in the fur of my neck. I lifted a hand in farewell to Crystaviel's companions and watched them go.

The smoke of their exhaust shaped itself into the wispy form of an elf woman in long pale robes. She looked at Florida, who still hid her face, and at me, and smiled. The exhaust dissipated. I blinked, unsure that I'd seen anything, yet I knew that no one would see the White Lady in Bordertown again.

A sleek expensive car rolled out from the Uriel-Greens' garage and stopped. Leander got out of the driver's side, and Strider out the passenger's; they had been prepared to follow Crystaviel if it'd been necessary.

"What happened?" asked Strider.

I sat down on the curb and exhaled in relief. Florida didn't want to be set down, so I shifted her to my left arm, pulled out my notepad, put it beside me, and scribbled an answer: FLORIDA AND I WENT TO MS. WU'S EARLIER. I TOLD HER THE KID WAS SELF-CONSCIOUS ABOUT BLEMISHES ON HER SHOULDER. THE MARKS ARE UNDER HER SHOULDER BLADE NOW, AND I'LL BE MAKING A COUPLE OF HERB-GATHERING EXPEDITIONS TO THE NEVERNEVER TO PAY MS. WU.

I added: YOU DECIDE IF MS. WU'S TRUSTWORTHY. SHE SMILED AND SAID NOT EVEN AN ELFLANDS MAGICIAN WOULD NOTICE SUCH A TINY ALTERATION. Then I added, IN CASE YOU HADN'T GUESSED, FLORIDA FOLLOWING ME HERE WASN'T PART OF THE PLAN.

They all read it. Leander said, "You needn't pay—"

I grabbed the pad back. I WANT TO. MS. WU'LL PROVIDE

THE SUPPLIES I NEED TO GO EXPLORING. IT ISN'T THE TOUGHEST PRICE FOR ME TO PAY.

Strider said, "How long'll Crystaviel stay in town?"

Leander turned his head to one side. "Hard to say. But I think she'll only get suspicious if she connects me with Florida." He squatted to look at her. "Which means I may not see you for some time, Your Highness. But I only stay away so we'll both be safe."

Florida let go of me and stepped into the street, then nodded. "Wiseguy take care of you. I take care of Woofboy. Everyone safe."

"Yep," said Strider. "Put her on the throne, and we'll change the world."

"Time to go home?" Florida asked.

I grinned.

Strider glanced at me, then said, "Say, Wiseguy, hear anything from Leda?"

She wrinkled her brow. "She left for Faerie this morning. Had her good-bye celebration last night. I was invited, but I don't like her when she's with her new friends. She'll be gone for a few years. Why?"

"Just curious." He gave me a look that said he'd done all he could and was sorry at the way it'd turned out.

A few years in Faerie could be my whole life here. I shrugged, nodded to Leander and Wiseguy, and headed toward the front gate with Florida.

Halfway down the path I heard Wiseguy call, "Wolfboy!"

I glanced at Strider, who said, "We'll wait."

I went back alone. Wiseguy, standing in the doorway, said, "I knew this kid once who was about your size. He had your posture, and he'd lean his head to one side and scratch behind his ear when he was puzzled, like you." She looked away, toward the last rays of the sunset, then back at me. "And Florida trusted him."

I started to lift my hands, maybe to protest, but I dropped them again.

"I think," she said, "that the judgment of children and animals is overrated."

I shrugged.

"But in this case, Florida may be right. I just wanted to say that."

I nodded.

"Mooner—" Her voice tightened, and I knew there was nothing I could do or say to help her. "He may've used you, but he liked you, too. For what that's worth." She looked down. When she looked up, her face was perfectly composed. "I hope you'll visit us again, Wolfboy. Truly."

I nodded and walked away. On the street I glanced back at the house. The curtains had not been drawn yet, so the gaslights made each window look like the setting for a play. Leander stood at one window, watching us or the sunset. Wiseguy ran up to him, and they embraced, a single shape in the window frame.

I stood there for a few seconds, feeling oddly sad and happy, then ran to catch up to Florida and Strider.

What more should I tell about that day? Goldy had kept some dinner warm in the oven, meatloaf covered with salsa, with carrots and a baked potato on the side. While I ate, Florida read aloud from *Treasure Island*, the chapter that I would've read to her months ago if Castle Pup hadn't burned.

Later that night, in the guest room that Mickey said was mine as long as I wanted it, I wrote three notes.

The first one read:

Dear Sparks,

There are enough people who'll tell you I'm a dink that you don't need to hear it from me. But I thought you might like to hear that I've realized I'm a dink. I'd like to take you to Godmom's to show you how much I've changed.

—Ron
c/o Elsewhere

I set that one aside because I'd ask someone to deliver it for me. Then I wrote:

Dear Mom and Dad,

A postcard isn't the best way to resume a relationship, but there must be worse ones. I just wanted you to know that I'm alive and well and happy, and I hope you are, too. I'll write a proper letter soon.

With love,
Ronnie
Bordertown

I put a stamp that I'd borrowed from Mickey on that one. The other side was an ancient publicity photo of Lon Chaney, Jr. as the Wolfman. I wrote: Hi, folks! next to him and enclosed the greeting in a word balloon.

Then I wrote my third note:

Tony-o:

They better give you a pair of wings.

The Kid.

I folded that one into a paper airplane and sailed it out over the streets of Bordertown. A breeze caught it, carrying it north toward Faerie. Something shimmered there. I thought I was seeing the northern lights much too early in the evening, then realized that I was seeing the Border itself. It moved like water or electricity or fireflies, a gentle, constantly changing form.

I watched the Border for a long time. That night I slept very, very well.